D0181138

Sweetbriar Autumn

Also by Brenda Wilbee
Sweetbriar
The Sweetbriar Bride
Sweetbriar Spring
Sweetbriar Summer
Shipwreck!
Taming the Dragons
Thetis Island

Sweetbriar Autumn

Brenda Wilbee

C5

Fleming H. Revell
A Division of Baker Book House
Grand Rapids, Michigan 49516

Published by Fleming H. Revell
a division of Baker Book House Company
P.O. Box 6287, Grand Rapids, MI 49516-6287

Printed in the United States of America

Library of Congress Cataloging-in-Publication Data

Wilbee, Brenda.
    Sweetbriar autumn / Brenda Wilbee.
      p. cm.
    ISBN 0-8007-5661-4 (pbk.)
      1. Denny, Louisa Boren—Fiction. 2. Frontier and pioneer life—Washington (State)—Fiction. 3. Women pioneers—Washington (State)—Fiction. 4. Denny, David Thomas—Fiction. 5. Seattle (Wash.)—History—Fiction. I. Title.
PS3573.I3877S915 1998
813'.54—dc21
                                                98-12726

Scripture quotations are taken from the King James Version of the Bible.

For current information about all releases from Baker Book House, visit our web site:
                              http://www.bakerbooks.com

Affectionately dedicated to my
"brother" Bruce Wiggins
Without whom . . .

Contents

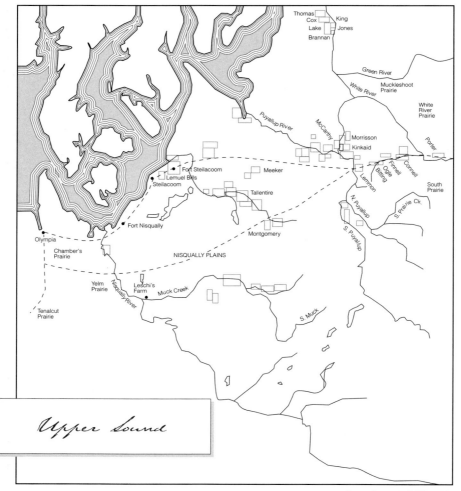

Thomas
Cox
King
Lake
Jones
Brannan

Green River

White River
Muckleshoot
Prairie

White
River
Prairie

Puyallup River

McCarthy

Morrisson
Kinkaid

Porter

Finnell
Ogle
Bitting
Cornell

Fort Steilacoom

Lemuel Bills
Steilacoom

Meeker

Lemmon

South
Prairie

Fort Nisqually

Tallentire

N. Puyallup

S. Prairie Ck.

S. Puyallup

Olympia

Montgomery

Chamber's
Prairie

NISQUALLY PLAINS

Yelm
Prairie

Leschi's
Farm

Muck Creek

Tenalcut
Prairie

S. Muck

Upper Sound

Composite map by B. Wilbee '98

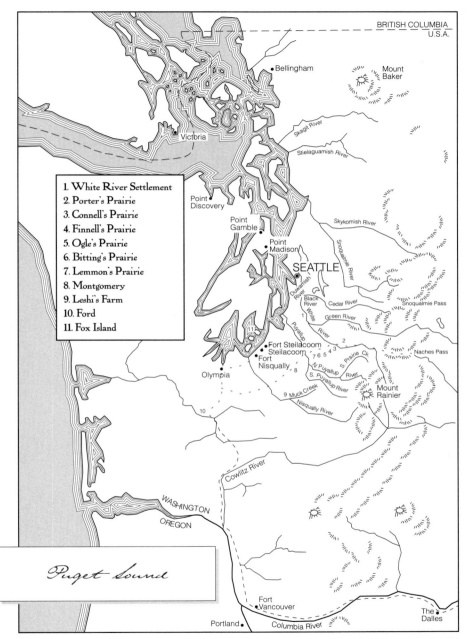

1. White River Settlement
2. Porter's Prairie
3. Connell's Prairie
4. Finnell's Prairie
5. Ogle's Prairie
6. Bitting's Prairie
7. Lemmon's Prairie
8. Montgomery
9. Leshi's Farm
10. Ford
11. Fox Island

BRITISH COLUMBIA
U.S.A.

Bellingham

Mount Baker

Victoria

Skagit River

Stielaguamish River

Point Discovery

Point Gamble

Point Madison

Skykomish River

SEATTLE

Duwamish River

Black River

Cedar River

Snoqualmie River

Snoqualmie Pass

White River

Green River

Puyallup River

N Puyallup River

S Prairie Ck

Naches Pass

Fort Steilacoom
Steilacoom

Fort Nisqually

S. Puyallup River

Olympia

Muck Creek

Mount Rainier

Nisqually River

Cowlitz River

WASHINGTON

OREGON

Puget Sound

Fort Vancouver

Portland

The Dalles

Columbia River

Composite map by B. Wilbee '98

THE BORENS AND DENNYS

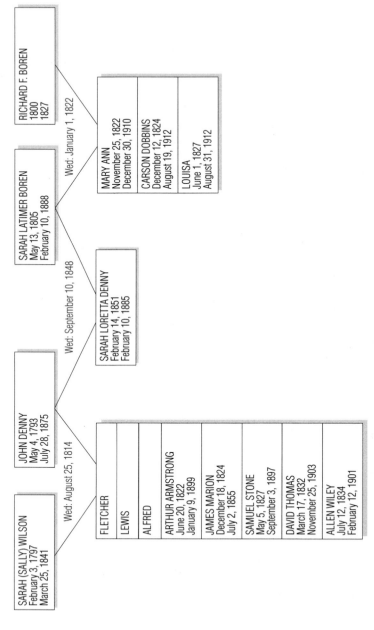

SARAH (SALLY) WILSON
February 3, 1797
March 25, 1841

JOHN DENNY
May 4, 1793
July 28, 1875

SARAH LATIMER BOREN
May 13, 1805
February 10, 1888

RICHARD F. BOREN
1800
1827

Wed: January 1, 1822

Wed: September 10, 1848

Wed: August 25, 1814

MARY ANN
November 25, 1822
December 30, 1910

CARSON DOBBINS
December 12, 1824
August 19, 1912

LOUISA
June 1, 1827
August 31, 1912

SARAH LORETTA DENNY
February 14, 1851
February 10, 1885

FLETCHER

LEWIS

ALFRED

ARTHUR ARMSTRONG
June 20, 1822
January 9, 1899

JAMES MARION
December 18, 1824
July 2, 1855

SAMUEL STONE
May 5, 1827
September 3, 1897

DAVID THOMAS
March 17, 1832
November 25, 1903

ALLEN WILEY
July 12, 1834
February 12, 1901

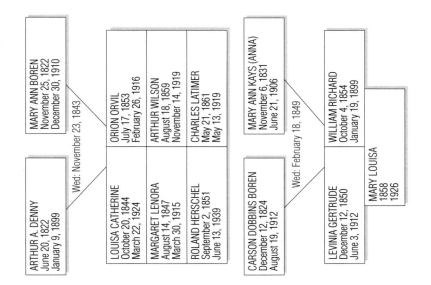

LOUISA BOREN
June 1, 1827
August 31, 1912

DAVID THOMAS DENNY
March 17, 1832
November 25, 1903

Wed: January 23, 1853

EMILY INEZ
December 23, 1853
Unknown

MADGE DECATUR
March 16, 1856
January 17, 1889

ABBIE LUCINDA
August 25, 1858
June 25, 1913

JOHN BUNYON
January 30, 1862
Unknown

ANNA LOUISA
November 26, 1864
May 5, 1888

DAVID THOMAS JR.
May 6, 1867
October 4, 1939

JONATHON
May 6, 1867
May 6, 1867

VICTOR W. S.
August 9, 1869
August 15, 1921

ARTHUR A. DENNY
June 20, 1822
January 9, 1899

MARY ANN BOREN
November 25, 1822
December 30, 1910

Wed: November 23, 1843

LOUISA CATHERINE
October 20, 1844
March 22, 1924

MARGARET LENORA
August 14, 1847
March 30, 1915

ROLAND HERSCHEL
September 2, 1851
June 13, 1939

ORION ORVIL
July 17, 1853
February 26, 1916

ARTHUR WILSON
August 18, 1859
November 14, 1919

CHARLES LATIMER
May 21, 1861
May 13, 1919

CARSON DOBBINS BOREN
December 12, 1824
August 19, 1912

MARY ANN KAYS (ANNA)
November 6, 1831
June 21, 1906

Wed: February 18, 1849

LEVINIA GERTRUDE
December 12, 1850
June 3, 1912

WILLIAM RICHARD
October 4, 1854
January 19, 1899

MARY LOUISA
1858
1926

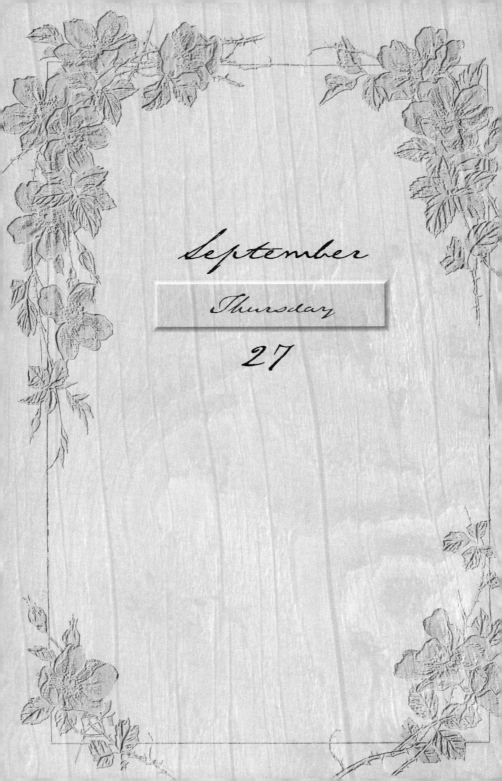

September

Thursday

27

Prologue

evening

All accounts of Seattle's part in the Indian War begin with the experience of Allen L. Porter of White River.

—Roberta Frye Watt, Katy Denny's daughter
in *Four Wagons West*

ifty miles southeast of Seattle and nestled into the foothills of the Cascade Mountains, Allen Porter knew he'd be the first to be molested when the Indians came through. His ranch sat just inside the high, narrow pass near the headwaters of White River in a picturesque valley called Porter's Prairie. Stretching downriver some sixteen miles were several other claims, clear down to Mox La Push where the White and Black Rivers converged to form the slow-moving Duwamish. When Porter learned the brutal fate of two neighbors from Mox La Push who'd gone into Yakima country last summer, he'd begun looking over his shoulder wherever he went and sleeping with two loaded guns at his bedside. But when news came September 23rd that the Yakima had murdered their Indian agent, Porter could no longer content himself with a wary eye and ready fire. He took to sleeping outdoors, away from his cabin. He did not want *his* throat slit while asleep.

On the 27th, Thursday evening, he came in late from his fields having searched in vain for missing cattle. The night was quiet. An autumn chill hung heavy in the air. The moon held little light and the young bachelor thought to himself that he really ought to start carrying a compass. But not to worry, not tonight, there was his house, the roofline a stark silhouette.

Suddenly he noticed movement around his home. Visitors? At this hour? He hurried forward, wondering who'd come to visit his humble ranch at such an ungodly hour. Perhaps they needed shelter. He was cutting across the back field, coming up alongside the barn when it came to him that these were no ordinary visitors. They were stationing themselves strategically around his house!

Crouching low, he darted forward, gun in hand. Dart and duck, dart and duck. Finally he reached the dark shadow of his barn. Catching his breath, for it came in short, suppressed gusts, he edged up to the far corner and peered around, careful to keep his body hidden.

Indians!

He pulled up straight, heart pounding, back pressed tightly against the wall. The Indians were here . . . at his house . . . everything he'd feared. But somewhere in all this he'd never considered what to do when it happened! What *do* I do?

He had to abandon his ranch. He had to head downriver and warn his neighbors as he went. *Like Paul Revere of the Revolution eighty years ago . . .*

Quickly he retraced his steps, away from the house, the barn, back out through the trees. He took the long way down to the river, then had to furtively creep back along the riverbank, up past his house, to where his canoe lay upside down on a sandy shore. He wrestled it over and into the water. He pushed off. Trembling, he eased down along the boat's narrow bottom. If the Indians spotted the canoe, they might think it just worked loose from its mooring.

He started to count to twenty, the rushing waters quickly carrying him away. At twenty he would sit up and start paddling. At the count of ten he heard an owl. At fifteen another owl. At eighteen he bolted straight up, heart in his throat— a knee-jerk reaction to the bloodcurdling war cry ripping through the night, stopping his heart and nearly wrenching off his ears. He scrambled onto his knees, canoe rocking, grabbed his paddle and dug in. Jim Riley! He had to get to Jim's place; he had to warn him!

All night long down the river—through cascade and calm and portage. Riley. Corcoran. David Neely and family. Robert Beatty. John Thomas and bride. Henry Adams. Joseph Lake. Arnold Lake. Sam Russell and family. William Cox and family. Moses Kirkland and daughters. Enos Cooper. Harvey Jones and family. George King and family. Joe Brannan. Will and Elizabeth Brannan. At Mox La Push, where the White and Black Rivers melded and vanished into the Duwamish, he let Charles Brownell take over. Brownell could warn the Duwamish River farmers, he was too tired.

He was too tired to get in and out of his canoe anymore, too tired to stumble up to yet another darkened house, too tired to rasp out one more time, "The Indians are coming! The Indians are coming!", too tired to even keep his head up as he paddled down the Duwamish to the little village of Seattle on the Sound.

He must have slept, the current carrying him, because when he woke it was daylight. The canoe bobbed in the Duwamish River mouth. In the near distance, across the bay five miles to the northeast, was Seattle and safety.

If there was such a thing as safety.

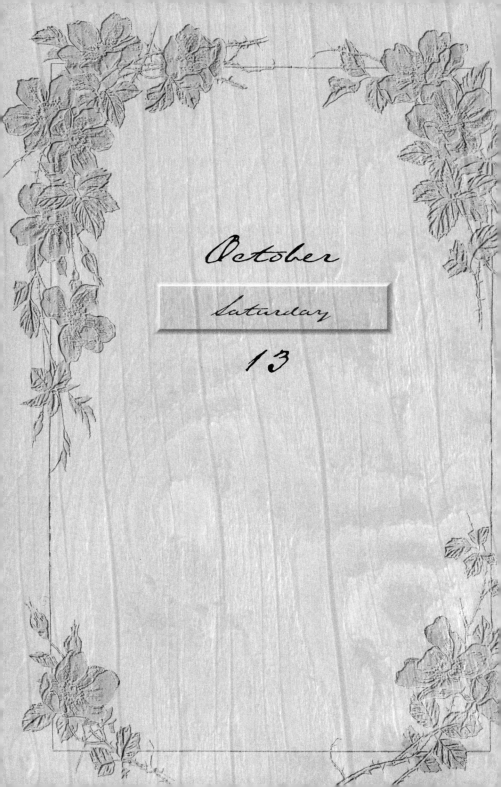

October

Saturday

13

1

noon

By gentlemen just arrived from Seattle, we are informed that
fears of an eruption of the savages prevails to such an extent
in our neighboring county, that nearly if not quite all the families residing upon the Duwamish and White river, have left
their farms, and fled to Seattle for safety and mutual protection. This is a very painful state of things.

—*Puget Sound Courier*
Friday, September 28, 1855

ouisa Boren Denny knew as well as any that Seattle's
merchants were getting rich off the White River settlers. The Yakima Indians of eastern Washington were at war,
and the families living closest to the mountain pass had fled
into town on the heels of Allen Porter a fortnight ago. They'd
arrived with nothing more than the clothes on their backs,
they'd rented every available accommodation in town,
squeezed in with friends, many even tented on the sawdust
in front of the mill. And they needed everything. Everything

from clothing to hairbrushes to blankets to pots and pans to food to put in them.

To say nothing of the sailors. Ninety men in jaunty uniforms plied the shops, looking for razors, whisky, souvenirs. They'd arrived a week ago, one week after the White River folk, sailing briskly into Elliott Bay in their sloop of war, backing off her yards at Yesler's wharf, firing off her guns and scaring half to death the women who'd gathered to pray for rescue from the Indians. Some folk believed the timely arrival of the *U.S. Decatur* an answer to those prayers. Others thought luck closer to the mark.

Either way, Seattle overflowed with outsiders and new prosperity; and Louisa, a pretty woman, twenty-eight years old, with raven black hair and light brown eyes, found herself wishing at times that she and her husband owned a store downtown. Dr. Williamson's mercantile; Denny, Horton & Phillips; Bettman & Bros.; and Plummer & Chase were all doing a booming business. If she and David had their own store, why, they'd be able to offset last summer's loss in less than a month! For Seattle—because of and despite the Indian uncertainties—was paradoxically enjoying profitable times.

No one, however, dismissed the Indians. Rather, having survived that first fearful week following Mr. Porter's arrival, when every forest sound heralded a gruesome end, the unexpected protection by the U.S. Navy buoyed new and exuberant confidence. How could the Indians dare strike now? Not here, not in Seattle! *Not with sixteen guns pointed off the water into the woods beyond!*

Also, word had come from Olympia, their territorial capital at the head of Puget Sound, that Major Rains of the Puget Sound Militia was sending two armies into eastern Washington to punish the murderous Yakima. The killing of gold miners last summer and then the ghastly, audacious murder of Indian Agent Bolon was not something the U.S. Army would overlook. From the southeast corner of Washington

Territory, Major Haller and a hundred and two men marched north. From Fort Steilacoom just south of Seattle on Puget Sound in the west, Lieutenant Slaughter with forty-eight soldiers marched east. Up past Porter's Prairie Slaughter would cross through the high mountain pass, then rendezvous with Haller in the Yakima Valley. Together they'd hunt down and punish the guilty Yakima who'd been murdering and plundering and whose head chief, Kamiakin, boasted a war of extermination against all whites. It was only a matter of days, everyone in Seattle felt sure, before Kamiakin was defeated. His brazen warriors would no longer be able to bully or threaten the local Indians, and the refugees could all go home. In the meantime—protected by the providential sloop of war—Seattle was doing a landfall business!

At noon, Saturday the 13th of October, Louisa Denny, herself a refugee, tied a pink bonnet under the chin of her twenty-two-month-old daughter.

"Where My go?" the child asked, an articulate little girl with her own sense of syntax.

"*My* goes to see Papa," said Louisa, tweaking her daughter's nose and giving her an amused smile.

Emily Inez smiled back and ran outside.

"Wait for me," Louisa cautioned. She stepped carefully around the six loaves of bread rising on the front stoop of her "inside" house, the small board cabin she and her husband had built two years before during Seattle's first Indian scare. Forced to abandon their claim two miles north of town, they'd only recently returned because of the new trouble, and living with them in the crowded, one-room, "inside" house were refugee friends from White River—Will and Elizabeth Brannan and their baby daughter.

"You're sure you won't come along, Elizabeth?" Louisa asked, turning back to see her friend in the shadowed room.

Elizabeth sighed, and in her pronounced English accent, said quietly, "Someone needs to mind the bread."

"Elizabeth," said Louisa with pity. "You needn't be afraid of the Indians in town. They're all friendly. No one in Seattle has to worry, they'll never hurt anyone. And we do have the *Decatur*." But one look at poor Elizabeth's face revealed the terrifying fear that could not and would not be assuaged. So Louisa simply said good-bye, took Emily Inez by the hand, and set out to find David.

They took their time walking into town, south down the short incline of "Front Street"—a glorified name for the narrow three-block trail ridging the ocean cliff directly to their right. They passed a few log cabins along the way and the cluttered Indian camp, and, in two blocks, the newly finished blockhouse crowning a ten to twelve-foot bluff. From here the land sloped quickly to sea level—and Mr. Yesler's sawmill straight ahead.

From where she stood one block away Louisa could easily hear the high whine of the whirling saw and see the flurried activity within the triangular, sawdust-covered clearing the Seattle pioneers simply called the "Sawdust." Fronting the Sawdust was Elliott Bay of Puget Sound. Directly behind, a densely wooded hill rose almost straight up. An old Indian trail cut up this steep incline, switchbacking through the trees for nearly a mile, and Mr. Yesler—upon whose claim the trail zigzagged—had straightened and widened the lower portion so he could skid timber from the back of his claim down to his mill at the front.

Local Indians, plus many of the White River refugees, were manning the mill today—alongside old regulars like Mr. Clarke and Mr. Butler. Some of the men, Louisa saw, were carefully guiding a stout trunk of Douglas fir into the huge whirling saw. Others stacked and measured cut lumber. Still others burned trash or hauled sawdust. Tents belonging to the refugees littered the ever-growing circle of sawdust, and on the beach several Indian dugouts had been nosed in to shore. A large cargo ship had come in late the night before and was tied up to Yesler's wharf. This morning sharp orders sang out over the shrill whine of the saw as crewmen and shorehands managed the laborious task of onloading the vessel, bound for San Francisco and beyond . . . China, Australia, the Sandwich Islands. Farther out in the harbor, rocking gently on the peaceful water, guns gleaming, was the heaven-sent *Decatur. How quiet and safe things are now,* thought Louisa, so very grateful to God and Captain Sterrett for their providential protection. *If only Elizabeth could feel more secure,* she thought sadly to herself.

Her gaze returned to the mill and Sawdust and scattered tents to follow the formless road bridging over to the small peninsula south of the mill. For many reasons the Point, pushing up from mucky tideflats, had become Seattle's downtown.

Suddenly, from the cookhouse tucked in behind the mill a man burst out, quickly followed by a tight escort of armed soldiers.

Who are they? wondered Louisa as the uniformed strangers, making no nonsense of it, marched across the Sawdust, got into half a dozen of the Indian dugouts, and paddled off. From the cookhouse a swarm of men and marines followed, their babbled arguments floating up the bluff. Louisa scooped Emily Inez into her arms and hurried down.

The acting governor, she found out, had just been to White River. "He made lie to everything Mr. Porter said!" exclaimed her friend, Ursula McConaha Wyckoff. Ursula, of course, had heard it all. "Mr. Mason talked to all the Indians out there, he says everyone is friendly and wants to be friends with the *Bostons.* He even went to Mr. Porter's house! He says nothing was disturbed!"

Louisa found this hard to believe.

"But nothing was touched!" argued Ursula, a strong, handsome woman with golden brown hair, worn in a single braid down her back. "You'd think that if the Indians meant to kill him, they'd have at least stolen his guns!"

25

"That is strange," agreed Louisa, puzzled by the odd contradiction. "Did Mr. Mason say if anyone's heard from Governor Stevens?"

"No. He's a thousand miles away. Making more of his stupid Indian treaties. For all the good they do," she added.

"So what does Mr. Mason suggest *we* do?"

Ursula swung her braid over one shoulder, and laughed. "He says the White River farmers should all go home. The Indian trouble, he says, is on the other side of the mountains. That may be, but I tell you, Louisa Denny, I wouldn't leave my pet canary at White River and expect to find two feathers when I went back!"

"Where's Eugenia?" Louisa asked suddenly, wondering if her friend's three-year-old might have wandered off.

"At the smithy with Lewis. Where are you going?"

"Arthur's store. I'm taking David his lunch." Louisa held up her basket. "Arthur and Mr. Horton hired him. Temporarily. To keep the shelves stocked. Help out when there's a big rush, things like that."

"I'll walk with you then. I'm on my way home!" declared Ursula. She led out, tucking her arm through Louisa's, pinching Emily Inez's cheek and laughing when Emily Inez shouted *"No!"* and pushed her away. "Saucy little thing!" said Ursula.

When they crossed the spit toward the Point it occurred to Louisa there were a lot of Indians in town. Though they weren't Chief Seattle's people, who visited often. Or any of Suwalth's small band for that matter. "Who are they?" she asked as Dutch Ned, the town simpleton, trundled up behind them with a wheelbarrow of sawdust. He all but dumped it on their feet.

"Who?" asked Ursula, leaping out of Dutch Ned's way.

"All these Indians."

Ursula gazed ahead to the new Indian camp. "They came in yesterday. Afternoon, I think."

"Who are they?"

26

"Some of Pat Kanim's Snoqualmie. His brothers, Thlid and John, brought them. Mostly women and children."

"I thought Pat Kanim took his tribe up north."

"He did. But John and Thlid say the Haida are on the prowl. Pat Kanim wanted the women and children brought here, just in case."

"First the Yakima, now the Haida." Nervously Louisa glanced over her shoulder, beyond Seattle and into the dense forest to the north. "The Haida won't trouble *us*, do you think?"

Ursula laughed and started up Commercial Street onto the Point. "Haida bothering white folk?"

Louisa relaxed in the rich peal of her friend's laughter. The Haida in British Territory had terrorized the local Sound Indians for generations with their swift, sudden forays out of their own northern waters into that of the Sound. They killed with a vengeance and went away with women and children to be used as slaves. But the Haida, for all their boldness, carried a healthy respect for the British "King George" authority and, consequently, American "Bostons." Which was why Pat Kanim, chief of the Snoqualmies, wanted his women and children in Seattle, thought Louisa. In Seattle they were safe.

She bid Ursula good-bye outside Denny, Horton & Phillips. Mr. Phillips's brass bell jangled when she entered, a rush of distinct smells reached her nose. Fresh-cut lumber. Leather, richly oiled. A hint of lavender, licorice, sugar. The itchy smell of stiffly starched cotton.

Emily Inez spotted her father. "Papa!"

Louisa let her down and watched with pride as Emily Inez hurtled across the wooden floor. David, his soft brown eyes lighting up when he saw his daughter, told his customer to mind a minute, then went around the glass counter to swing her into his arms. He held her way high and pretended to bite her toes. She kicked and squealed, and when he finally relented and brought her down for a hug she lavished him with kisses, babbling away in her own quaint way.

Meeting Louisa's eyes, David said, "Can you stay and eat with me?"

She nodded.

"I'll be a minute."

She wandered through the store, always able to find something new. Arthur and his two partners sold everything from silver thimbles to crosscut saws. *Needle to an anchor,* she thought to herself with a smile. She stopped to admire a small red coffee grinder, saw the price. Quickly she put it down. Whew! David would have to work a whole week to pay for that!

She passed into the back through a curtained doorway, entering a dark, narrow hall. Two doors opened off it. She popped her head into Dexter Horton's office first, bid the accountant hello, then went on to Arthur's and David Phillips' office. Mr. Phillips was not in. Arthur, however, looked up from his desk, and smiled.

"Mary Ann says you don't want lunch today," Louisa told him. "You must be trying out Mr. Plummer's new restaurant?"

"I am," said her husband's older brother, who happened to be married to her older sister.

"You're wasting your money," Louisa chided, teasing him a little, "eating out instead of taking lunch."

"Shall I tell you if the food is good? Hello, Dave," he added, for David, Emily Inez on his shoulders, had come in.

"Can you take over out there? Dexter can't. He says he's got a tangle in his numbers."

Arthur, ten years older than David and as blond as David was dark, laughed. "Dexter's always got a tangle in his numbers!" He stood easily and came around the corner of his desk. He helped himself to Emily Inez on his way past.

"Shall I keep her while you two have your lunch?" he asked when they reentered the main part of the store.

Louisa couldn't remember the last time she'd had David to herself, and jumped at the chance.

"That was nice of him!" she said as they stepped back into October's thin sunlight.

"Mary probably put him up to it. How are you feeling?"

Yes, that would be like Mary Ann, thought Louisa, taking David's hand to let him know she was feeling just fine. Still, she thought gratefully, no one made Arthur do anything unless he wanted to. "Where shall we eat?" she asked.

They sat behind the store. David rolled a weathered log against the siding and they spread out their sandwiches on a hanky Louisa had brought along. Before them lay the bay—and, across the water, the snowcapped Olympic Mountains of the distant peninsula. They ate without comment, shoulders touching, happy to be together and leaning lazily against the store, staring at the familiar, yet eternally different, landscape of mountains and sea.

When David swallowed his last slippery peach he licked the spoon clean, then reached forward to pack the empty, sticky jar into Louisa's basket. It came to him this was a contradictory moment. On the surface, everything idyllic. Yet in the shadows, where none could see, the future loomed ominously uncertain.

He leaned into the wall, tucked his hands in behind his head and wiggled into a comfortable position. Content to rest in this momentary mirage of peace, he let his mind wander. Was it a whole year ago he and Henry Smith put up Arthur's shingles? If he closed his eyes he could still see the grandeur of the country the way it had loomed that day from the rooftop of his brother's two-story commissary. The tide behind and below them, at its brim, flooding the beach. The shoreline nosing up, capped by immense evergreens. The land pushing up from there; up, up, swell after swell, hill after hill, piling itself into the great Cascade mountain range fifty miles inland—reflective of the Olympic Mountains across the Sound. He swiveled his head suddenly to squint at Louisa, and grinned. "Baby moving yet?"

She clapped the crumbs off her hands. "Not yet."

"Isn't it about time for a little kicking around in there?"

She shrugged, content in her pregnancy and unworried. "One of these days, I expect."

Angry voices suddenly erupted behind them. David leaped to his feet and pressed his face against a salt-streaked window above them. He motioned for Louisa to climb onto the log beside him and together, like naughty children, they watched in astonishment as Captain Sterrett of the *Decatur*, who had up until now presented himself a conscientious, mild-mannered man, lit into Arthur with sharp, accusatory words. ". . . false alarm, meant to line your pockets! The Indians aren't hostile, never have been! They have no intention of attacking you or anybody else! You and every other land shark in this town have used me shamelessly! *Shamelessly!* You fed the hysteria; you played me a fool; you tied up my ship in your harbor to keep an easy business with my fast-spending sailors!"

Arthur remained seated, staring at his hands.

"I have been grossly deceived," said Captain Sterrett, leaning over the desk. "You are cowards and squatters, the whole lot of you, and I've been victimized by you for the purpose of trade! But let me tell you—" He leaned closer. "I do not propose to be hoodwinked another day! Mr. Mason tells me I can with all propriety leave you, a spider in your web! I tell you I will, just as soon as I hoist anchor and set my sails. I wish to God—" He broke off.

Arthur leaned back in his chair. Solemnly he regarded the furious man before him. Louisa, breathless, pushed her nose tighter to the window. What would Arthur do? No one *ever* spoke to him like that! "David, do you think you should go in?" she whispered.

But Arthur had begun to answer, slowly, softly. "If you, to whom we have the right to look for protection," he began, "choose to desert us in our extreme danger, I have no power to prevent your doing so. But, Captain Sterrett, I say this with all due respect. If our people, who have come to Seattle for safety, allow themselves to be seduced by Mr. Mason's assurances and return to their homes they will all certainly be murdered within the month."

Louisa glanced frightfully at David. Their eyes met. She turned back to the window. Captain Sterrett was pacing up and down in front of Arthur's desk. He kept rubbing the back of his neck. *He musn't leave us!* Louisa thought in a panic. *None of us will be safe! It'll be the same as before! Oh, dear God, please don't let him leave us to the Indians!*

"I don't know!" Captain Sterrett finally cried out, wheeling around to face Arthur. "You seem so earnest! How can I tell whom to believe?"

Arthur remained silent.

So did David and Louisa outside the window.

Captain Sterrett sank into the opposing chair. He sighed wearily and said, "I will stay then, and find out for myself. I will stay and find out who is the deceiver, and who is being deceived."

2

still noon

Some of us tried to induce those who were here to stay, but a number of them came to the conclusion that Porter was alarmed without cause, and that Mason ought to know best and must be right; and so returned to their homes. It may now seem strange that there could be any doubt of the true situation, when it is remembered that the fact was known to all that Walker and Jamieson had been killed, and that Eaton and Fanjoy were missing, with no reason to doubt that they had shared the same fate, yet many of the citizens were ready to agree with Mason, and ridicule those who had given timely warning, calling them timid and even cowards.

—Arthur Armstrong Denny
in *Pioneer Days on Puget Sound*

It was still noontime when Elizabeth Brannan picked up her baby and went to the door of David and Louisa's tiny cabin. "What do you mean we're going back to White River?" she asked her husband fearfully.

32

"Just what I said!" panted Will Brannan, for it had been a fast run up the trail. "Never was any danger! Never were any Indians at Porter's house! Living too long by himself, got spooked. Spooked the rest of us too." He grinned wildly, happy to have the matter resolved.

The matter was not resolved for Elizabeth. "What about the missing gold miners last summer? You can't tell me they all just vanished! Mr. Jamieson and Mr. Walker we *know* were killed! And Mr. Fanjoy and Mr. Eaton have been missing for months! No one's heard from them! Mrs. Fanjoy even sold the sawmill at Mox La Push to Mr. Plummer—soon as she heard at least eighty miners were murdered!"

"That's a bit of an exaggeration, don't you think?"

"And if *she* thinks her husband's dead!" Elizabeth barreled on, "and is going back to Ohio—"

"We've been through all this before," Will interrupted impatiently. "Whatever happened, happened *east* of the Cascades. Not here."

Elizabeth pushed past her husband, needing to get away from him, and walked over to the cliff a few feet away. The draw of the mountains across the water was strong, and she stood staring at their lofty height, a distant range of snow-capped mountain peaks framing the far western shore of the Sound. If only she could go over there, where it was safe, where Chief Seattle and many of his people had gone. *Chief Seattle,* she thought to herself. *So unlike Chief Nelson near us. Or the Yakima! Threatening every day to come through the Cascades! She* believed their threats! Why didn't anyone else? *Why didn't Will?*

She heard him come up behind her. "I don't want to go," she told him, biting her lip, staring determinedly at the mountains.

"Mr. Mason says there's no Yakima, or any other hostile Indians anywhere near our place."

"And if he's being deceived?" she asked, turning to face him.

33

"No one is being deceived. Come on, the *Water Lily* is warming her engines. Charles Terry is taking any of us who want to go upriver. What do we need to pack?"

"I don't want to go!" she burst out, backing away from him, clutching her baby. "I *won't* go! You can't *make* me go!"

"We can't keep taking David and Louisa's charity," he told her sternly.

"We'd do the same for them."

"A man's got to take care of his own."

"Will, please. Another week. Wait just one more week, please . . ."

"No. You know as well as I that David hates working at his brother's store. But someone has to put food on the table. No, I'm not going to accept their charity any longer."

"It's not charity!"

"It is when Mr. Mason says we can all go home!" Tears streamed down her face.

"Elizabeth," he begged. "Mr. Mason went up with some of the soldiers from Fort Steilacoom. They *swear* nothing at home is amiss! You know I'd never take you anywhere I thought was dangerous! You *know* that!"

"Do you think the Indians are stupid?" she all but shrieked.

He stared at her, not understanding.

"Do you think they'd tell a whole squadron of soldiers their *real* intent? I don't *care* if they're Indians," she cried. "They are *not* stupid!"

He grabbed her shoulders with both hands, hands that normally gave comfort and assurance. "Lizzy, you've got to learn to trust people."

"The *Indians?*"

"No," he capitulated, smiling tenderly. "Just your husband."

Emily Inez hardly gave her parents a glance when they returned to the store after lunch; she'd found a large, shiny bucket, a perfect toy. Captain Sterrett hardly gave them a glance either, and very nearly bumped into them because of it. "Oh!" he said, startled; then, his better nature asserting itself, he said, "Good day."

"Good day," responded David quickly, stepping back to open the door for the uniformed officer.

"Do you think he saw us?" Louisa whispered. "Looking in the window?"

"Nope. He was too angry."

Arthur came out. "You heard all that?"

"Yes," said David.

"Then I don't have to waste my time repeating it. We're closing up shop. My guess is that half the White River farmers are already packing. You've got to find Will before he has Elizabeth and that baby halfway back to White River."

David went over to pull Emily Inez out of the bucket. "He's the farthest out," continued Arthur, grabbing his hat off the hat rack. "He'll be one of the first killed."

"Where are *you* going?" Louisa asked, alarmed by the anger in Arthur's face.

"To find Mason. Before he goes back to Olympia—if he isn't already gone. I want to know who he talked to out there. Obviously he didn't talk to Nelson or Leschi!"

There was a brief discussion between David and Arthur, all of which Louisa had heard before. The warring Yakima coming through the mountains was an unrelenting fear, but a more immediate danger—at least in the brothers' minds, to say nothing of her own!—were some of the Upper Sound Indians. Since last winter's treaties they'd been pounding on their war drums. Louisa honestly couldn't blame them.

Leschi's Nisqually near Olympia at the head of the Sound had particular reason to be upset. Last Christmas Governor Stevens had assigned them a small reservation high on a stony bluff—a barren outcropping of land with nary a river or creek running through. No reasonable person could expect them to live up there, and Leschi, a wealthy and well-respected man appointed by Governor Stevens to be the Nisqually chief, had refused to sign. Enraged, Stevens ordered him off the council grounds, declaring that because Leschi was half-Yakima he couldn't be chief after all. Yet, curiously, on the treaty a large "X" marked Leschi's name. Even more curious, the editor of the *Pioneer & Democrat* had reported the Indians fully satisfied. It wasn't until early summer, when war drums started up, that the settlers began to figure out the truth. By mid-July it was common knowledge that Leschi had refused the reservation assigned him and was continuing to farm his own land—considerable acreage at Muck Creek, where it flowed into the Nisqually River. And as summer progressed, rumor had him first here, then there, finally all over the map, fomenting trouble. But to any who asked him, he was, he said, waiting for the governor to return. He had no quarrel with any of the settlers. Only the government.

But the Nisqually, Louisa knew, weren't the only unhappy Indians. The Muckleshoot, the Puyallup, even some bands of Chief Seattle's Duwamish had reason to be angry, and their chiefs and subchiefs—men like Nelson of the Muckleshoot—weren't quiescent like Leschi. In fact, Nelson was famous for his ugly temper.

What made everything worse, and what worried David and Arthur, *and* her, was that Kamiakin of the Yakima Nation had let it be known to the Upper Sound Indians that when he crossed the mountains—which he swore he'd do—he'd treat as enemy all those of his own race who refused to join his war against the whites. This put undue strain on the already unhappy Indians. The brothers were lamenting again Arthur's convictions that Mason probably hadn't spoken with either Nelson or Leschi when Arthur abruptly jammed on his hat and went out.

The first of the White River families were already hurrying past the store, headed down Commercial Street for Mr. Plummer's new pier and the *Water Lily,* the little side-wheeler running through her engines in preparation to cast off. "Looks like they've made up their minds," said Arthur dourly.

"Probably too late to turn the tide now." But he headed north anyway, against the flow.

"Boat's leaving in fifteen minutes!"

"Hey, Joe! Where're you going?" hollered out David.

"Headin' home, Denny!"

"Is that wise?"

Will Brannan's older brother chuckled. "Allen Porter's some kind of yellow! Mr. Mason says the only thing wrong out our way is our fruit crops! Says they're all rotting in the sun! Feeding the flies! And that's food, he says, for the soldier boys come winter—if they're to keep them rascal Yakima behind the mountains! Mason's willing to pay too!" hollered Joe, breaking into a run, knapsack bouncing on his shoulder. "For whatever we can salvage!"

David shifted Emily Inez in his arms and grabbed Louisa's hand. They'd hardly gone ten yards when a man blocked their way. Louisa remembered Mr. Ben Wetmore. Mr. Wetmore—amongst others, mostly newcomers—had openly mocked David a month ago for giving away a year's worth of his timber to build the blockhouse.

"Hey there, Denny," Mr. Wetmore said now. "Didn't I say there ain't no reason to be scared? You and your brother and some of them other fellers—like Smith and Yesler? You can all go back to minding your own business, I guess, and leave off worryin' the rest of us."

"I wish we could," said David carefully. "But I keep hearing the war drums."

"Pht," spit Mr. Wetmore. "All that ruckus is to keep guys like you and Porter checking yer pants!" He chuckled maliciously.

David pushed past and hurried on.

"Hey, but *I* don't skeer worth a cent!" Wetmore hollered. "There ain't no one gonna find *me* running down to Steilacoom to hide behind no army skirts like Porter just done!"

"Stupid man," muttered Louisa, catching up to David. "Oh, David, they're *all* going back!" she panted when they came off the Point onto the Sawdust. Tents were going down so fast the dust flew. "Even the Joneses! Look, David!"

He veered over. "You're not going back, are you, Harvey?" he asked worriedly, watching Harvey's hired hand, Enos Cooper, pull up the tent pegs.

"Sure am!" declared Harvey Jones, a slightly built man with clear blue eyes. He tossed odds and ends into a pack. A smile lit his whiskered face. "Mr. Mason says the coast's clear!"

"That's not what the locals report."

"What locals?"

"Suwalth. Salmon Bay Curley. Chief Seattle."

"Mmph. What do the *Siwash* know?"

David winced. "You don't think the *Indians* know what's going on out there?" he asked, letting the slur pass. He thrust his chin toward the surrounding forest. Dark, forbidding, completely impenetrable to most white men.

Harvey Jones laughed. "There ain't no Siwash this side of the Cascades what's going to put up a fight—and I don't care if their feathers *are* ruffled. I only come into town 'cause Mr. Porter got his shirt in a knot. But now Mr. Mason—who's in position to know, I guess—says there ain't no Yakima this side of the pass and that our own Indians are friendly enough, why then there ain't no reason to stick around here, is there? 'Ceptin' maybe if yer a coward?"

David let that one go too. "The local Indians have their own reasons for taking potshots at white folks, Jones, and you're sitting in the heart of Muckleshoot country. Are you saying Nelson's *not* been hanging around your place, sullen and cranky?"

"Hey, Johnny!" interrupted Mr. Jones, hollering over to his six-year-old stepson playing in the sawdust. "Come get your brother and sister! Boat's leaving any minute and they're bothering the daylights out o' yer ma! She can't get a lick o' work done with them tugging on her skirts, hear?"

"Yes, Sir!" Johnny King, a spry, eager little boy, rushed to his mother.

David and Louisa knew they'd been dismissed. They bade good-bye and went on, but not before Louisa gave Eliza King Jones a warm hug. "I'll be praying for you," she whispered.

"Thank you, Ma'am," whispered Mrs. Jones.

Louisa gave her a smile, then ran to catch up with David, carrying with her the haunting sadness in Mrs. Jones's resigned face. *What made some men ignore the fear in women's eyes?*

When they crested the slope north of the mill, David detoured down around the brand-new blockhouse to where a few rude Indian huts, separate from the majority crowding the trail, hugged the bluff between the blockhouse and beach. All were built of cedar planks fastened to uprights with a combination of nails and rope. Mat hangings, woven from various marsh grasses, covered the doorways. Suwalth, a middle-aged Duwamish subchief who'd been living in Seattle with his small band from the very beginning, sat on an upturned barrel in front of his own nondescript shack, watching the comings and goings with an amused expression on his face.

"What do you think of all this?" David asked him in Duwamish. Louisa, who only knew Chinook, the local trade jargon, could nevertheless tell that Suwalth thought everyone had gone plumb crazy.

"He says Nelson and some of the other headwater Indians are laughing at how gullible the soldiers are," David translated.

"They think *'big trick!*,'" Suwalth told her in English. "But I say, big trouble!"

"Nelson's laughing at the soldiers?" gasped Louisa. Last January at the Mulkiteo treaty signing she'd seen Nelson, many times, and had spoken with him. Always a lover of children he'd played with Emily Inez and chuckled over her antics. But he'd also been furiously angry. His band of

Muckleshoot were being deprived of their river dwellings in the Cascade foothills and shipped across the Sound with the saltwater Duwamish. And although Chief Seattle, allied chief of all the tribes in the area, told Nelson it was high time he learned to get along with his redskin brothers, Nelson said getting along was one thing, *living* with them was another.

"David," she said urgently, tugging on his hand, "the Brannans live just south of the Joneses! We have to go!" But he kept on talking. Too anxious to wait, she abandoned him to Suwalth and scrambled back up to the blockhouse, then zigzagged around the stumps and clumps of bracken that littered the narrow path of Front Street. In minutes she arrived at her sister's house. Mary Ann was outside, throwing apple peels to their chickens: Louisa's Rhode Island Reds, Mary Ann's Leghorns.

"Did the Neelys leave?" Louisa asked, panting, referring to the family Mary Ann and Arthur had taken in.

"Yes, I'm afraid so," sighed Mary Ann with telltale resignation. "Though I tried to stop them." She dumped out her apron, and the chickens fussed and clucked at her feet and each other, squabbling over the scattered peelings.

"And the *Brannans?*" asked Louisa.

One more shake of the apron, and Mary Ann looked up. She need not answer; the frown on her face was enough. Louisa bolted for her own little house next door.

Her bread was just as she'd left it, undisturbed on the stoop. But inside the cabin, the clutter of two families sharing a confined space was completely gone. Dismayed, she spun in a circle. Gone!

David ducked in a moment later, Emily Inez on his shoulders. He looked around at the eerily empty room. "They leave a note?"

She handed him the scrap of paper she'd found on the table.

Dave, thank you—Soon as I bring in the harvest you and
Louisa must come visit. W/gratitude, Will.

"We shouldn't have stopped to talk to Mr. Wetmore or the
Joneses," said Louisa, trying not to cry. "They probably
passed right by us . . . and we didn't even see them . . . Oh!
David!"

He regarded her tenderly. "I don't think we'd have had any
better luck with the Brannans. The farmers are pretty desperate to get back to their crops. I can hardly bear to think
about the Swale myself, everything going to seed . . . and us
not there."

Louisa brushed away a tear. "We'll never see them again,
will we? Arthur said they'll all be killed—"

"Liza, let's not take the dim view," he interrupted, refus-
ing to let her dwell on what they feared the most. He set Emily
Inez onto the floor. "Lieutenant Slaughter and Major Haller
will soon get the Yakima under control. When they do, the
Indians around here can settle down. And we can all go
home. One more week. A fortnight at the most. Think about
it, Liza. We'll be back at the Swale in no time, sweeping down
the cobwebs and cleaning out the mouse droppings—What
is it?"

She was smiling.

"Liza?"

"The baby just moved!"

He reached her in two strides. With new energy he pulled
her into his arms, a small woman who stood no more than
five-foot-two, weighing scarcely a hundred pounds. He
grinned happily down into her radiant face, brushed back a
strand of her glossy black hair and wiped away her tears with
the back of his fingers. Worry for their friends fell away as
they beheld each other in awe and wonder, lost for the moment in their own personal happiness and love.

"No more running up the hill, Liza."

"I wasn't running."

41

"You *were*," he argued gently, laughing a little. He swung her up off her feet. She squealed in surprise and threw her arms around his neck.

"I just thought of something," he whispered.

"What?" she whispered back, delighting at the smile in his eyes.

"We have the house to ourselves tonight."

Their eyes held, but then together they glanced over to Emily Inez playing with her blocks under the table.

"Well, almost," he corrected, laughing.

"Do you think she's old enough to spend a night with her cousins?"

"We could find out."

This time Louisa laughed. Worry and fear had its place. But so did love.

October

Sunday

14

3

evening

It was understood that when Major Haller's command would start from Fort Dalles for the Yakima country that another force would be sent from Fort Steilacoom on the Sound to meet him on the east side of the Cascade range and cooperate with him in bringing to justice the refractory Yakimas. In accordance with this understanding Captain Maloney, in charge at Fort Steilacoom, sent Lieutenant Slaughter, with 48 men, to perform that duty.

—Ezra Meeker, pioneer and historian
in *Pioneer Reminiscences*

usk of Sunday evening the following day had already fallen by the time Acting Governor Mason finally arrived back in Olympia. Bone tired and irritated by all the hysteria he'd encountered in Seattle, Arthur Denny's especially, he sat down wearily behind his desk to read a waiting dispatch from Fort Vancouver. While he read, he unconsciously inched forward in his chair until he was sitting straight up. *Haller had been routed?*

Mason tugged off his glasses and mopped his brow, vaguely aware of the pounding in his chest. When President Pierce appointed him territorial secretary two and a half years before, he'd not envisioned this kind of duty—crises boiling over, the governor a thousand miles away. Where *was* the governor anyway?

The twenty-five-year-old secretary—and current acting governor—put his glasses back on and read again the hastily written, but lengthy, document from Major Rains, commanding officer of the Puget Sound Militia. Last Sunday, forty miles north of The Dalles, Kamiakin with an unexpected force of fifteen hundred warriors had taken Haller's advancing column by complete surprise. A three-day fight ensued, leaving five of Haller's men dead and seventeen wounded, one fifth of his entire command. Forced to spike his howitzer and turn loose all the pack animals and provisions belonging to his troops, Haller had fled back to The Dalles by night.

Mason's first cogent thought was of the small command under Lieutenant Slaughter. They'd left Fort Steilacoom two weeks before to rendezvous with Haller. *Where were they? Had they crossed the mountains?*

His second cogent thought frightened him. If Slaughter *had* crossed the mountains, then he was advancing right into enemy territory—completely unaware of Haller's defeat! *How many in the command? Forty-eight? Up against how many? Fifteen hundred?* Mason glanced quickly back at the dispatch. *Yes, fifteen hundred!* He mopped his brow and glanced again at the dispatch.

If they were to contain the war at all, Rains wrote, it was imperative the fighting be kept east of the Cascades where the fewest settlers lived. To that end, Rains was immediately leaving Fort Vancouver in southern Washington to take over the field command at The Dalles in eastern Washington. He'd already notified General Wool—commander of the U.S. Army's Department of the Pacific, unfortunately located in

46

California—of their precarious state of affairs. He'd also notified Captain Maloney at Fort Steilacoom, and given him orders to take what remaining force he had left to go after Lieutenant Slaughter—wherever he was. But with or without Slaughter, Maloney was to continue into Yakima country to rendezvous with Rains. "Haller's thwarted objective *will be accomplished!*" Major Rains directed. "The refractory Yakima *will be punished!* They *must!* Already Kamiakin is marshaling all of the eastern tribes into a singular Confederacy—the Cayuse, Walla Walla, Palouse, Shoshone, etcetera."

Jesus, Joseph, and Mary! thought Mason, a staunch Catholic. *Bring the Walla Walla into this, the very devil will have to be paid!* How to pay the devil though, he had no idea. In all of the territory there weren't more than six hundred soldiers.

A tap on the door brought him up short. Washington's surveyor general stood in the open doorway. "Yes, Tilton?"

"News just came in, Sir. Fort Steilacoom, Captain Maloney, Sir."

Mason snatched the dispatch. Quickly he scanned the directive. Things were escalating so quickly he could hardly keep up. "He doesn't have enough regulars to go after the Yakima and still mind the fort," he mumbled to Tilton. "He wants two companies of *volunteers.* He suggests one from Olympia, another from Vancouver."

"To do what, sir?"

"Stand home guard. Patrol the passes once he and the regulars vacate for eastern Washington."

"We're on our own then, are we?"

"No. He says Second Lieutenant Nugen will stay behind at the fort with a small squad."

"Great," said the surveyor general with biting sarcasm, "that's a relief."

"Well . . . we'll have the volunteers—"

47

"Volunteers?" yelped Tilton. "Farmers around here can't shoot the moon off an *outhouse!*"

"That'll be your job," said Mason, grim-faced. "Here on in, you're adjutant general, in charge of volunteers. You'll get what guns and ammunition they need; you'll make sure they *can* shoot straight!"

"Where's Governor Stevens?"

"Blackfoot country."

"If and when he decides to come home he's gonna walk right into Kamiakin and his warriors swaggering around. Someone's got to warn—"

"Just a minute . . ." Mason was reading again, concentrating on Major Rains's conclusion. "For the safety and protection of the majority of our settlers who live west of the mountains it is *essential* we keep the hostiles—the whole Confederacy if we must!—behind the Cascades lest they mingle with and incite the Puget Sound Indians who shall, without doubt, *be emboldened by this disastrous Yakima triumph!*"

Mason pursed his lips.

"What?" asked Tilton sharply.

"Leschi. Where is he?"

"Chief of the Nisqually?"

Mason nodded.

"Last report, doing his fall plowing. Why?"

"He's half Yakima, Tilton. His mother was a Yakima princess. Which means Leschi's related directly or indirectly to every chief and subchief of the Yakima Nation."

Tilton sucked in his breath. "Holy smokes, but that changes a few things."

"The way I see it, he could either join his cousins or—"

"Or what, Sir?"

"Kamiakin's victory may be all the encouragement he needs to throw caution and good sense to the wind. What if he decides to declare his own war? *This* side of the mountains?"

48

"Maybe you shouldn't have told those White River folk to go home. Sir?"

Mason had swung his chair around and was staring fearfully out the window. The deepening gray of the sky had turned leaden. Night was upon them, rain coming down hard. Just where in Blackfoot country was the governor? Where on his trail was the express rider that had been sent a fortnight ago with news of Indian Agent Bolon's murder and Kamiakin's formal declaration of war? *All of which is hopelessly old news . . .*

But this kind of thinking wasn't doing him or anybody else any good. Stevens was out of the picture, that was that. Mason forced a realignment of mind. Four thousand settlers lived in western Washington. All were dependent upon him to fence the Yakima and keep the peace this side of the mountains. *Someone* had to seize control. He leaped to his feet. "Post that call for those volunteers Maloney wants!" He started around his desk, toward the door. "And I want Leschi! He and I need to talk!"

"Shouldn't we send someone after the governor, Sir?"

Mason looked at Tilton like he was loose a few screws. "I should think that was understood, Mr. Tilton!"

October

Saturday

20

POSTSCRIPT—HALLER DEFEATED!

By the mail which has just arrived, we hear further particulars of the Indian war. Major Haller has been attacked by the Indians, about 40 miles from The Dalles, on Sunday morning the 7th inst, about 5:00. As soon as the first gun was fired, the command was completely surrounded, and the fight began in earnest continuing until dark. Five men were killed, and 17 wounded—one-fifth of the command. A howitzer was spiked, and left on the ground. The Indians took nearly all the pack animals and provisions belonging to the troops, who were in consequence without food or water, and under arms for 50 hours. Indian losses not known. Lieutenant Day started to his aid with the remaining troops at The Dalles. Major Haller arrived at The Dalles on the 10th inst., having to fight his way through until within 5 miles of The Dalles. It is estimated there were 1500 warriors.

—Puget Sound Courier
Steilacoom, October 12, 1855

ithin twenty-four hours news of "Haller's Defeat" had swept the Sound, spreading like wildfire. The initial reaction amongst the pioneers was, at first, stunned dismay.

53

The U.S. Army *defeated?* By *Indians?* Then came fear and its questions: Where were the soldiers from Fort Steilacoom who'd gone out to meet Major Haller? Had the Yakima turned on them? Where was the governor? Was he trying to get home? *How* was he to get home? Worse—when, how soon— would the Yakima come through the mountains? Finally, in reaction to their mounting fright, outrage. The majority called for immediate retaliation and the *Pioneer & Democrat* boldly headlined their cry for revenge.

WE TRUST THE YAKIMA WILL BE RUBBED OUT

BLOTTED FROM EXISTENCE AS A TRIBE!

A minority, however, felt pressure should be brought to bear *not* on the Yakima but Governor Isaac Ingalls Stevens himself—wherever in the world he was. A Whig newspaper, begun out of Steilacoom the previous May in opposition to Olympia's *Pioneer & Democrat*, named the governor as "sole cause" of the resultant Yakima eruption, and the editors placed entire responsibility on the shoulders of "King Stevens I.I." The Indians, the *Puget Sound Courier* reported, had been treated as brutes and robbed of their land by a governor who'd paid nominal amounts "because he wished to be known as the man who'd bought the most land, in the least time, for the lowest price."

Whether this was true or not, David Denny did agree that Governor Stevens had left them with a lapful of wrongs and little authority to right them. What any of them could do about the wretched state of affairs, he wasn't sure. Except somehow defend themselves and pray for the best.

More to the point, what were he and Louisa going to do? Haller's defeat put into pi all thought of returning to the claim, which they needed to do. To say nothing of defaulting on the residency and improvement laws required to gain title to their land. Would they lose everything? Everything they'd come west for? *Because without the land they had nothing.*

Visiting his brother's house for the afternoon, he was rekindling the fire for his sister-in-law when an idea came to mind regarding the governor. The proslavery element in Kansas had persuaded President Pierce to remove Governor Reeder. Maybe the same thing could be done here in Washington. No, he quickly decided. Kansas was battleground for polarized politics and President Franklin Pierce was a southerner. Pierce had a vested interest in making Kansas a slaveholding state. He had none in a territory which granted donation claims to men of color.

David's eldest niece sat listlessly in her mother's rocking chair beside him, watching as he tried to coax the tiny flames into something more promising. He noticed a shadow of sadness resting in her eyes and wondered if it had anything to do with the latest unrest, despite the fact they were all trying—best they could—to carry on as usual.

"You don't like turning eleven today, Katy?" he asked, reaching over to tug her big toe. When she didn't answer, he said, "Two more years and you can get out of those braids you hate so much."

She slumped farther into the chair, legs dangling, swinging over the edge. "Doesn't seem like my birthday," she finally told him.

"Maybe because we haven't gotten to the cake yet, or the presents. When your pa gets in it'll be your birthday all right."

"No . . . that's not it," she said with a long sigh.

He fed another log into the fire. The flames hissed, sizzled. Smoke billowed and swirled. The flames shrank back. Quickly he leaned in, blowing with short quick puffs to feed the fire. Outside, he could hear the heavy rain drumming against his brother's windows. Indian summer was definitely over.

"I miss Gerty and Wills," said Katy suddenly.

Ah, so that's it, Anna's children, thought David, easing back on his heels. Last summer Katy's Aunt Anna had run away and taken the children with her. Her husband—Louisa and Mary Ann's brother—was out looking for them now.

"You getting too big to sit on your uncle's lap?" he asked.

She gave him a little smile.

"Come on then. Climb on up."

They watched the birthday preparations in companionable silence: Louisa and Mary Ann mashing potatoes, making gravy, cutting pickles, buttering bread; Katy's eight-year-old sister, Nora, helping their two little brothers drape streamers off the loft; and Emily Inez climbing endlessly up and down the loft ladder, pleased with herself and singing in her own kind of monotone a menagerie of nursery rhymes: "Polly Put the Kettle On," "Little Robin Red Breast," "Ba-a Ba-a Black Sheep." A bedticking sat rumpled on the floor at the foot of the ladder, a permanent fixture ever since the little boys had started sleeping in the loft. Handy as well for "Mynez." She'd already fallen. Twice.

"Wills' birthday was a whole fortnight ago," said Katy quite suddenly. "Same day as when the *Decatur* came in."

"How's that?" mumbled David, comfortable in the cozy warmth of the two families, the smell of good food to come, the steady tick of Mary Ann's fancy grandfather clock in the corner.

Katy twisted a little in his lap to meet his eyes. "We missed his very first birthday, Uncle David. His *very* first. He doesn't even remember us anymore, I bet," and she crossed her arms and flopped back against his chest. "I am desperate to see him, I really am."

He had to smile, she did have her exaggerations. "Maybe Aunt Anna will decide to come home. Do you think?"

"No. She hates Seattle. She hates Uncle Dobbins. She *despises* him. She wishes she'd never married him."

What she said was true, though David didn't agree out loud. Fact was, if water and oil didn't mix, neither did pretty Anna Kays and somber Dobbins Boren. They'd had no business marrying each other, and David actually felt sorry for them. Anna mostly. Being a man's world she suffered the worst. Suddenly Moreover, Mary Ann's black Labrador hound, one eye shut before the fire, snapped to attention, ears perked. Louisa's dog, Watch, one of Moreover's early pups, did the same.

"Pa's here! Pa's home! Time for my party!" screamed Katy, sliding off David's lap and racing for the door. Nora and Rollie and Orion scampered halfway down the ladder, then leaped off midway to avoid knocking Emily Inez into the bedticking.

"Happy birthday, Woodpecker!" sang out Arthur at the door, greeting Katy as she bounded toward him. Wind and rain swirled around his shoulders. The lamp on the table flickered. He stepped in quickly and closed the door, shutting out the wet world.

"You're all wet, Pa! A-a! Even your lips are wet, Pa!"

"My *bones* are wet! A man could wring me out like your ma does the bedsheets on wash day, and get enough rain to take care of the garden all summer."

"You're being silly again," said Nora, squeezing in for her own kiss, squealing too in a fall of rain spilling off Arthur's hat.

"Hey there, Upstart. My, what's all this? A party?" and he leaned over to pick up the little boys, Rollie, three and a half, Orion, two and a half, one in each arm.

"We did it oursel's, Papa," announced Rollie.

Orion plucked his thumb out of his mouth long enough to point out the streamer of gingerbread men hanging off the loft rail.

"You sure did," agreed Arthur, "and a fine job too," but he winked at Nora.

"We're ready to eat," called out Mary Ann, "just as soon as you wash up!"

"I need a few minutes, Mary. Still have a few chores."

"But you're already late!"

"It's all right," reassured Louisa, looking pretty and pink from the heat of the stove. "We can manage."

"It'll go quicker if Dave helps me," said Arthur.

"Right," said David, stirring himself.

He put on his oilskin, wondering what chores had to be done this time of day.

Outside, the rain lashed at their faces and a stinging wind whistled around their ears. "Whew!" whistled David. "It's gotten mean out here!"

"Fat's in the fire," snapped Arthur.

So much for chores. Something had happened. They passed the back corner of the house, apparently headed for Arthur's shed where they could talk without alarming the women and children. David plunged down the narrow, dim trail after his brother, mud sucking at his boots, ferns slapping at his shins and drenching his pants, cedar boughs overhead dropping icy sheets of water down his neck with every gust of wind. Arthur grumbled something about building a covered bridge in his spare time, then shouted over his shoulder, "Mason's made out a warrant for Leschi's arrest!"

David stopped cold in his tracks. "He joined the Yakima?"

"Nope!"

"But—" David got a move on. "If he didn't join the Yakima, then why—Did he commit some kind of crime?" he panted when they reached the shed.

Arthur shot back the door bolt. The chickens inside let out a squawk. Arthur stumbled in. David followed, nostrils pinching shut on the smell of wet feathers.

"He commit some kind of crime?" he repeated.

"Nope," said Arthur from somewhere in the shadows straight ahead. David heard the scratch of a match. "Grab me that lantern, will you?"

Following the line of his brother's chin to somewhere just behind his own left ear, and in the dim light of his brother's single match flame, David spotted a lantern hanging on a

58

tenpenny nail. Even in the near darkness he recognized the rusty lamp as one they'd used on the Oregon Trail.

"Hurry up," grumbled Arthur. "I'm about to burn my fingers here!"

The wick eagerly took the flame. Gigantic shadows climbed up and down the walls.

Burrr, but it's cold, thought David. He rubbed his hands together, then gave it up and shoved his fists up under his warm armpits, listening to the rain beat harshly on the shakes overhead.

Arthur kicked a bale of hay onto its side and sat down, set the lantern on the floor in front. Shadows shifted. "Things are heating up fast, Dave. Mason ordered the volunteers from Vancouver into active service under Major Rains at The Dalles. He sent Olympia's volunteers to Naches Pass after Captain Maloney—and Lieutenant Slaughter if they can find him." Arthur snatched off his cap, raked a hand through his thinning, sandy-blond hair. "I sure hope they find him. Anyway, come Monday, Mason's calling out four more volunteer companies, one *specifically* to go after Leschi."

"What's Mason want with Leschi?"

"Wants to keep him in 'protective custody' while the regulars are gone. Maloney left one squad at the fort, twenty men, maybe. Maybe twenty-five."

"What's this got to do with Leschi?"

Arthur sighed and shook his head. "Since Haller's defeat, too many people figure war or peace this side of the pass hinges on whatever Leschi decides to do. He *is* half Yakima."

"So?"

"That scares folks, Dave!"

"Leschi's not going to do anything! He's waiting for the governor to get back—"

"Yeah?" interrupted Arthur furiously. "So where's he going to do his waiting? Jail—or with his Yakima cousins? Hobson's choice, David! You tell me!"

David's mind suddenly felt crushed under the weight of something too monstrous to believe. From the very beginning Leschi, the wealthy chief of the Nisqually tribe, with his vast herds of cattle and horses and several acres of wheat, had made it clear he'd *never* give up his home or wealth. Nor would he ever allow his people to starve on that barren outcropping of rock the governor had assigned his tribe! *But he'd also made it clear he preferred peace!*

"Mason's not stupid," argued David, trying to explain—though he knew it wasn't Arthur who needed any explaining done. "Mason ought to know that going after Leschi can only force him to take sides! Is he *asking* for war?"

Arthur leaned forward, elbows on his knees, and rubbed the back of his neck with both hands so strongly that his skin turned pink.

"Arthur?"

"That's just not the way he sees it . . ."

David plopped down on the hay bale beside his brother. "How *does* he see it then?"

"Figures if he can hold Leschi hostage it'll take the starch out of his warriors. They'll feel the pinch, he thinks, and put away their war drums."

"It doesn't work that way. It'll only make them madder. It'll *enflame* them!" David found himself staring at the tenpenny nail. Suddenly, among the crushed bits of thought in his mind, he saw the full shape of everything being destroyed. "This is crazy, Arthur! Leschi does *not* want to go to war; he wants peace! He and his elders have been waiting for Stevens to get back, to see about negotiating a new treaty!"

"Well it's not going to happen now!" snarled Arthur with fresh fury, and he snatched a piece of straw off the dirt floor and flung it away from himself.

It was icy cold in the shed. Every word drove the cold deeper into them, and the rain outside kept pummeling the shakes overhead like shot. David started to shiver. "So what's going to happen now?" he finally asked, getting up to walk a bit, to get the blood moving again in his feet.

"I don't know. I thought the White River folk were in danger. Hey, we *all* are. You know what Captain Sterrett just told me?"

David shook his head dully.

"The governor of Oregon just called out *eight* companies. Do you know how many *men* that is?"

Probably a thousand . . .

"And every single one of them is headed for The Dalles!" said Arthur. "Because the whole east side—the Walla Walla, the Cayuse, the Palouse, the Snakes, the Spokane, the Umatilla—they've all joined the Yakima. A regular club," he said sarcastically. "Chief Peo-Peo-Mox-Mox is even boasting to keep Stevens out of Walla Walla or have his scalp. *And now we got Mason going after Leschi?*" Arthur snorted in open scorn. "Mason would do better fighting fire with kerosene!"

An idea played in David's mind. Chief Seattle and Leschi were friends. Kin of sorts. And Seattle hated Owhi and Qualchin, chief and war chief of the Yakima Klikitats, also brother and nephew of Kamiakin, head of the Yakima Nation. If he remembered the story right, years ago Owhi had murdered one of Seattle's kinsmen. In revenge, Seattle and Suwalth had taken five canoes of warriors up White River and in a surprise attack killed ten men without loss to themselves. "Do you think we can get Seattle to help out?" David asked his brother. "Maybe he can talk to Leschi, convince him that further forbearance is the only answer. Discretion the better part of valor . . ."

"Won't hurt to ask, I suppose," grumped Arthur. "But Seattle's satisfied with his own treaty. From his corner there's not much to be gained for the meddling."

"Keeping the peace is to everyone's advantage."

Arthur shrugged.

"Seattle's satisfied, sure," David pressed. "But not all of his subchiefs are. I don't see either Nelson or Suwalth herding their bands over to the peninsula like they're supposed to. And they *are* subject to the treaty terms Chief Seattle signed last spring."

"True . . ."

"But if Seattle can work with Leschi the governor's bound to sit up and take heed. Together they represent probably four or six thousand Indians."

"You have a point."

"Align Seattle and Leschi, Stevens is obliged to listen. Leschi—and Seattle's more agitated bands—can then renegotiate. And I, for one," said David emphatically, "will rest easier knowing Nelson has nothing to complain about. That guy scares me."

"He scares all of us. A regular chameleon. Okay, so when are you going over to see the old man?" Arthur asked, his mental sorting finished.

"*Me?* I can't go over to the peninsula, to Port Madison, not with Louisa in her condition, I can't."

"She looks fine to me."

"I'm not going, Arthur."

"Well I can't go. I don't speak Duwamish."

"What about Doc Maynard?"

"Yeah, great idea, Dave. Is he sober?"

David ignored the jibe.

"Okay, so we'll ask him," Arthur grumbled. Suddenly he slapped his wet cap back onto his head, stood, and picked up the lantern. The eerie shadows tilted and slid across the ribbed walls of the shed. "By the way, I sold my share of the store to Horton and Phillips this morning."

"You what?" The change caught David off guard. "Come again?"

"Sold out."

"Why?" David stammered, hardly able to adjust his thinking.

"Tough times ahead. I don't want to get stuck holding an empty bag. Don't worry, you still have your job."

"But what are you going to do?"

"For starters, get Yoke-Yakemen to help me clear out the burn. Need some kind of meadow for my cattle."

"*Dobbins's* cattle," David reminded his brother.

"Dobbins isn't coming back," said Arthur matter-of-factly, referring to Louisa and Mary Ann's brother who'd gone out looking for his wife and children. "Hey, what are we standing here for? It's Katy's birthday, we have a party. The least we can do is give her a good time." Arthur started for the door, braced himself for the plunge—they could hear the wind whistling outside, waiting for them. "Sorry to dump this on you, Dave. Fact is, when I got home I found myself so hoppin' mad I figured if I didn't leak some steam I'd pop my lid." He blew out the lantern, fumbled along the wall and hung it back up.

"I'm the sacrificial lamb?"

"Sorry."

Cheerful notion, thanks, thought David, following his brother into the storm.

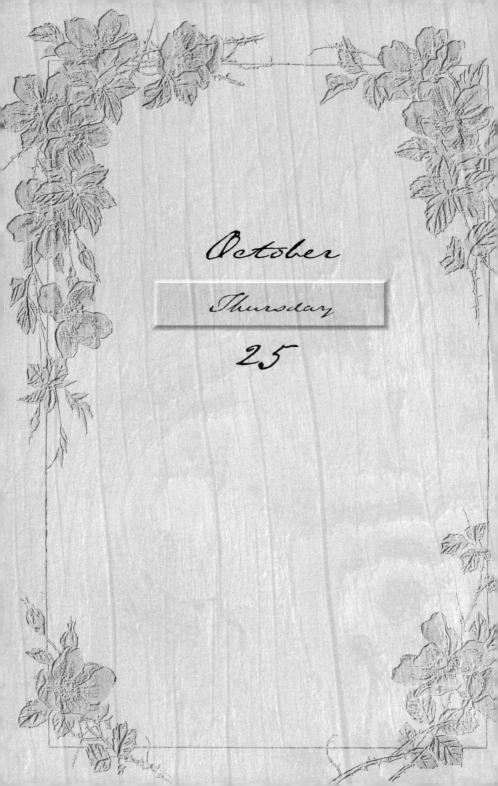

October

Thursday

25

5

afternoon

On request of Captain Maloney, then in command of the United States troops at Fort Steilacoom, Acting Governor Mason, on the 14th of October, 1855, issued a call for two companies of volunteers to operate against the Yakima tribe of Indians, one company to be recruited at Olympia, the other at Vancouver. This was the first official act of the war on the part of the Territory, and was the direct result of the defeat of Haller by the Yakima Indians. . . .

On the 22nd of October Governor Mason again issued his proclamation, this time calling for four additional companies. . . .

—Ezra Meeker, pioneer and historian
in *Pioneer Reminiscences*

*O*ver the next four days Louisa watched with growing anxiety the threat of war escalate, drawing ever closer, and involving more and more people. The regular army had gone out to meet Major Rains east of the mountains; the two volunteer companies as well. Monday last Mr. Mason had posted another call for four more, and several were mustering in. A second company in Olympia, one in Steilacoom, three in Vancouver, one in Grand Mound, one in Port Townsend. Wednesday, forty men in Seattle signed up for their three months of service—including David. *This isn't supposed to be happening,* Louisa kept thinking. *Major Haller is supposed to have stopped Kamiakin. We're supposed to be going home!*

The very sound of the word brought tears to her eyes, and suddenly she wanted to be at home more than anything else in the world. Home in her dear new house in the Swale, embraced by the luxuriant meadow, her gardens, the awesome view of Mount Rainier to the south. Home, where at any moment Madeline and Salmon Bay Curley might stop by for a visit—or one of Uncle Tommy Mercer's girls might yoo-hoo across the creek and come running through the grass with a basket for eggs.

But home wasn't going to happen. Not now, not with "Haller's Defeat." For the first time Louisa realized just how much she'd been banking on Major Haller to stop the Yakima war, yet the Yakima had triumphed, and now David said there were even more Indians—the Walla Walla, the Cayuse, the Palouse, *even several tribes from Oregon!* Indians *everywhere* seemed to be rising up, and with each new rumor the prospects of going home diminished. *And if Major Rains is defeated?* she wondered, worrying, fear attaching itself to her like a shadow, lengthening and darkening with each passing hour.

As for Leschi, she dare not think of his arrest. But she couldn't help it. *Was it done? Or had he escaped?* If he *was* caught, would the Nisqually retaliate? If he escaped would he really go and help Kamiakin? *Or would he rally his own warriors?* She nearly dropped her cup of flour all over the floor and herself. *Would he start his own war?*

She tried reminding herself that Chief Seattle might yet have a solution. Doc Maynard had gone to find out. *But was it already too late?*

So many questions, persistent and unrelenting, and behind it all the nagging, horrible fear—*this is only the beginning.*

Company H in Seattle elected Christopher Hewitt, Seattle's newest attorney, captain. David Neely, whose wife had insisted only the day before that he remove them from their claim on lower White River back into Seattle, was made first lieutenant. John Henning became sergeant, David Denny corporal. Louisa knew how deeply Arthur would like to join them, but he'd been elected to the House for the third time in a row and would be leaving for Olympia in a few weeks. First of December the territory's third Legislative Assembly would convene, and so he was excluded from military service and regretfully stood on the sidelines, watching, while the others began their training under the guidance of Captain Sterrett's four lieutenants.

Oddly, a few of the settlers, led by Misters Wetmore and Woodin, owners of the tannery up on Mr. Yesler's Skid Road, stubbornly maintained that Indian trouble in these parts was unlikely. They refused to participate, and they derided the majority in an attempt to justify their position. Louisa hoped and prayed they were right. Though she couldn't help but notice that the Do-Nothings weren't as adamant as before. Haller's defeat and the news that Leschi was to be arrested had given them something to think about.

As for herself, this long week following Katy's birthday was one of ominous adjustment as she fought back her fear that grew stronger each day. How welcome the propitious arrival of the *Decatur* had been. How comforting to hear the marines make their rounds and call out "all's well" at each sentry post. But now? Listening to her own husband and other men she knew well, drilling, training for defense?

"Squads, left wheel!"

"Company, halt!"

"Present arms!"

Lieutenant Drake's commands came up off the hill, echoing and reechoing through the trees; and as she went about her daily tasks of scrubbing and cooking and cleaning she found that she leaned into the scrub board and punched down the bread and swept with her broom to the beat of each command. "Squads, left wheel!" *Punch.* "Company, halt!" *Sweep.* "Present arms!" *Scrub.* She tried fighting the rhythm with a hymn, with memorized Scripture or poetry. It was almost a relief when the shouting stopped and target practice began; at least the crack of gunfire was sporadic.

Things took a dark turn in her mind when David came home Thursday afternoon with the news that most of Seattle's men didn't have working guns or ammunition. The majority had let their supply of ammunition run low. Over a period of time, many had even given their rifles and muskets to the Indians in exchange for fresh game.

The four stores on Commercial Street, he confided, were low as well. Nearly everything in way of arms and ammunition had gone into eastern Washington with the gold miners the previous summer. "Dexter Horton says he put Dave Phillips on the *John Hancock* for San Francisco today. They've decided to buy up what they can, with what money they have. But until he gets back, the Indians probably have more guns than we do."

She didn't want to think about that. "Do you suppose Arthur regrets selling his interest in the store?" she asked instead, looking up from her ironing to watch David clean his rifle, parts and pieces laid out on the hearth.

"If Dexter and Dave make money I expect he will."

"Oh!" she said, suddenly remembering, "did Charles Terry get away?" Charles and his brother Lee were part of the original pioneers. Mossbacks, the newcomers called them now—though none knew Lee. He'd left not long after he and David had built that first cabin over at Alki.

70

David looked up, gave her a puzzled look.

"Don't you remember? Lee's got consumption. Charles has been fixing things so he can get back to New York before he dies?"

"Sorry . . . wasn't listening. Yes, he got off all right. Said to say good-bye." David blew down through the muzzle. "You know, Liza, the way things are going I wonder if it isn't a good idea for *us* to board some boat and get away."

She pushed the tip of her iron into the rumpled corner of a hanky, fighting the tears that came all too easily these days. Get away, where? *Oregon?* If anything, it was worse down there. *California?* With what money? She folded the hanky, lay it aside, and took another from the ironing basket.

A half-mile north of town, deep into the woods, Captain Sterrett of the *Decatur* stepped into a burn. "Hey, Denny!" he hollered. Arthur Denny followed through with his swing, ax blade whacking into the smooth bark of the alder he was trying to fell. He gave a quick back yank to clear the blade. Only then did he look up.

"Hey, there, Captain Sterrett!" he rejoindered. Dusk lingered. In the sky to the southeast, a point or two off the captain's right shoulder, Mount Rainier glimmered pearly gray, holding fast to the last rays of sunlight.

"Looking real good out here!" Sterrett hollered out to Arthur, coming on and casting an approving eye over the cleaned-up acreage Arthur and his hired hand, Yoke-Yakeman, had been working on all week. "How long before you get some real grass growing in here, do you think?"

Arthur laughed. "If I was to bet what comes up first, grass or alder—" He hit the skinny tree beside him with the blunt end of his ax. "—I'd put my money on *these* weeds any day of the week!"

"They're pretty trees," commented the captain.

"Yeah? Well, maybe so, but they take over worse than the blackberries, and I got to have some space for my cows to have a stretch. But you didn't come all the way out here to inspect my burn. What's up?"

The captain glanced over at Yoke-Yakeman. For a moment he studied the squarely built Snoqualmie man piling more and more brush onto a roaring fire. Obviously a hard worker—and a conscientious one. He was of medium height, twenty-three or four years old, a broad face, intelligent eyes. He wore a hickory shirt and Kentucky jeans similar to Arthur's—tucked into moccasins "Californy" style. Unlike Arthur, he wore the round conical grass hat common amongst the Indians instead of a white man's woolen toque. "Well," the captain said, turning his gaze back to Arthur, "I'd like to have a word with you if I may. Privately."

"Whatever you have to say to me, you can say with Yoke-Yakeman around."

Sterrett hesitated.

"Have a seat," said Arthur with just enough shortness in his voice to let the captain know there was no arguing. He pointed out a fallen log and sat down himself. "Must be pretty important for you to come all the way out here."

Sterrett sat. "Just how far out are we?" he asked, still uncomfortable about talking in front of Yoke-Yakeman, though the man seemed to be paying no mind, his energies focused instead on the task at hand.

"Oh . . . half-mile or more. See down yonder?" Arthur spoke with pride, and pointed west, southwest. "'Course, in this light you might not be able to see it. But out on that bluff is my *first* cabin." He laughed suddenly and took off his toque, mopped his brow, and slapped the hat back on. "You know, when I platted this, I had that little house sitting right on 'Spring Street.' And see up there?" He pointed west, northwest. "'Bout where Yoke-Yakeman is now?"

"Yeah."

"Near as I can figure, that'll be the intersection of Pike Street and First Avenue someday. Yes, sir," said Arthur with keen satisfaction, "whenever I come out here, I can see it all.

We're just waiting for that transcontinental railroad. Once that comes through, and terminates here on the Sound, this town'll turn into a seaport overnight. We got the shortest route to China, the deepest harbor on the west coast. Sure as God watches us all, this'll be a major shipping center someday!" Arthur proudly swept his hand over the burn. "Can't you see it, sir? Bigger even than New York? Ah, but until then," he said, reality catching up to his dreams, "it's a good place to feed my cows. But hey, we're gabbing again and you've got something entirely different on your mind."

"I do."

"Spit it out, sir."

"All right then. Your acting governor's ordered me to arrest Pat Kanim's brothers. And any other Snoqualmie men in town. He wants them put in irons."

Agog, Arthur swung around on the log to face the captain directly.

"I know, I know," said Sterrett, holding up his hands in agreed confusion. "Which is why I've held off. But Mason's insisting. Wait, hear me out, he does have a reason. Though I did want to run it all by you before doing anything so drastic."

"Drastic!" Arthur managed to blurt out. "That's hardly the word! What's gotten into Mason anyway? Arresting everyone peacefully disposed! He's got so many brush fires started we'll have a regular forest fire on our hands!"

"End of September, Slaughter sent word down to Mason saying that Chief Pat Kanim was harassing his soldier boys every night," blurted out the navy captain. "Spooking his horses. Firing into their camp. Howling and yipping and I guess generating an all-round rumpus. Mason didn't think much of it at the time—so long as not much more than that was going on—but when he was here and saw all those Snoqualmie camped on the Point he got to thinking. And now, since Haller's defeat, and no one's heard from Slaughter—"

73

"He's thinking that if Kamiakin didn't meet up with Slaughter, and wipe him out," Arthur interrupted, "Pat Kanim did?"

"Well . . . it's possible . . ."

Arthur shook his head in disgust.

"He's of the opinion that if I arrest the Snoqualmie boys it'll force Pat Kanim to withdraw."

"Now why doesn't that surprise me?" said Arthur angrily.

"Well, that's why I wanted to talk with you. You seem to be the only one with a pulse on what the Indians are doing around here."

Arthur stared past Yoke-Yakeman to the setting sun. Dusk was coming on fast. "Then you need to believe me when I say Pat Kanim's nowhere near Lieutenant Slaughter."

"Where is he?"

"Steilaguamish River, to hunt bighorn sheep."

"You're certain?"

"Of course I am! Last summer Pat Kanim came by the house on several occasions to warn me of trouble ready to break. Late August he stopped in to say things were about to rip, that he was taking his people up to the Steilaguamish, out of the way. He had no wish, he said, to get entangled in any conflict between his race and ours. None whatsoever."

"Where's Steilaguamish River?"

"Three days north. Maybe four. About as far from trouble as he could get without bumping into the Lummi and Sno-homish up near Bellingham Bay."

"Yet his brothers are here in Seattle."

"Yes," agreed Arthur. "Because Pat Kanim was worried about the Haida. He had his brothers bring the women and children down for safe keeping, plus some of their less able-bodied men. Figured here in Seattle they'd be out of harm's way."

"Nice arrangement," commented the captain dourly. "We look out for his women and children while he and his warriors raise cain on the battlefield?"

"That, sir, is grossly unfair."

"Just looking at every angle."

"Then look at this one. The Haida have been prowling the Sound in big numbers all fall—as you know. What you don't know is that since we settled in this area the Indians have come to depend upon us to keep the Haida in line. Chief Seattle on down—including Pat Kanim."

"Fear of the Haida I understand. Scared of 'em myself," Sterrett grinned suddenly.

"If you don't mind my saying so," said Arthur, "we have enemies enough to look after without attacking our friends. And I *know* Pat Kanim. His word is sterling. What he says I'd endorse with my life."

"You seem to feel strongly—"

"I do. As to why, shall I give you an example?"

"Do."

"Two years ago a man was murdered out on my brother's claim. Turned out to be a white man, with a couple of Snoqualmie boys responsible. Pat Kanim, of his own accord, brought them in to see that justice was done. I regret to say it was not. Pat Kanim would have been perfectly entitled to turn on us. He did not. Another time, last winter, he led me to yet another murdered man. A case of retaliation this time, Indian against white. Only this time we couldn't determine the murderer. Nonetheless, it was Pat Kanim who—"

"I get the picture. Do you have any suggestions? As to what I can do to keep Mason happy, without throwing a snake into an ant's nest?"

"I'm willing to accept full responsibility for their actions."

"That doesn't do me any good if someone gets killed up on the pass."

"Suppose I prove Slaughter wrong about Pat Kanim."

"How?"

"I go out to his camp, bring him in."

Captain Sterrett leaped to his feet. "I can't have you risking your head!"

Arthur stood. "It's no risk."

"How about sending one of your Indians instead?"

"I suppose," said Arthur. "You got anything against Yoke-Yakeman, Sir?"

Yoke-Yakeman, sensing he was under discussion, paused and looked up, dusk and shadows racing over his face.

"No, I guess not. Not if you don't," said Sterrett. "How soon can he have Pat Kanim here?"

"Steilaguamish River!" hollered Arthur over to Yoke-Yakeman. "Pat Kanim's camp! How long? There and back?"

Yoke-Yakeman propped his rake against a darkened tree and ambled over, hands in his pockets. "A week?" he guessed. "Ten days?"

"Will that work for you, Captain?" Arthur asked.

"That'll work."

October

Friday

26

6

moon

On the Friday preceding the outbreak Nelson, one of the chief men of the Indians in the vicinity, came to visit us. I remember that that day he was unusually quiet and uncommunicative. Mother kept on with her household duties, passing before and around him, as occasion required. His talk was mostly in monosyllables, and then only in reply to some question or suggestion. Finally he left, and said in mixed Indian and English, that "it would not be very long until Indian be gone and white man have all the land around here."

—Dr. John King, written years later
to Ezra Meeker, pioneer and historian

*T*he fear that the Indians might have more weapons than the settlers was confirmed the very next day when James Tilton, territorial surveyor general, now adjutant general for the volunteers, arrived in Seattle to ask Captain Sterrett for the loan of whatever arms could be spared from the *U.S. Decatur.*

"The whole Sound is short," David announced to Louisa glumly when he and a new friend from the *Decatur* came up to the house at noon to report Tilton's arrival and request. "Even Fort Steilacoom has only four hundred rounds of ammunition."

"Was Captain Sterrett able to help at all?" Louisa asked, feeling her nerves begin to fray. She sat on a footstool next to the woodbox, and with her wrists she rubbed the thin film of perspiration from her forehead. All morning, desperate to keep her mind off the "Squads, left wheel!" coming uphill from the Sawdust, she'd arranged and rearranged her cramped little "inside" house—as if by merely shuffling furniture she could, in some way, shuffle the bigger things beyond her domicile. "Are you eating with us today?" she asked the young middy.

"Well now, Ma'am—" The middy hid a self-conscious grin. "—your husband did say something mighty fine about your clam chowder."

"I don't know that my chowder is any different from Mrs. Horton's down at the cookhouse, Mr. Corbine."

"Well now, Ma'am, if you say," though he smiled conspiratorially at David.

David had thrown himself onto the bed and was staring overhead at the cedar shakes, the hanging onion bunches, the jerked venison, drumming his thumbs against his chest. Emily Inez tried to climb up beside him; absentmindedly he reached to help her.

"*Was* the captain able to help out?" Louisa repeated. Her fingers, she noticed, trembled on the soup ladle.

"If yer talkin' 'bout Cap'n Sterrett, then yes sir, Ma'am," said Corbine, sliding loosely into the rocking chair by the fire. "Muskets, carbines, pistols, swords, percussion caps, carbine ball cartridges, pistol ball cartridges. Just about gave away the store. Why thankee, Ma'am, this does smell good."

The list frightened her. *So much weaponry, and its only purpose to kill.* "There's biscuits and coffee," she said. "Help

80

yourself. Mynez? Climb down now, darling. Father has to eat."

"But Mynez not hungry."

David rubbed her head. "That may be, Missy Mynez-Inez, but *I'm* hungry." He swung her off the bed, dropping both his feet onto the floor beside her. "You can sit on my lap, if you want, and lick the spills off my shirt."

"You're spoiling her," warned Louisa.

"Of course." He tweaked her ear on his way past.

She waved him off and went back to the footstool. With a critical eye she gazed at her morning's work. Maybe if she lined the shelving in the corner with some white muslin it would lighten things a little. She caught Corbine watching her. "My ma," she told him, "says change is good for the soul."

He flashed a smile. "That's right, Ma'am. And my ma says, change for changie. Turn a back parlor into a front kitchen."

She laughed. It felt wonderful.

David said, "We ran into Suwalth on the way up. He says Leschi eluded Eaton's Rangers—"

"He *did?* Where? How?" she asked excitedly. Then, *"Who're Eaton's Rangers?"*

"The volunteer company ordered to arrest Leschi. But Leschi gave them the slip two days ago," David went on while her heart pounded and the laughter died in her throat. She said nothing. Her eyes must have begged the question, though, for David answered, "No, he's not with the Yakima. Not yet anyway."

She swallowed, and managed, "Where then?"

"Holed up in the foothills, no doubt."

"Lit out so fast," Corbine told her from his side of the small room, "he left everything behind. His cattle, his horses. Even his plow. Went and left it standing midfurrow."

"Which means he'd been in the middle of fall plowing," said David. "Does that sound like insurrection to you?"

She felt a little weak all of a sudden.

81

"So now Mason's figured out—" David spoke bitterly, his mouth full, "—that Leschi's intentions were peaceful by driving him to war."

"But we don't know he's gone to war!" she countered. "Maybe he's just hiding!"

"Oh, he's hiding," agreed Corbine, "and if he's smart he'll stay that way. Mason's ordered the Rangers to keep after him. Charlie Eaton even helped himself to fifteen of Leschi's thoroughbreds to make things easier—"

"They're using his own horses to capture him?" interrupted Louisa, amazed and startled at the same time.

"They do mean to goad the bee's nest, don't they, Ma'am."

"And if they keep it up," added David, "Leschi and his warriors won't have any choice but to strike back."

"But has he any warriors?" argued Louisa. "It's all just rumors!"

Corbine suddenly stood up, and took his bowl over to Louisa's wash basin. "I do thankee, Ma'am. Dave, you comin' back with me?"

David slurped up the last of his chowder, grabbed a biscuit and shoved it into a pocket. He eased Emily Inez over to her own chair. Louisa just had to ask. "Do you think the Brannans might come into town then, David? The Neelys did."

"The farmers on the upper river, Liza, have no idea what's going on. The Brannans, the Kings, the Joneses—they live too far out. But I expect Elizabeth is safe enough," he added, heading out the door after Corbine.

"Why do you say that?"

"The Indians have too much respect for the Hudson's Bay. They'll never hurt anyone English."

"But what about Will? He's *Boston,* like the rest of us."

David hollered after Corbine to wait up a minute, then stepped back into the room. He pulled Louisa to her feet. Gently, firmly, he cupped her face in his hands. "Don't borrow trouble. One day at a time. Remember?"

"But the days are adding up!" she broke out, fighting her tears, her anger, her fears, everything that was keeping her family from getting on with their lives. "It's almost the end of the month and Arthur said that if the White River settlers went home—"

"Shh!"

"What about Nelson?" Her nerves were fraying so fast she *couldn't* be quiet. "This business with Leschi is only going to infuriate him! You know how he is! Remember when he and Pat Kanim—"

"That was a long time ago."

"What if he and Leschi—" She stopped cold, horrified by the very thought. "Oh, David, what if Nelson *and* Leschi join forces?"

"No 'what ifs'! We've said that, we promised each other!"

"Oh, but David, if they—"

He silenced her by setting his finger against her lips.

Her nerves snapped. She grabbed his hand and pulled it away. "It's the end of the month! And Arthur said, he said if they went home they'd all be killed!"

The pain-filled look in David's eyes made her spin around. Emily Inez sat woodenly in her chair. Instantly Louisa regretted her panic. She pulled Emily Inez into her arms and with trembling fingers brushed her daughter's soft brown curls away from her round little face. "It's all right, darling, it's all right."

"Mama scared?" whimpered Emily Inez, looking to David uncertainly, her bottom lip wet and quivering.

"Yes, Mother was scared," agreed Louisa. "But not anymore. See?" and she smiled. Playfully she hugged Emily Inez and kissed her sweet little nose to make her forget the tension. She fluffed her daughter's hair and hugged her again. *If it weren't for the* Decatur *anchored offshore—Why oh why?* she wondered in fresh worry, hugging and kissing her daughter. *Why won't Will bring Elizabeth in where it's safe?*

"Louisa, don't," cautioned David.

He was right, she had to stop this. For Emily Inez's sake. She forced a smile to her face. "David, go back to work. I'll be fine. *We'll* be fine. Don't worry."

"What will you do?"

"We'll visit Widow Holgate. She's always a balm for the soul."

David nodded.

"Oh, kiss me!" she said brightly, "and be off! Corbine's waiting for you!"

Worry stirred in his eyes.

"I'm fine," she insisted. "Just kiss me, do that and I promise to be fine!"

His kiss, though, when it came lightly, sweetly, to her lips, was so cold she shivered. David, she understood now, was more alarmed than she.

Twenty miles away in a rich grassy meadow bordering the circled loop of White River, where the river all but turned around on itself, stood a prosperous orchard and farm. A mossy log cabin hugged the high riverbank just after the river made its pigtail turn. Used now as a storage shed, this one-room cabin was where Harvey Jones and his family had lived two years ago when first getting started. Now they lived in a large frame house a few rods to the north, surrounded by a vast orchard of 2,500 fruit trees.

The family consisted of Harvey and Eliza Jones; six-year-old Johnny King, a son from Eliza's first marriage; and the Jones's two small children, a little girl not yet four years old and a boy not quite two. Enos Cooper lived there too and helped Mr. Jones with the work; and for neighbors they had the Brannans on an adjoining claim to the south, Mr. Lake on a claim directly west, away from the river, and George and Martha King and their five-year-old son—no relation to Johnny King—to the north. The Thomases lived even farther north—two miles.

Their other neighbors were the Muckleshoots, a dirty, rough-mannered tribe, many of them untidy, even repulsive. They often stopped at the fancy house near the river loop. They rarely knocked; instead, they made questioning grunts until someone opened the door and let them in. Then they'd sit around visiting or poke their noses into whatever captured their interests, always eating whatever tidbit of food Mrs. Jones might offer them.

Their chief, Pialse, was a stocky man the Hudson's Bay Company had nicknamed Nelson years before. He didn't look much like a chief for he habitually clothed himself in dirty blankets, and his long, unbraided hair was permanently matted. But he was a friendly sort of man, usually, in a restrained sort of way. He was intelligent. He spoke English. And he had money, for the Hudson's Bay Company, even some of the settlers, employed him to run errands up and down the rivers. And if Nelson resented Harvey Jones and Enos Cooper as intruders on Muckleshoot Prairie he never let on.

But this last Friday of October his visit to the large frame house on the river loop struck Mrs. Jones as being remarkably different. She was baking bread in her big Dutch oven— one loaf at a time—when he arrived. Bread was a treat for her guests, yet when she offered a slice to Nelson he simply grunted *wake*, no, and continued to sit on the bench by the fire, staring into the flames, hugging his Hudson's Bay flintlock musket between his knees.

"Have you been hunting?" she asked, trying to draw him out.

"*Wake.*"

She gave up. Nothing more said, she worked around him, trying hard not to let his sullen demeanor alarm her. He stayed longer than his usual half hour, but when he finally left, he paused a moment at each child and gently rested his hands on their heads. But like everything else about his visit today, so at odds to his normal, the words he spoke belied the kindly gesture. "Soon the Siwash will be gone and the *Bostons* will have all the land," he said with bitterness feeding each word.

"My stars, whatever is the matter with him?" gasped a distraught Eliza the moment Nelson was gone.

Johnny looked up from his slate. "I expect he's sad, Mother."

Eliza bit fearfully down on her bottom lip, so hard she broke the skin and tasted blood. *Sad turns mad.* This is what her first husband, Mr. King, used to say. Even a whining dog, he said, will in the end bare its teeth. Eliza King Jones lifted her heavy Dutch oven off the fire and with suffocating fear set another loaf of bread on the table to cool.

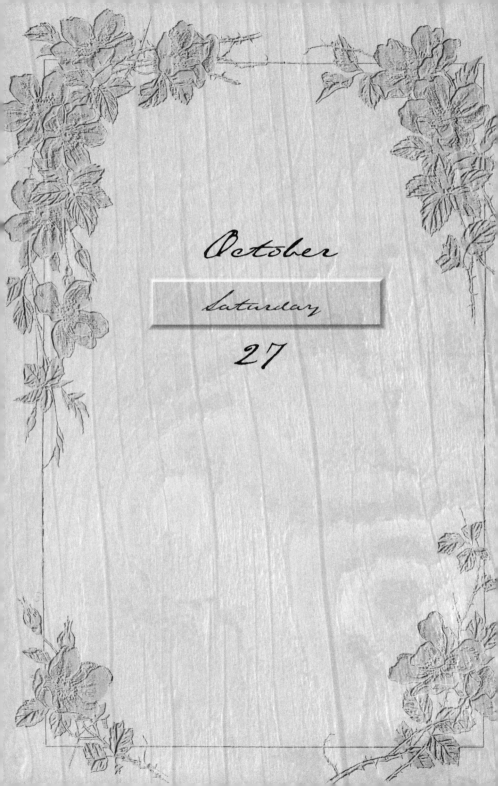

October

Saturday

27

7

midday

The company left Mr. Eaton's, nineteen strong, on the 24th inst., in quest of the whereabouts of Leschi, a Nisqually chief, half Klikitat, and whom, it was apprehended, had for some time been preparing his band for active hostilities against the settlements. Leschi is an Indian of more than ordinary wealth and power. He is in possession of farming land, which he has heretofore cultivated, near the Nisqually River, between Packwood's Ferry and the crossing of that stream at Yelm. He has some good, substantial houses on his place. As Eaton's command passed his farm, the command found that the bird had flown . . .

—J. W. Wiley, editor
Pioneer and Democrat, October 30, 1855

The first day's pursuit of Leschi, Wednesday the 24th of October, had taken Eaton's nineteen Rangers up Muck Creek to where Leschi had his ranch and farm, then north over the Nisqually plains. They'd ended up that night out at Frank Montgomery's big log cabin, all but sitting atop

Military Road eight miles shy of the Puyallup River. In the morning, Thursday the 25th, Eaton took the road east, into the interior country. Because soldiering was new to his boys and the road so bad, it took them most of the day to cover their eight miles, wade the milky Puyallup, then finally, after another mile or two, reach the first real uplands.

But here, in the uplands, was a view. Standing on the crest of Elhi Hill in the shadows of an abandoned cabin on Bitting's Prairie, and looking down onto the broad valley below, a man could see for miles. Autumn's yellows and russets stretched mile after mile, reaching back to the Sound and the evening's brilliant sunset. *This is a sight that can stir a man into thinking it country worth fighting for,* Jim McAllister thought to himself that pearly evening of the 25th. But he knew there was no need to fight. Which was why he was riding with the Rangers. Fact was, he'd been friends with Leschi far too long to let things get out of hand like this. If he could but find Leschi and explain things, they could all go home and relax.

Right after sunrise the next morning, the 26th, Eaton had divided their group into two sets of ten. Eaton led one group, McAllister the other. They spent all day Friday searching both sides of the Puyallup, upstream and down, but when night came on, no Leschi. No sign of *any* Indian, for that matter.

It was Saturday morning, the 27th, when Eaton sent five of his crew back to Olympia with the mule train for more grub, and three other men, on foot, to Grand Mound for more recruits. He sent the Indian scout—Stahi, Leschi's brother-in-law—up the road to report back anything remotely smelling Indian. The remaining men, with nothing else to do, took opportunity to strip down and scrub the previous day's mud from their clothes. A thin sun held, giving just enough warmth to tempt them to go naked while their shirts and trousers decorated nearby huckleberry bushes, and bent the boughs of one or two low-lying salal shrubs.

Midafternoon, Eaton was just giving his corduroys another feel to see if they were dry when Stahi trotted back into camp.

"Found Leschi!" Stahi reined in at the cabin—nothing more than a cage of unpeeled logs with a roof. The young Nisqually slid effortlessly off his spotted Cayuse. "Camped up at Connell's!"

"They're holed up at my place?" burst out Mike Connell—like he wasn't quite sure he believed it, or maybe didn't want to believe it.

Eaton grabbed his cords off the huckleberry bushes. Dry or not, he shoved one leg in. "You're sure it's Leschi? Hey, McAllister! Come over here!" he yelled, hopping up and down on the one leg, fighting his damp trousers. "Stahi's found our man!"

"Camped on the far side, down by the river crossing," Stahi explained, breathless but in perfect English, when McAllister, dragging his wet clothes with him, got close enough to hear. "Leschi, Quiemuth, and a whole bunch of Puyallup. Even some Green River Klikitat."

"Klikitat?" yelped Eaton, forgetting his fight with his trousers. "You saying we got Yakima over here now?"

"Just a small band. They live in the headwaters," said Stahi with a shrug. "Kanasket's bunch."

"How many warriors, do you think?" McAllister asked while gingerly poking his arm into a wet, wrinkled shirtsleeve.

"Altogether? All the tribes? Hundred maybe," Stahi answered.

"Usual mob? Kids, women, dogs?" questioned Mike Connell, and McAllister thought he could see the cogs turning inside Connell's brain, trying to figure how many carrots and beets might be left by the time all this was over.

Stahi nodded.

"So maybe thirty warriors," murmured Eaton. "What are they doing up there?"

"Fishing."

"He's lying," said Clipwalen suddenly, squeezing in beside McAllister.

"There's no reason to disbelieve him," said McAllister, turning sternly to the seventeen-year-old Chehalis boy he'd raised for ten years.

"I tell you, he's lying!"

"Nope, fishing," insisted Stahi. "Good place. All you need's a bucket."

"But if Leschi and Quiemuth have *Klikitat* with 'em," debated Eaton, his russet, freckled face puckered in thought.

"I told you," said Stahi, "only a small band."

Charlie Eaton's bushy red eyebrows knit over the bridge of his blistered nose. Suddenly he hitched his britches. "Don't like it," he said, buckling his belt. "A trained soldier couldn't have picked a better spot on the Sound—if his aim was to aid the Indians, that is."

"How so?" asked Jim McAllister.

"Where Leschi's sitting now? Why, he's got command of the only road through the mountains. He's sitting on Maloney's rear, blocking supplies or reinforcements needing to go through. And if Maloney meets defeat? God forbid," Eaton hastily added. "No one'll get back through alive! It'll leave the road wide open to hostiles from both sides of the mountains! No, sir, Leschi picked Connell's place on purpose. He aims to fight, all right."

"You mean *you* aim to fight."

"You're darned right I do! Though I think it best we wait until we get our own reinforcements. No sense stirring up trouble we can't handle. Thirty warriors . . ."

McAllister wiggled his other arm into another wet sleeve. "Bring in the cat, Eaton, you scare the mouse."

"What's that supposed to mean?"

"The Nisqually aren't fighters, Eaton. There's no need to bring in the guns. They're the most peaceful tribe on the Sound. So gentle I could lead them over a cliff—"

"Yeah, yeah," interrupted Eaton, waving his hand at McAllister. "You can lead them over a cliff with nothing more than a cane—they're so meek and mild. We've heard it all before."

"Well it's the truth," said McAllister defensively. Then, "Come on, Eaton. Let me just talk to Leschi. I'll explain what's what, why we need his cooperation. Let me do that and I reckon we can all go home tonight."

"I'll take you!" Stahi offered, leaping quickly onto the back of his spotted pony.

"It's a trap, don't you see?" implored Clipwalen, turning now to Eaton.

"I don't like it, McAllister," Eaton agreed. "Don't like it all."

"Even if it *is* a trap," answered McAllister, determined to seize the opportunity and make of it what he could. "Leschi's not going to shoot me. I'm Nisqually myself. He adopted me into the tribe. We're brothers, he and I."

"McAllister," warned Eaton. "You are *not* going."

"I'm going as a friend. No harm in that. Here, take my rifle."

"No harm if you don't mind getting your head blown off."

"It's my head."

"I won't allow it!" huffed Eaton, getting redder and redder in the face.

McAllister started to chuckle for he could see Eaton's freckles turning green from his pinking up. "Hey, don't worry, Eaton. Don't forget, I know these Indians. I've lived with them ten years. I know Leschi. He's no renegade. He's a law-abiding man—"

"I know what he is!" exploded Eaton all of a sudden, so mad he didn't realize he'd accepted McAllister's gun. "I've lived here *eleven* years! And I'm *married* to his daughter, aren't I?"

At that McAllister laughed right out. "Which is why *I'm* going and not you, Charlie! I don't have to worry about my wife not talking to me when I get home!" All the men laughed at that. Eaton sputtered. McAllister slapped him smartly across the shoulder blades and started over to the horses hobbled a few hundred feet away. He turned around. "Eaton, I'm willing to take a chance on going in alone in hopes we can avoid war our side of the mountains. If it's worth the risk to me, what's the skin off your nose?"

"You come back here. I'm the captain. I order you to come back!"

Suddenly Eaton was holding Mike Connell's rifle as well. "Hey! Where do you think *you're* going?"

Connell shrugged. "He needs someone to ride with him."

Eaton gaped in disbelief. *"There's a war on!"*

"Not yet! Not unless you start one!" hollered McAllister, still headed for the horses but easily overhearing Eaton.

"It's my place," explained Connell to Eaton. "I know the country. Jim don't."

McAllister heard that too. "Connell, you saying I can't follow a road without falling off it?"

Connell laughed suddenly. "If I thought so, McAllister, why, I'd have Eaton come along! He and me, one on each side, keeping your sorry carcass right side up!"

McAllister chuckled and shook his head. "Well, come on then. If you're coming."

Five minutes later the remaining Rangers, just nine of their original nineteen, stared as two more of their number headed out.

"You're doing this against orders!" shouted Eaton one more time. "All right then, McAllister! Sundown! Do you hear me? *Sundown!* I want you here by *sundown!*"

McAllister turned around and waved. "I will! If alive!"

October

Sunday

28

8

predawn

Louisa threw her arms around her friend. "It's a lovely thought . . . straight from God, I think!"

"We *will* meet again, Liza! If not here, on the other side."

Louisa nodded, tears streaming down her face. She hugged her friend for the last time, then turned and ran. The seeds were fisted tightly in her hand, and when she had passed through the gate she stopped and opened out the cloth. The seeds, the promise of spring, of life, lay in a small heap, so tiny and insignificant. Quietly she made her decision—she would place the seeds between the pages of her Bible until she reached the Promised Land of the West.

—Brenda Wilbee
in *Sweetbriar*

he very next morning, Sunday the 28th, Louisa awoke disoriented. One minute her dearest friend and springtime, the next a chilly autumn morning lying in bed with her dear husband. For awhile she lay quietly in this mix of time and distance. The dream had been so real she could still smell Pamelia's sweetbriar. Yet she could smell the sea as well. Two lives, coexistent? Then, now? Illinois, Puget Sound? Half-consciously she knew she'd been here before, caught between the two worlds. Always in her mind a road led back home and to all of yesterday. Yet the road led forward as well and sometimes in sleep she got turned around. She waited as gradually the worlds separated. She was here. Here in Puget Sound—staring at her ceiling layered in shadow.

The sun was obviously not up, the cabin dark, and now that she was fully awake, fearfully cold. The fire, banked the night before, glimmered red with coals that gave scant warmth. She slipped from the covers, shivered in the waiting chill, and reached for her shawl.

In the past this had always been her favorite time of day: David asleep; Emily Inez curled in her trundle bed; the world quiet, not even the gulls awake and cawing. She liked the solitude, the time alone to think. But lately all she'd been able to do upon rising was wonder in fear what the day might bring. Today as she let the dog out, then stoked the fire and started the coffee, she deliberately put the worry from her mind and thought instead of Pamelia. Their sweetbriar, their tryst.

To her death Louisa would remember the date, April 10, 1851. For that was the day she and her dearest friend on earth had parted. How their hearts had nearly broken, and oh! how they'd wept! How they'd clung to each other, neither able to say good-bye, the terrible word that would separate them forever—until Louisa remembered the sweetbriar seeds they'd gathered and saved the year before. "You have them in your bureau!" she excitedly told Pamelia. "Give me half! As soon as I get my own home in the Promised Land I'll plant them and send word to you, then you can plant yours! It'll be a tryst between us! In that way we'll never, truly, be apart!"

A tryst it had been. Tucked into the pages of her Bible, Louisa had safely carried her portion of seeds to the Promised Land—to Puget Sound. When she married, David took her out to the claim. There she planted the precious seeds on both sides of their cabin door. And last spring when she and David moved out to the Swale, deeper into the woods, away from the sea, she'd taken the sweetbriar with her. Now the transplanted bushes grew in front of her pretty new home, all along the porch railing. *"Sweetbriar will always bloom, Louisa! Spring will always come!"* Pamelia had said when they'd last embraced. *"We'll not be parted forever! Joy will follow our sorrow, we shall meet again. If not here, on the other side!"* Yes, a tryst. Even when the letter had come two years ago telling of dear Pamelia's death.

For this is *our hope,* thought Louisa gratefully, scooping two spoons of coffee grounds (made of roasted green beans from her garden) from an old butter firkin into her kettle. She and Pamelia *would* see each other again—in a world where they'd never be called to part!

Outside, beyond the warped glass of the small window, the morning's faint light had begun diffusing itself over the sky while inside the cabin shapes and shadows slowly took form and color, separating themselves, defining what they were. Shoulders of bacon, chunks of jerked venison, bunches of onions, all hanging from the rafters. David's rifles over the mantel, the sugar barrel behind the stove, the hats on the back of the door. Louisa laid another stick onto the fire. *What a wondrous word, "hope!"* she thought to herself while her eager little fire seized the new wood with crackles and spits, and dozens of "fireflies" clicked and popped and floated upwards out the flue. Furniture shadows flickered over the walls in elephantine proportions. Her own shadow loomed larger than life when she let Watch back in and helped herself to the bucket of milk Arthur had taken to leaving on her stoop each morning before sunup. Now that Arthur had taken on Dobbins's cows and gotten them to produce, it was nice—

wonderful in fact—to have fresh milk each day. Happily she skimmed off some of the cream for her coffee. Soon as it was light she'd skim the rest for butter.

She sat down at the little table before the window and propped her elbows on the puncheon top. Coffee cup warm in her hands, she stared past the rising steam, past the interior gloom of her cabin to the world outdoors. *Hope!* Hope brought peace to the troubled. Hope encouraged the discouraged, comforted the sorrowing, assured the fearful. Hope was nothing less than a gift from God, enabling them all to take life as it came—because God was bigger than their lives. He redeemed all things, even death. And this was what Pamelia had known and seen symbolized in the sweetbriar they shared. The wonder and power of eternal hope.

Dawn hovered now, around the edges of the world. It was not yet light, but then neither was it dark. The blackness of the sea had given way to tarnished silver, and soon the silver would brighten, another day. In this growing light Louisa's thoughts left the past and drifted into the present with all its attending trouble. *No,* she resolved, *I mustn't think of this. We're in God's hands. And is it not in him,* she asked herself, *that we place our hope? Redeeming and eternal? Even in death?* That thought scared her. She didn't want to die! She didn't want anyone else to die either! Not her own David, or Emily Inez!

Under her elbows, lying in disarray, was the *Puget Sound Courier*. Both David and Arthur had switched from the *Pioneer & Democrat*. They'd gotten perfectly weary of Mr. Wiley and his constant editorials on the "debase" nature of the "contentious" Indians. "The man's almost as bad as Reverend Blaine," David had complained.

If I were a man, if I could vote? Louisa set down her coffee. She'd be a Whig. Definitely! Whigs stood for temperance, for suffrage, for abolition. Whigs believed in equality and dignity for every man, woman, and child, light skin or dark skin. But right now (and she was grateful to have the distraction) she wondered if anyone had answered Lemuel Bills's advertisement.

Last month a Mr. Bills had informed every *Courier* subscriber that he lived comfortably on a prosperous farm outside Steilacoom. He had chickens, a cow, twenty acres of wheat. Furthermore, he'd platted the west end of his claim into town lots, and they were up for sale. He lacked but one thing to make a good life—*Was anyone interested in becoming his wife?*

Arthur thought the whole thing a preposterous joke, a gimmick to sell papers. But Judge Landers, who used to live in Steilacoom, said there really was a man by the name of Lemuel Bills. And that advertising for a wife sounded *exactly* like something the white-haired, ruddy-faced, built-like-a-barrel Lemuel Bills would do.

What's this? Louisa bent in, closer to the window. Tiny print all but jumped off the page. *Mr. Lemuel Bills my dear Sir—* She glanced quickly down the column. Ellen Brooks? *A quote from Lord Byron?* Good heavens! Someone *had* responded!

Mr. Lemuel Bills my dear Sir—

Please forgive the presumption of a POOR LONE woman in thus unceremoniously addressing a stranger. Perhaps your letter will somewhat excuse my boldness at this time. Words of mine could not express the emotions of my heart while reading that simple request. A presentment at once took possession of my mind, telling me in unmistakable language that my destiny was ere long to be united to that of another, and that one none other than Lemuel Bills! I speak of you as a stranger. You are not a stranger! Oftentimes, have my mesomeric eyes beheld your noble form. I fully appreciate your commanding talents and noble-heartedness. Oh! Lemuel, it seems almost sacrilegious to attempt to place upon this cold sheet the sentiments which are now awakened within my heart. To say, I love you, is too common place. To say I worship you is not enough. I will not—I dare not—express my emotions.

> Be assured, dear Lemuel; that since the event above mentioned transpired, my heart has beat strangely wild. O, how often since then have I called you, MY OWN, MY LEMUEL! How often have I imprinted upon your noble brow a burning kiss, and, oh! how your warm embrace thrilled my every nerve with more than electric power. How often in my imagination have I officiated as matron of your humble domicile. How often have I prepared the frugal meal, and how often has our humble repast been sweetened with domestic bliss.

Louisa started to giggle. Imagine! Such rubbish! And sent to a newspaper? Scandalous! And there was more!

> You do not ask for beauty. You do not ask for wealth. I am not possessed of either qualification. On me, Nature has not lavished her charms with a prodigal hand. You may consider this epistle as sickly, sentimental and unworthy of notice; if so FORGIVE AND FORGET. Of Myself, perhaps it is foolish to speak. Suffice it to say, I am 35, and homely. I am not in this country HUSBAND-seeking. I came here on an errand of mercy, not even wishing to change my state of single-blessedness, as it is termed. YOU are the only gentleman who has ever made an impression upon my hard heart, but you have succeeded, and that too in a very singular way and indirect manner. Should you consider this brief, simple, but sincere effusion worthy of reply, please direct a letter to Ellen Brooks. P.S. "I love you, and you can't help it! Oh! Lordy, how I do love you!"—Byron

"What's so funny?"

"David, you're awake!" Louisa looked up, smiling. She gathered the paper together and went over to the bed. "Do you remember Lemuel Bills?"

David snorted. "Don't tell me someone wrote him!"

She nodded knowingly.

He sat up.

She started to giggle again.

"Who?"

"Shall I read it to you?"

He grinned and flopped back down on the cedar bough mattress. "You're going to do me the honor anyway, aren't you?"

"You don't want me to?" she asked, genuinely hurt.

He laughed. "Coffee ready?"

9

In early October, Rains, who had been commissioned a Brigadier General of Volunteers by Acting-Governor Mason, "a bit of hocus-pocus" that was sarcastically denounced by Lieutenant Philip Sheridan, . . ."

—Clinton Snowden
in *History of Washington*

"Sorry to haul you out of bed like this, but we got a problem—coffee's good and strong, though," announced Second Lieutenant Nugen of Fort Steilacoom. He handed Billy Tidd, Steilacoom's carpenter and coffin maker, a mug of the piping hot coffee about as soon as the older man came through the door at army headquarters.

"I should hope so," mumbled Billy Tidd, looking sleepy in the flickering light of the shadowed office. He glanced out the window to a sky only now relinquishing her stars. He gave the coffee a sniff. "Hot too," he said. Then, "Where to today?"

The question sounded as though he expected to be sent off to some farm—maybe Lemuel Bills' place, or Judge Chambers', maybe Mr. Chapman's gristmill—to fetch a sack of vegetables or a crate of eggs or a bushel of ground wheat for one of the merchants in town. Not to deliver war correspondence. But Tidd was a quiet man, unassuming, the very last to be taken for an express rider.

"Acting Governor Mason reports that Rains is held up at The Dalles." Nugen slipped around behind his desk to ease his knobby body, rail thin yet rock hard with muscle, into his chair.

Rains hadn't left The Dalles? This was serious. Tidd parked his own lean frame into the opposite chair.

"There's been a squabble with the Oregon volunteers. Said right out they won't sign with the army. Don't want to take their orders from Rains. Rains turned around, said he wouldn't give 'em any guns." Nugen leaned back, chair squeaking. "The dispatches flying back and forth these days, well . . ." He buzzed his lips. "What a mess."

Tidd waited.

"Course, there's no reason Rains has to take over like that. He's got no business bossing volunteers from Oregon. But Rains needs to be a big shot, and Nesmith—head of the Oregon boys," Nugen explained. "Seems he's a colonel—"

"I get the drift." Tidd had another go at his coffee. "Colonel outranks major . . ."

"So Mason's decided to promote 'His Royal Highness' to 'Brigadier General' over *our* boys. All I can say is, I hope that bit of hocus-pocus does the trick. But all this is taking time."

"Which is why he's still sittin' on his duff—"

Nugen shot forward. "Sittin' on his brains! We got Maloney and those volunteers trailing Slaughter straight into oblivion, while Rains plays king of the castle—"

"No word at all from Slaughter?"

Nugen started to swear but stopped short. Tidd was a praying man—one didn't swear around folk like him, not in

105

these precarious days they didn't. "Here's the picture," he said, starting all over. "We got a hundred and seventy regulars and volunteers—not counting Slaughter—Hey! Why not count him? Maybe he *did* get wind of trouble and got the h— got out of there! Means we could have as many as 225 men up against Kamiakin's—what is it?—three thousand? No, six thousand," he amended, "what with Peo-Peo-Mox-Mox and his Walla Walla now. Every single one of 'em no doubt armed to the teeth. And what do *we* have? His Royal Highness putting on a pout for no better reason than some Oregon commoner, heaven forbid, has more stripes on his shirt than he?"

Second Lieutenant Nugen started rifling through the spread of papers on his desk. "Adds up to one big scalping for our boys, Tidd, if we don't get word to Maloney to put on the skids."

"What's he supposed to do? Come back? Stay put?"

"I don't know. I'm not the boss." Nugen found what he was looking for and handed the dispatch across the desk. "All I know is we're supposed to let him know he's the bull's-eye this week. Let him make up his mind what to do. How fast can you ride?"

Tidd had already been figuring this out, but faced with the question straightforward he set aside his coffee, just too hot, took the dispatch, and stuck it down inside his shirt pocket. "Maloney's bound to have reached the pass by now, so we're talking ninety miles at least," he said, thinking out loud and scratching his head. "Fifty of 'em through the mountains. Snow maybe. I don't know. Forty-eight hours? Give or take?"

"Can you do it?"

"Live or die."

When the sun at last cast a sleepy peek over the Cascades this last Sunday of the month, housewives throughout the Sound began to stir and set their houses in order.

In Seattle, Louisa poured off her cream.

Next door, Mary Ann called up the loft to her children. "Sunday today, dears! Remember to dress for church!"

South of the Sawdust, Ursula Wyckoff pulled her pillow over her face. "I'll get up! I will too!" she mumbled at Lewis.

Up at White River, Mrs. Cox squeezed into her corset. "I don't want to hear no more about women keeping silent in church, Mr. Cox. If Will Brannan so much as breathes a word about it, I'll give him a mean poke in the ribs."

Two claims away, Mrs. Thomas was saying, as sweetly as she could, "What do you think, dear?"

"Why you all dolled up?"

"It's Sunday!"

"You's only going out to feed the chickens."

"Yes, well, I was really hoping you'd see your way clear to letting us go over to the Brannans' this morning."

"Yes, soon as I get them apples picked and you get them juiced, I guess we can all go to Sunday school. Fact is, Bible says, 'don't work, don't eat.' And you know that. Told you a thousand times."

Near the loop where White River almost turned around on itself Elizabeth Brannan stoked her fire. "Help yourself to the coffee," she called over to her husband, still in bed. "Doris is shivering. I need to get her out of the tub."

"Hope it's good and strong," mumbled Will, staggering out of the bedsheets, reaching for his clothes.

Elizabeth knelt beside her shiny new tin tub to rinse the soap off her daughter. "Isn't it always?"

"Need it stronger than usual," yawned Will. "Couldn't sleep last night, Lizzy. Too many owls. Don't ever remember them being this bad before."

It wasn't owls keeping them awake; it was Indians. But no point in telling him. He was the ostrich, head in the sand. "If you don't like it, let it sit awhile."

"What's that?"

"The coffee!"

107

"Oh! I guess so, but this should be good enough to get me started. So long as you made plenty!" He smiled at her while he stretched, then took the cup over to his chair by the fire. "When're the others coming over?"

"An hour or so."

"Lizzy, you're worrying again. I wish you wouldn't."

As if I can help it. But then maybe today it'll all be over! she thought, daring to smile hopefully. She and Mrs. Cox were planning a mutiny. Instead of Sunday services they were going to insist their husbands take them to Seattle!

"Come on, Doris!" she singsonged, "Upsy-daisy!"

The cabin door suddenly banged in with a violent crash. Elizabeth leaped to her feet. Will too. Kanasket, notorious chief of the Greenwater Klikitat, a small band of renegades living high in the headwaters, stood on their stoop. He was a brutal-looking man, vicious scars skewing his face, a man who made good the dreaded reputation of all Klikitat in the Yakima Nation. He possessed the strength of three warriors. His voice was such that when he boomed a command everyone leaped to obey—and woe to any with whom he grappled. Seeing him on the doorstep, decked in vermilion war paint, Elizabeth's heart all but stopped.

"Take the baby, go to the wood," he snarled at her in Chinook. *"Klatawa!"*

She looked over to Will.

"Better do as he says," said Will quietly, going white around the mouth.

"But Will—"

"Do as he says!"

She looked into her husband's eyes and saw something she'd never seen in him before. Stark fear.

Hastily, with trembling hands, she pulled Doris dripping wet and slippery from the tub. She hesitated. "Will . . ."

"Do as he says," Will repeated.

Somehow she made a start, wondering that her feet could even obey. Yet they did. By some miracle, she got her shawl around Doris and both of them over to the door without stumbling. When she passed Kanasket, breath held and wondering if she dared turn back for another glimpse of her white-faced husband, the painted war chief reached out and seized her arm above the elbow. She must have made a cry, for he silenced her with a harsh, hissing "shoosh!" then propelled her roughly off the stoop.

He continued to hold her arm as he hurried her across the yard, past the chicken coop, past the well. He spoke rapidly in his own language. She understood nary a word. She tried turning around, to look back at the house, to see if her husband followed, but Kanasket shoved her forward so violently and so swiftly into the first fringe of woods she all but lost her balance. Doris let out a scream, or was it her?

He steered her unmercifully down the narrow trail leading to the river. Not until they were well into the woods, thickets snagging her skirts, branches slapping her face, did he let go of her arm. Here the world was dark. Here the trees grew thick and tall, sunlight all but barred from this heart of darkness. The chief pointed straight ahead. *"Klatawa!"* When she didn't move, he set the flat of his hand on her back and gave her a hard push.

Obviously she was to go to the river. With her baby naked? Without her husband? She started along. Kanasket, satisfied, stepped off the path into the trees. In seconds he was gone, swallowed by the woods.

Alone, she stood terrified in the silence. The Yakima were coming, Kanasket had come to take her away, this much was clear. The rest was not. Why me? Why not Will? Where is Will? Why didn't he follow?

"Will?" she called out, trembling. "Will?"

The dark purple trunks of the forest trees seemed almost to draw together in the trail before her, around her, behind her. There was no escape from these austere woods. "Will!" she shouted in panic. "Will!" Only silence, and the awful quiet completely unnerved her. Panic mounting, she broke into a run back through the trees, tripping over the roots that clawed the ground, dodging, ducking the grasping branches, Doris crying now in her arms.

She had to get Will! Before the Indians came! She needed him! She and Doris couldn't escape by themselves! Oh, why didn't he come? Why didn't he follow? *Because he's the ostrich, head in the sand. Oh but I can tell him!* she thought. *I can tell him, he'll believe me now!*

"Will!" she sobbed, voice catching in her throat as she broke out of the trees and into the sunlight. Suddenly she stopped in her tracks, breathing hard, lungs desperate for air. What was she doing? She couldn't let Doris come to harm!

But there'd been no gunfire, no war cries. There was still time. She started to run again. "Will! Will!" Oh, if she could just run fast enough, if she could just get to the house before the Indians did, yes, they could all escape! Will would take her to Seattle now! He wouldn't argue with her anymore! "Will!" she sobbed, passing the well, the chicken coop, the world and everything in it reduced to blurred teary images seen from the corners of her eyes.

Elizabeth plunged up to the doorstoop, staggering. "Oh, Will! The Indians are coming! You must take me to Seattle! Please take me to Seattle," she begged, and she burst through the door.

The Klikitat had a close-combat knife they liked to use, made from a saw file. By grinding the end to a point and then sharpening the long edge like a razor, these blades were lethal and inflicted terrible damage.

A mile away the Jones family sat down to breakfast.

"Mother, when's Father going to be better?" three-year-old Laura asked from her end of the table just as soon as her mother had said grace. "I don't like it when he's sick."

"Well neither do I," declared the hired hand, seated opposite her. "Makes more work for me. But that don't change things none." Enos Cooper slapped a thick slice of ham onto her plate, and gave her a wink. "There y'are, Little Girl. Eat up."

"When, Mother?" Laura insisted, still pouting.

"I don't know, Little Girl," sighed Eliza Jones, trying to find a smile for her daughter. Only eight in the morning; already she was dog-tired. Her husband was sick again, with pleurisy this time. He'd kept her up all night what with one thing or another. Mostly thirst. Perhaps after breakfast, when she got the dishes washed and put away, and if Mr. Cooper was agreeable and would oversee the children's catechism, she might have a nap. Suddenly there was a scuffle at the door. "Now, who do you suppose that is?" she wondered out loud.

The children crowded around before she could even lift the latch.

"Hey, no one here!" exclaimed Johnny, poking his freckled nose out from behind her skirt.

She was about to shut the door when from the corner of her eye, she saw someone standing off to the side, a runty man, no one she knew. She was about to step out, to say something to him, when Johnny stiffened. Instantly she saw what had frightened her son. Another Indian, half hidden behind the old house across the yard, had the tip of his rifle braced on the crossed logs at the back corner. His face was pressed against the butt, hand near the trigger. She gasped, slammed the door. The gun exploded. Instantaneously there was a thud at the door and the sound of splintering wood. Then a high, bloodcurdling "yip, yip, yip!"

Through the southeast window she saw them coming. Whooping. Jumping. Swinging their tomahawks. They seemed to rise out of the very ground. Some had flintlock muskets. These, she knew, carried an ounce ball, and did terrible execution. She rushed the children to their bedroom, gunfire ripping the air outside and coming now from every direction. The glass window in the bedroom shattered, a thousand shivering pieces; a bullet whizzed past, splintering the partition between the two rooms. She lifted the down-filled feather mattress, panting, heart pounding. Johnny understood. Quickly he lifted his small sister, then his baby brother onto the roped webbing that cradled the mattress, then crawled up himself. *God knows this is the best I can do,* thought Eliza King Jones, letting the full softness of the mattress fall down over them. *God be with them.*

Not too far away Joe Lake was standing on the front stoop of Cox's log house having a smoke and admiring the clean new day when he heard the crack of gunfire. He was waiting for Mrs. Cox to finish her dishes; he and Mr. and Mrs. Cox were to walk over to the Brannans' together this morning. Today was his turn to lead Sunday's discussion, and he was debating whether or not to pursue last week's argument about women being allowed to pray in church when the gunfire startled him. *No one out hunting,* he thought to himself, *it's Sunday.* Scaring off a cougar? Suddenly a whole volley of gunfire. A bullet whistled under his crooked arm, a hot, burning wind.

"Indians! They're attacking!" He bolted round back for the trail to the river. A bullet caught his shoulder. The pain all but blinded him. Mrs. Cox, still holding her dish cloth, raced past. Mr. Cox seized Joe's other arm and together they ran for the river where Mrs. Cox already had the canoe flipped up and ready. Joe leaped in. Mr. Cox leaped in, pushed off. Everyone gripped the gunwales with white-knuckled desperation. The canoe caught the current with a lurch . . . and forward rush.

morning

They attacked the front of the house and began firing through the door and windows. I shall never forget the sickening sensation at the report of the guns, the sound of the shivering glass. Mother took us into the northwest bed room, and, bidding us to get into the northwest corner of the room, as that was the farthest from the point of attack, covered us with a feather bed. She did this, I suppose, to take advantage of the fact that it was a difficult matter to send a musket ball through a mass of feathers, especially the old flintlock musket ball.

I became tired of my confinement and peered cautiously from beneath the bed. I noticed the direction of the balls was more upward than horizontal; they were coming through my step-father's room, and tore huge slivers from the partition between the rooms . . .

> —Dr. John King, written years later
> to Ezra Meeker, pioneer and historian

When little Johnny King peeked out from under the mattress he immediately noticed the direction of the balls—more upward than horizontal. They were coming through his stepfather's room, tearing huge slivers from the partition and lodging just over his own bed. He waited a moment, then crept out and along the floor where it was safe, to look through the door opening onto the larger room. His mother and Mr. Cooper both had guns, and were furiously firing out the windows, each from a different corner. In the middle was the lonely breakfast table, the chairs pushed back as though everyone had politely excused themselves. Movement caught his eye; his stepfather was out of bed and had come to his own bedroom door to stare into the larger room. Suddenly he staggered and leaned more heavily against the casing. "Oh, dear God, I am shot!"

"Oh, Harvey, don't say so!" Johnny's mother dropped her five-shooter and ran over to support his weight. Right arm over her shoulders, he opened his shirt, exposing a huge gaping hole! Sickened and in terror Johnny flew back to his hiding place, yet from beneath the mattress, heart pounding so loudly it filled his ears, he could nonetheless hear his stepfather's prayers and last hurried advice, his mother's terrible despair. Johnny plugged his ears—still he heard. Nothing stopped the sound of their parting good-byes, his mother's broken sobs. Not even the heavy firing and the crash of musket balls tearing through the partition could stop the desperate sounds. But then his stepfather's prayers changed to moaning. Johnny unplugged his ears, the moaning ceased. His mother spoke to Mr. Cooper. "It's hopeless," she said, and he knew his stepfather was dead. "Try to escape," his mother told Mr. Cooper.

Johnny pushed up the mattress again. Mr. Cooper had come into the room and was using an ax to pry off the window stop. He moved the lower sash, hesitated, looked outside first one way and then the other, then leapt from the window.

In a few minutes there was a lull. Everything quiet. Johnny heard footsteps, they were not his mother's. He peered out again. Everything was much lighter than before. The sun had come out. Indians swarmed through the house. One carried a loaf of bread in his hands. The man saw him, pointed and shouted, and Johnny found himself straightway being hauled out from under the mattress. In the large front room the splintered walls twinkled with pinpricks of thin sunlight. He was dragged on past them all and out through the demolished door. A swarm of Indians and yet more Indians met his eyes. Then he saw Nelson.

The chief was seated on a tree stump a few feet from the door. He wasn't silent and morose as he'd been on his last visit. He was directing all the Indians and seemed to know exactly what must be done. "Don't be afraid," he said to Johnny. "Nelson don't let them hurt you."

Johnny stopped crying instantly. If Nelson said not to be afraid, then he didn't need to be; and when Laura and Frederick were brought from the house he told them everything would be all right because Nelson had said so. Nonetheless, they whimpered and cried. Nelson patted Laura on the head. "Shh."

He kept the three of them close while the other Indians, all strangers to Johnny, carted blankets and bedding, clothing, anything flammable out of the house, and stuffed it all underneath. Nelson talked to Johnny with guarded kindness. Occasionally he shouted and gestured at the others. Someone fired into the hidden cache beneath the house, then another fired, and another. Flames flickered. Smoke curled up from the foundations and in minutes the whole house was ablaze. *Mother! Mother?* Johnny panicked.

"Go to Thomases'," Nelson whispered.

Johnny gulped. He went to school there every day; he knew it was a long way away. Could his little brother and sister walk that far?

"You must be careful. No wait . . ." Nelson held Johnny back with a restraining hand. "Not yet, not safe. Wait, I tell you when."

He shouted more orders. Numbly, Johnny watched as first one Indian and then another tossed flaming torches onto the roof of the little cabin down by the river. He'd helped his mother store the potatoes inside, and the big firkins of butter. Quite suddenly the Indians all left. Only Nelson remained—and a mean-looking man with circles of vermilion war paint on his wrinkled face. And the hot fires with their terrible heat; and all the loud snapping and sharp crackling and popping; and the high swirling smoke that pinched his nostrils and stung his throat and made his eyes cry. The little fire in his mother's hearth had always been like a pet kitten, purring with warmth and ready to play, but this fire. . . . This was a snarling cougar, ready to attack!

"He will take you to Thomases' now," said Nelson. "Go. *Klatawa.*" He strode away. Johnny blinked in astonishment and confusion, trying to understand. They were to go with this mean-looking Indian?

The Indian seized his hand and began dragging all three of them—Johnny had Laura's hand and Laura had Frederick's—the wrong direction. "No!" resisted Johnny. The Indian insisted. He half led, half dragged, them over to a low spot in the fence near the barn, a few rods from the house. Suddenly he let go of their hands and the children reeled backward and fell into a pile. The Indian upbraided them viciously, muttering harshly and for a long time in his own language. Finally he waved his hand as though he didn't care what happened to them, crawled under the fence, and was gone.

Johnny sat in a cocoon of misery, huddled with his sister and brother, equally miserable, while the world and everything burned. Things were happening too quickly. His mind couldn't comprehend the whole. It was as though he'd been turning the pages of a familiar storybook and come unexpectedly upon a colored picture he'd never seen before; a picture of houses ablaze, the page too hot to turn. He didn't know what to do. Suddenly the roof in the burning picture caved in with a roaring crash. Flames shot skyward, whistling in the swooshing wind of the horrific fall. The noise startled Johnny out of his fog. Laura was begging for something to eat.

He decided instantly that the Thomases lived too far away. He would take the little ones the other direction, to the Brannans' house. The Brannans lived only a mile away. Mrs. Brannan would give his sister something to eat.

As he went along he shouted for Mr. Cooper, for it occurred to him Mr. Cooper might be hiding in the woods and could help them. But when he heard his own echo come back at him from the silent copse of trees he stopped, frightened by what he'd done. Shouting would only attract attention from Indians lurking about!

It didn't take long to realize he'd do better without Laura and Frederick. He couldn't go faster than his nearly four-year-old sister, and she couldn't go faster than their nearly two-year-old brother, who did not care about walking at all. What a long time it would take to get to the Brannans' like this! He would have to leave them and go alone for help. Looking about, he spotted a round depression in the ground and into this hole he tucked his sister and brother, covered them over with brush, and told them not to move until he came back. "Do not come out, the Indians will kill you!"

Half an hour later he cautiously approached the Brannans'. Everything was deathly still, not even the tree boughs seemed to move. He drew nearer. The door stood wide open. The windows in the house were all broken. Chairs, table, other furniture, everything inside broken and strewn about. The bedticking, the pillows, torn open. Feathers floating here, there. Too terrified to enter the house, to even call, he turned and ran rapidly back across the yard to the wooded trail, heart thudding louder than his footfall on the bloodied ground.

He found Laura and Frederick as he'd left them. Only now they were all hungry for it was nearly noon. Not knowing what else to do, he took them back to the ruins of their home. All that remained were a few blackened studs, erect and smoking. The little log house was but rubble itself, smoke spiraling up off the chaotic pile of partial walls and blackened log spill. He hardly dared approach. But they were hungry. The potatoes, he discovered, were nicely roasted and there were streams of butter from the charred firkins. He salvaged what he could and soon their stomachs were full, and it was time to think again about going to Mrs. Thomas's.

He took his sister and brother on a circuitous route around the barn, when suddenly out from shadows—"Rover!" screamed Laura in almost hysterical joy. The half-grown pup bounded over, tail wagging. He nearly knocked Laura off her feet. She laughed and giggled. Frederick, too. Johnny joined in, happy to see a friendly companion! But then he remembered his task. "We have to go," he told Laura and Frederick. "We have to go to Mrs. Thomas's."

"Can't he come with us?" asked Laura.

He was inclined to say yes, but on second thought knew the dog would betray them. So he told Laura no. When the dog wouldn't go back to the barn, he did the hardest thing yet. He picked up a stick—and drove the dog away. Tears stood in his eyes to see the hurt in Rover's face. "Come on," he told the others. "Give me your hands, let's go." He forgot himself and started calling again for Enos Cooper. The only answer received was the lonely echo of his own voice.

As he passed along he unexpectedly came across his mother. The sight of her startled him out of his wits for she lay prostrate on the ground some hundred feet away from the blackened house, her hair disheveled and eyes full of pain. He fell to his knees, overcome by what he saw.

"Johnny," she whispered with a breathless, little voice, trying hard to give him a little smile. "God has been kind, he answered my prayers . . . you're all alive. But why are you still here?" she chided gently, looking up at him with glazed concentration. "You must hurry, you must help the children escape."

"I can't leave you," he whimpered, leaning in, trying to figure out why she lay so still and so white. "I don't want to leave you. I won't leave you."

"Darling, I'll soon be in heaven with God. You must do what you can for the children. Take them, leave quickly, Mrs. Thomas will take care of you."

"No," he cried, wishing he could throw himself on top of her and bury himself in her arms. Child though he was, he could see this would be her end. So he lay instead on the cold hard earth beside her and pressed himself as close to her as he dared. He put his cheek to hers. "Don't leave us, Mother," he wept. "Everyone is dead, Mother. Oh, Mother, don't die!"

She whispered so softly he had to stop crying. "If the Indians come back they will kill us. You must go. Take the children . . . Go now, darling," she urged. "God will keep you safe."

He had to go, he knew this. Quickly too. Heartsick, he pulled himself away.

"Johnny . . ."

"Mother?"

She smiled at them all so beautifully he thought for a moment she was an angel.

The trail to the Thomases' lay through heavy timber and dense undergrowth along a narrow and winding path for two long miles. Johnny carried his brother and let his little sister get along as best she could. Sometimes he had to put the baby down to catch his breath and rest his breaking arms, but the baby would do so little walking and so much crying that as soon as he could, Johnny picked him up again and staggered on. When they at last emerged from the trees into the clearing, they were startled to hear a cacophony of wild barking. A few more steps and three Indian dogs tore around the corner of the house snarling and snapping, their teeth bared, barking so fiercely the little ones cowered in fear and pulled at Johnny's hands, trying desperately to hide behind him.

"Mr. Thomas! Mrs. Thomas!" Johnny shouted bravely.

No answer. Now what was he to do? He started back, Frederick again in his tired arms. Only now he could not keep the baby quiet. Frederick cried inconsolably for his mother. Laura, too, began to whimper. He found that he could generally keep her quiet by telling her "Indians kill," but his brother was much too little to understand.

The day started to wane. By four o'clock they were hungry again. Johnny knew of some tree bark and an edible root that his mother had once shown him, and so he let the little ones stop for a rest while he searched the forest. He was, he knew, at least twenty miles from a white settlement, and that there was no real way to get there but by canoe. Maybe they could walk along the river bank. But what of the Indians? The cougars? The bears? An almost overwhelming sense of danger and helplessness swept over him. And when he thought of the night ahead . . . Frightened, he ran back to the children, gave them what little he had found, and started on again.

"An Indian," said Laura suddenly, pulling hard on his hand.

"Quick!" he hissed, dragging her into the high, dense underbrush. He dropped Frederick down beside her, the ferns and huckleberry bushes springing up around them, a soft green fence and canopy. "Don't move!" He put a finger to his lips and started backing out of the enclosure.

"Where are you going?"

"Shh! I'll be back!"

"Johnny!" Laura pleaded.

"Be quiet, Little Girl!"

He darted diagonally back to the trail, to come in farther along from where he'd left it, closer to where the Indian was. Most of the day he'd been in mortal fear of meeting an Indian. Now it seemed his only hope. Even if the Indian killed him, the little ones would be no worse off. To his surprise, the Indian was someone he'd seen frequently while attending school at the Thomases' house. Chopping wood. Grubbing stumps. Burning brush.

"Oh, Tom!" he cried, bursting out of the thickets. "Tom! The Indians—Everyone is dead!" he sobbed. "Tom, please will you help us?"

11

evening

There was nothing warlike in the appearance of the town on the evening of the 28th at the close of a quiet October Sabbath. Some of the settlers were attending evening worship in the little white meeting house; others were lounging about the cookhouse; the *Decatur* lay idly at anchor—when a canoe sped from the mouth of the Duwamish.

—Roberta Frye Watt, Katy Denny's daughter
in *Four Wagons West*

*E*vening stole over the Sound this Sunday night with nothing more ominous in the air than the dampness of approaching winter. Just another quiet October Sabbath coming to an end. In Seattle, a few of the settlers attended service in the little white Methodist Episcopalian church, others lounged about the cookhouse, smoking their pipes, discussing the war with off-duty marines.

"Leschi says to McAllister—"

"*Who?*"

"McAllister. Down by Nisqually. Feller what took his claim on the Nisqually council grounds back in '45."

"Fool thing to do . . ."

"Not if Leschi give it to you—Leschi, he made McAllister a Nisqually. But what I was saying was last week he says to McAllister no harm'll come by folk what stay on their own place and mind their own business."

"He gonna fight then?"

"If'n the soldiers want to fight, he'll fight all right. But his fight ain't with regular folk."

"No fight around here then! We ain't got no soldiers! Not no more we don't!"

"No? Where'd they all go?"

"They gone over to make angels out o' them Yakima devils!"

"Ha, ha!"

Outside, dusk hovered. Rosy hues reflected off Elliott Bay; the pebbled shoreline lay in a bath of gleaming twilight. The tide turned and started silently back out. The *Decatur*, anchored a few rods offshore, noiselessly swung around so that her bow pointed inland, past the twilight-lit sawdust and mill to where the forest behind Seattle rose up in a high wall of darkness.

On the beach David and Louisa—a part of the dusk and cold tranquillity—sat atop a smoothly polished log, speaking softly. Their log was large enough to let them draw up their feet and wrap their arms snugly around their knees.

"No-o-o . . ." Louisa corrected her husband, knees embraced, holding her small Bible out in front of her drawn-up legs.

"What is it then?"

"Like *un*to a man." The light was poor. She had to hold the Bible up and squint to be sure.

"Tut, tut," said David. He gave her a little nudge, making her smile.

"You keep doing that, I'll fall right off this log."

"All right, but you have to let me start over."

"Go ahead."

"For if any be a hearer of the word, and not a doer, he is like *un*to a man—"

"Good."

"—beholding his natural face in a glass: for he beholdeth himself, and goeth his way, and straightway forgetteth what manner of man he was."

David and Louisa had spent much of the day memorizing from the Book of James. David had done this earlier, on the Oregon Trail, but had long since forgotten most of it. A few weeks ago they'd both decided to learn it; but the day was to enjoy as well, so when Louisa had wearied of the memory work she'd started to read *Uncle Tom's Cabin* for a third time while David plowed through the stack of newspapers, catching up on the European War and the latest unrest in "Bleeding Kansas." The Free-Soilers, he found out, were holding their own convention and had called for a "legal" election in December—Kansas's spring election having been largely the stuff of Missourian Ruffians who'd crossed the border to vote proslavery. So was Kansas going to have *two* legislatures? he'd wondered. Proslavery *and* free-soil?

Now that it was evening the two of them sat outdoors, reciting what they'd managed to learn of James, chapter one; forgetting too, for a short time at least, the alarming state of affairs in their own corner of the world that required them to continue living in town.

They sat on the sea-polished log, bundled in their winter coats, shivering a little from the dampness that came through the log beneath them. They watched the weakened sun drop off, and listened to the quiet lap of the receding waves, the chattering of their Duwamish friends squatting around a blazing beach fire nearby, and the pleasing voices of their white friends singing in the church up the hill. *Such familiar refrains,* thought Louisa nostalgically, remembering her church choir in Cherry Grove, her memory but a momentary distraction. "My turn," she told David, handing him her Bible; glancing, too, at the crackling bonfire ten yards away and the red glow of flames reflected in the dusky cheek bones of familiar smiling faces. Mandy, Yoke-Yakeman's *klootchman*, had Emily Inez by the hand and was showing her how two or three men pushed the larger logs into the fire as they burned. Mynez tried doing this herself, to the amusement of her admiring audience, and Louisa smiled at the attention her daughter always managed to elicit from the friendly Duwamish living along Seattle's shore. When it became too dark to read her Bible, she and David would join the group for a few moments before going up to bed.

"I'm not done yet, Liza."

"What's that?"

"I'm not finished reciting." David pushed the Bible back at her.

"You mean you know more?" and she looked at her husband in amazement.

"I learned to the end of the chapter."

"You did not!"

"I did!"

"All right," she intoned with exaggeration to let him know she didn't really believe him. "But mind, I'm not giving any more hints. You make a mistake, it's my turn." She peered past the blazing fire and collection of Indians. "Wait a minute. Is that the Maynards? Are they back from Port Madison already?

"It's been a week," he said, following her gaze to the fire and beyond, squinting. The light from the fire rose up like a wall in the growing dark, and all but cut from view everything that lay behind. "I don't know, kind of hard to tell." He stood to his feet and ambled down to the water, hoping to get out of line from the spiraling flames. His boots ground harshly against the pebbles. He could feel his ankles twist a little when he got to the large stones.

"Hey, Dave, that you?" A familiar voice mingled with the soft break of tiny waves retreating farther and farther from shore.

"Liza! You're right!" hollered David, quickly starting down the beach, pebbles and stones grinding underfoot with each step. When the gap closed, he put out his hand to take the doctor's, pleased to see the rascal. "It's been a long week!" David exclaimed. "Mrs. Maynard, good to see you!" he acknowledged, giving her a smile. "Welcome home!"

"Home! What a nice thing to hear!" said Catherine Maynard, returning his smile tenfold. "And thank you! It *is* nice to be home!"

"What'd Chief Seattle say?" David asked, jumping right in, anxious to hear the outcome of their visit to the peninsula, their consultation with the most important chief on the Sound.

"He's here. Came back with us," said Doc.

"He is? *Where*—" asked David happily.

"Tête a tête with the captain just now. But he's anxious to see you—"

"What's he say about Leschi? Can he help?"

"Says you can't stop a rolling stone. But—"

Louisa arrived, breathless, looking pretty in the glow of sunset and her pregnancy. Doc broke off whatever it was he was going to say, blue eyes lighting up. Not even dusk could hide his pleasure in seeing her. "Mrs. Denny, didn't I warn you about swallowing watermelon seeds?"

If she had to pick a favorite pioneer, she'd pick Doc Maynard every time. She loved his irreverence, his boldness, his easy ability to irritate Arthur. She knew of no one who could get under Arthur's skin so quickly and tenaciously as Doc; it was a pleasure to watch. But mostly she loved him for his unequivocal kindness, to everyone. "Watermelon in these parts? More like a healthy-sized cucumber seed!" she shot back, smiling at Catherine, for Catherine had given her some very precious cucumber seeds last spring.

"Nope, watermelon," Doc diagnosed, and he patted Louisa's small protruding stomach.

"Now you stop that," scolded Catherine, slapping his hand. To Louisa she said, "Why do people always feel entitled to pat a woman's tummy whenever she's growing a baby? Do you know, Mrs. Blaine is quite sick of it. She says the bigger she gets, the more she gets patted. She says it's like being a dog!"

"Only when we get scratched behind our ears as well," Louisa corrected, hiding a smile.

Doc Maynard chuckled. "I said it before, I'll say it again. Good thing I got my own wife, Dave, or I'd be after yours!"

"You'd have to stand in line, Doc. George Seattle *still* asks if he can't make a trade."

"He does not!" gasped Louisa.

When David laughed and said he'd swear on a stack of Bibles it was true, she pretended to swoon and with exaggerated drama, declared, "Oh, by my mesomeric eyes behold *your* noble form, my dear! To say I love you is too commonplace; to say I worship you isn't enough, my own, my *dear*, my *Lemmmm-uel!*" They all laughed uproariously, happy perhaps to know they still could, and she felt pretty pleased with herself for making such a show.

Suddenly a muffled shout came off the water. Not the kind that meant hello, but a desperate, frightened kind.

The dozen Indians keeping warm around their beach fire heard the call as well. The singsong monotone of their chattering abruptly ceased and they hurried, more curious than alarmed, over to where David and Louisa and the Maynards stood trying to see through the thickening gauze of dusk. Seeing her father, Emily Inez toddled over and insisted on being picked up.

"They're coming in near the wharf!" shouted Doc Maynard. He and everyone else, Indians included, took off like a shot. David swung Emily Inez onto his shoulders, took Louisa's hand. Together they walked as quickly as Louisa could manage toward Yesler's wharf. The cookhouse was all lit up, men streaming out and rushing over the Sawdust. Church dismissed. Whole families ran to the beach.

"The Indians have attacked! The Indians are coming!"

Such buzzing, frightful words! For a moment Louisa stood quite still, a contraction of pain in her chest.

Mr. and Mrs. Cox and Joe Lake, obviously shaken, stood beside a large canoe.

"They sh-shot Joe!" Mr. Cox stammered, panting hard. "Right in front of the house! On the stoop! Show 'em, Joe!"

Joe Lake eased open his coat and it seemed to Louisa the whole crowd took a step back when they saw the large, ragged hole torn clean through. And when he painfully took off his coat, Louisa went wobbly all over. So much blood. *Oh dear God, Elizabeth . . .*

"What about the other families? What about the folk out by you?" Arthur asked. Oh, the anger, the fury in his voice!

"We warned everyone comin' down, Denny!"

"But the Thomases, the Brannans! The King family! I'm talking about everyone south of you! Do you know what's happened to them?" Arthur was frantic. So was everyone else.

"I can't say!" Mr. Cox pleaded.

Elizabeth . . . "I'm going to be sick," said Louisa. She bent in a rush. The entire contents of her supper came up so quickly she couldn't get her breath. Vaguely she was aware that David had handed Emily Inez over to someone else, that Doc Maynard was pushing people back, away from her.

"Someone else coming in!" came a high cry.

Mercifully, attention was diverted. Louisa stood weak-kneed and shivering, waiting to see what her stomach would do. "I think I'm done," she finally told David. He dug around in his pockets. Gratefully she took his hanky and wiped her mouth while Doc Maynard kicked sand over the mess.

"Liza, we've got to go home," David told her.

"Where's Inez?" she managed to ask, staggering over to a small log, gagging on the taste of bile still thick and stinging in her throat. When she sat, she fairly plopped, for she was trembling all over, she was hot, she was cold. She huddled over herself, trying to find some warmth and strength, to contain the terrible shaking.

"Catherine took her up to Mary Ann. Liza, please, we must go home—"

"I don't want to," she argued weakly. "I want to see if Will and Elizabeth come in."

Doc Maynard stepped onto the log, beside her.

"Aren't you going to go help Mr. Lake, Doc?" she asked him quickly, looking up, holding her stomach.

"If Mr. Lake hasn't bled to death yet, Louisa, he's not going to. Dave, if this isn't the Brannans coming in, take Liza home whether she likes it or not. Doctor's orders, Liza," he added, his mouth a stern line in dusk that no longer held back, but advanced quickly, darkening the world.

Dear God, she prayed fervently, *please let it be Elizabeth!*

David eased down onto the log, sitting on the other side of her. "Did you hear Doc?"

Please! Please let it be Elizabeth!

"Did you?" he repeated.

She nodded.

The crowd had grown quiet. Full meaning behind what was happening had begun to sink in, and the growing horror held their tongues. War had come to Puget Sound after all. The Indians had risen, their own Indians. But . . . who led them? The Yakima? Had they come through the mountains then? Or was it Nelson? Was it Leschi? *Who?* Which tribes? How many? Had they struck anywhere else? *Where?*

"What's happening?" Louisa asked, clumsily working her dry tongue and lips.

"Captain Sterrett and Lieutenant Drake are getting out a rowboat to go after those folks coming in," Doc Maynard told her. "They don't seem to be making headway. Tide's going out. Must be too tired to fight it, I guess."

Oh, dear God, please, please let it be Elizabeth, please, dear God. Ple-e-ase!

"Louisa, we *must* go home," David tried again. "This isn't good for you or the baby. You're shivering head to toe, you're as white as a ghost—"

"I *can't* go!" she snapped, though she was immediately sorry for her impatience.

John and Nancy Thomas, under tow, put in a few minutes later.

"The *Thomases?*" Louisa felt sick all over again. *Where was Elizabeth?*

The young couple coming in were so exhausted they had to be helped from their dugout. Neither could speak beyond a mumble. Nancy Thomas began to sob. Doc Maynard stepped off the log and went down. Whispers broke out.

"David? What is it?"

He hesitated.

"*Da*-vid!"

"John says they saw a lot of black smoke—"

Louisa looked up in panic.

"Spiraling out of the trees upriver from their place," David finished, looking away from her stricken face.

She burst into tears. Smoke meant but one thing. Bereft and heartsick, she leaned again over her knees. *Why oh why did Will take Elizabeth back there?* Tears coursed down her face and fell over her hands as she tried, failing, to keep them back. Elizabeth was dead. *If the White River settlers go back they'll be murdered within the month.* Arthur was right, he was always right. . . .

David wrapped his warm arms around her and pulled her in close. "No, Liza," he said, arguing her tears, for well he knew why she cried. "They wouldn't hurt her. Not even the Yakima or Klikitat would hurt anyone English."

But Elizabeth was dead and Louisa knew it as surely as she'd known last summer that David's brother James was dying.

Dark settled in for good now, swiftly, like a smothering cap, and the beach stood silent under the weight. Silent, but for the sound of pebbles grinding underfoot as the stunned crowd slowly dispersed. Silent, but for the soft murmur of cold waves curling their lips over the low wet stones before letting go on the outgoing tide.

12

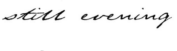

But when the second expedition under Captain Maloney and Captain Hays, with both regulars and volunteers, passed through their country and the Eaton rangers had driven or frightened Leschi and the disaffected Nisquallies to their vicinity they could be restrained no longer, and the outbreak came like a clap of thunder out of [a] clear sky.

—Ezra Meeker, pioneer and historian
in *Pioneer Reminiscences on Puget Sound*

Happily, other families from White River put in during the night. Unhappily, their stories presented an alarming state of affairs. The Indians—whoever they were and to what degree of success—were sweeping downriver as far and as fast as they could. Where they meant to stop, none could guess. Conceivably they could try coming all the way into Seattle—though Mr. Wetmore's Do-Nothings still insisted no. Wiser men hurried into the night to warn the pioneers living on nearby farms.

Bill Gilliam and Dexter Horton hastened out to Uncle Tommy Mercer's claim two and a half miles north of town. Mr. Plummer of Plummer & Chase paddled swiftly across the bay up to Smith Cove to warn his wife's brother and mother—Dr. Smith and Widow Smith. Walter Graham, a bachelor, headed down Beach Road to the Duwamish River mouth to go after his friend George Frye at the timber camp. And Captain Sterrett, no longer ignorant as to deceiver and deceived—his estimation of Arthur Denny rising astronomically high in his mind—ordered an immediate posting of double guards around the village and called for a meeting of minds. He wanted Chief Seattle and his two sons, Jim and George, plus Subchief Suwalth in attendance—and any other Indian who might shed light on the situation. Arthur of course was to be there. The four officers of Seattle's three-day-old militia as well. David, corporal of the volunteers, attended.

This left Louisa alone with Emily Inez, not even Watch to keep her company for he was down at the cookhouse with David. She found it next to impossible to hide her distress; such terrible images haunted her mind. Like everyone else last year, she'd read all about the Ward massacre near Snake River on the Oregon Trail—very near where they themselves had been attacked, and by some miracle escaped with their lives. Not the Ward train. Children roasted to death . . . mothers forced to watch . . . unspeakable tortures done to the women. Fortunately, tonight, Emily Inez was keyed up about the short visit with her cousins and noticed nothing of her mother's tension. She chattered nonstop, pausing only when Louisa tugged her nightgown down over her head, happily starting right back in, head emerging like a turtle.

"My know my ABC's, Mama! Katy 'n Nora teached me! See? A,B,C,D,E,F,G! Jesus died for you and me! H,I,J,K,L and Mmmmm! Jesus died for sinful men! Amen! O,P . . ." Louisa hardly listened; the forest was alive with its own sounds, all pressing against the thin walls of the cabin, permeating the weathered boards as stealthily and as surely as the damp night air. An owl. Now a raccoon gliding through the underbrush. Somewhere the distant cry of a cougar. But also, gratefully—like a clock chiming each quarter hour—the regular, reassuring footfall of Captain Sterrett's marines making their rounds, their hushed, base voices confirming "all's well." What would they do without the *Decatur?* How would they cope? wondered Louisa in dismay. As it was, she could hardly restrain her tears or still the trembling of her hands. And when she thought of Elizabeth? Dear, sweet Elizabeth. And sad Eliza King Jones? Was she alive? *Dear God, let their deaths be merciful, don't let them suffer.* The children, she wouldn't, couldn't, think about. She said, "Diaper time, Mynez."

Drawing the diaper's longest triangle end up through her daughter's legs and folding the tip in under the waist, Louisa tried desperately to recapture her morning's thoughts of Pamelia and their shared hope symbolized so wonderfully by the sweetbriar. But where was hope when people could wake and dress for another day, only to be murdered?

"Ouch!"

"You have owie?" asked Emily Inez, straining to lift her head off the mattress and twisting to see.

"Yes, I poked myself with the diaper pin!"

"My kiss you better?"

"When the bleeding stops. Lie down now, we have to get this diaper fastened."

Emily Inez did as she was told, though she kept her eyes carefully on her mother. The task done, she asked, "Now My kiss owie?"

Louisa offered her finger.

"All better?" Emily Inez asked, smiling, confident.

"Yes, darling, all better," said Louisa.

To keep her daughter amused she gave her a piece of butcher paper and one of David's large carpenter pencils—one of many used last spring when building their house in the Swale. A long time ago, a whole world away . . .

"My draw pichers, Mama?"

Was hope but an illusion? Was she fooling herself in thinking God had his hand in their affairs? But then what could God do, she had to ask, when people insisted on ignoring the obvious? Arthur TOLD them not to go back!

"My draw pichers?"

Where oh where is David? What's keeping him?

"Mama! My talking to you!"

"Yes, yes, of course, darling!" answered Louisa hurriedly, startled, called back to the present by the annoyance in her daughter's voice. "Yes, while I fix your cocoa you can draw a picture—" The door swung in. Louisa whirled. "Angeline!" she gasped.

Heart pounding, fear and relief collided. Louisa fell onto the bed beside her daughter, feet splayed, and waved her hand back and forth over her chest as if to stay the thudding. "Princess Angeline, for heaven's sakes! You near scared me to death!"

"Nika—Nika delate chockhut . . ."

With new alarm Louisa scrambled to her feet. Hastily she pulled the weeping daughter of Chief Seattle into the house. "Why are you broken? What has happened?" she asked, though her mind, numbed as it was by the attack at White River, could hardly imagine or bear new despair.

"Nika delate chockhut . . ." the middle-aged Indian princess repeated, wiping her eyes with the hem from one of her many skirts. Louisa guided her friend over to a chair and sat her down. Not knowing what else to do, she handed her one of David's clean handkerchiefs. "Shall I make some tea?"

Angeline nodded, blubbering into the hanky.

Emily Inez, clad in her gown and nightcap, slithered off the high bed and toddled over. She looked up at their guest with a troubled expression on her little face.

"Ach, memaloose, papoose—" With a broken sob, Angeline pulled the little girl into her arms and began to rock back and forth, switching from Chinook to Duwamish to croon

135

more easily her sorrow, tears coursing her wrinkled, leathery face.

"Angemeem sad?" Emily Inez asked, at last sensing something was terribly wrong.

"Yes," Louisa answered, though to her Angeline seemed more frightened than sad. She put some water on to boil and set out a few cookies. Emily Inez tried to show Angeline her slippers.

"Auntie Mary knitted them! You like pink, Angemeem? Mama, Angemeem no talk to My!"

"Sometimes we need to let people have their cry, darling," Louisa explained. "Sit quiet, be a good girl. She'll talk when she's ready."

But it wasn't until the tea had steeped its three minutes, and Mynez's cocoa was stirred, the lamp wicks adjusted to give better light, with Louisa seated at the table opposite, and pushing over a small bowl of sugar cubes, that Angeline finally, haltingly, and in broken English, began to talk.

"Your soldiers gone now. No soldiers here. So redskins kill the whiteskins at White River," she stammered out. She burst into new tears. "Everyone soon be dead!"

The Indians had been waiting for the soldiers to leave?

Goosebumps raced over Louisa's shoulders, down her back, her arms.

"So much killing, I am broken," Angeline wept bitterly. "My heart is broken. My people kill your people. Your people kill my people. No soldiers to stop the killing, no soldiers now . . ."

"But, Angeline," argued Louisa, desperate to give her friend some comfort, and to find her own, "we have the *Decatur!* We have Captain Sterrett—he has soldiers!" *Oh, thank God!* Louisa thought with renewed gratefulness, *we do have the warship and the wise captain!* And for the first time since the terrible words—the Indians have attacked!—greeted her on the beach her mind seemed to clear, to become her own again. Familiar thoughts, familiar beliefs. And with these, sanity, not fear. A stronger heart, not despair.

Angeline looked up and sniffed. "Soldiers on the big boat?"

"Big guns too."

Angeline blew her nose.

"In fact," said Louisa, "the boat with all the guns came when the ladies were praying to God for help."

Angeline looked up in surprise. "You pray? And Sahalie Tyee helps you?"

"Yes . . . Sometimes he does, yes."

"Then we pray now! We ask him to stop the killing! I can pray! I know the Lord's Prayer!"

"Mynez can pray too!" piped in Emily Inez, responding to the uplifted mood and wiggling around on Angeline's lap excitedly. "Mynez can say *Nesika Papa!*"

"I've been teaching her the Lord's Prayer in Chinook," Louisa explained.

Angeline smiled. Conspiratorially she whispered something in Emily Inez's ear. Emily Inez nodded gravely and clasped her hands. "Mama, shut eyes," she instructed.

Louisa did.

"Nesika papa klaxta mitlite dopa sahale." Angeline started, but Emily Inez quickly chimed in, and goosebumps of a different sort altogether spread over Louisa's skin, a thrilling sensation, as she listened to the strained, breaking voice of her frightened friend guide the simple, trusting words of her child. At the prayer's end, Emily Inez said, *"Kloshe kahkwa,"* and then, with a very pleased smile, looked up into Angeline's face.

"Amen," repeated Louisa.

"Every day I pray," said Angeline, her fear and sorrow considerably subdued.

"Yes, I think we need to always pray these days." Louisa smiled over at Emily Inez, and was about to say time for bed when Emily Inez, knowing exactly what her mother was going to say, argued, "My no go to bed!"

No hayseed growing between her ears, thought Louisa. "Angeline, would you like to help me tuck her in?" she asked, hoping this might simplify things.

"You tell me story?" Emily Inez asked hopefully, swiveling around on Angeline's lap.

Angeline nodded.

"You tell 'Swallow House,' Angemeem!"

"Please," Louisa reminded.

"Peeze?" Such a sweet, tiny voice.

"Mm-m," said Angeline. "Maybe you like new story?"

"No-no, 'Swallow House!' Long long time 'go when earth all new, all animals have houses . . . a'-sept birds. Angemeem, you tell rest!"

With Emily Inez tucked into bed and Angeline seated on the ground beside her, Louisa hurried outdoors to see about more stovewood. Tonight the stars glittered clear and bright against their velvet blanket. The silver-white moon stood high, nearly full, luminous. Yet when she sniffed the air, she smelled rain. Suddenly she was thinking of the dead settlers at White River. It would be dark there too. Everything cold. Were their bodies lying exposed to the elements? *Someone has to go out there and bury them. Someone has to bury Elizabeth.* She started to cry in the cold moonlight.

"Good-bye," said Angeline suddenly, coming out the door.

"But I was going to make more tea!" Louisa objected, hastily wiping her eyes and wondering how long she'd been standing outdoors, shivering to death.

"My father's fire will go out if I don't put on more wood," Angeline explained.

"Well then if you must," Louisa acquiesced reluctantly, wishing Angeline could stay, at least until David got home. "You'll give my regards to your father? And Jim and George? Oh! Did George bring his new wife this trip?"

"Wake." No.

"Next time?"

Angeline shrugged.

For a minute or two Louisa peered down the trail after her friend, hoping to see David come along. Where was he? What was keeping him? Did he know the Indians had been waiting for the soldiers to leave? But what was she doing out here, shivering like this? She'd catch her death!

One more glance to the dark trees, and she gave up. No sign of David. She picked up her cumbersome, heavy sticks of stovewood and staggered back inside. Emily Inez, secure in her own little world, lay fast asleep. Louisa deposited her armful of wood and went over to kneel quietly by the small trundle bed. With aching love she looked down into her daughter's sweet, innocent face. *Oh, dear God,* she prayed, *don't let anything happen to our little one.*

13

nighttime

At parting [Eaton] particularly admonished McAllister to return that evening, and he had replied that he would do so "if alive."

—Clinton Snowden
in *History of Washington*

"I t's true! A watched pot never boils," laughed Louisa a few minutes later, relieved and happy to see David at last. She held up the teapot. "I made it for Angeline, but she had to leave. Want some?"

"I know. I ran into her on the trail." David shrugged out of his coat and tossed his toque onto its hook on the back of the door. Wearily, he flopped into his chair at the small table.

"It's too late, I take it," said Louisa carefully, realizing her short moment of happiness had come and gone, "for Chief Seattle to work something out with Leschi?"

"That's putting things mildly."

She held the teapot up again. He frowned. Not in response to her but to everything that plagued him. She went ahead and poured him his tea. "Has anyone else from White River come in?"

He nodded.

She had to ask. "The *Brannans?*" The china cup in her hand rattled against its saucer.

Hastily he reached for it. "No. No one out past Nancy and John Thomas, Liza. John Bennett and his children got in, though."

She pulled up a chair and sat with him at the table. "What about the Russells?"

"They just got in. Though Mrs. Russell," he added sadly, "is in a sorry state."

"What do you mean?"

David took a shallow sip of his tea. "They nearly didn't make it. If Mr. Russell hadn't built a tunnel out to the river . . . Well, it was a narrow escape, and Mrs. Russell is half out of her mind with terror."

"He built a tunnel?"

"A while back. Started it, he said, when they first moved out there from Alki."

"Why that's just like in *Uncle Tom's Cabin!*" *Why was she talking about that?*

"Liza. It's war. The Indians are breaking out everywhere."

Her stomach hurt.

"Leschi killed a couple of Eaton's Rangers yesterday."

How could she feel any further alarm when she already felt so saturated, body and soul, by fear? Sweat dripped down her back, down her chest bone.

David ran his thumb around the hot rim of his china cup. "He had no choice. The Rangers had him cornered. He was camped at Connell's Prairie—fishing someone said. Across from Porter's place, up near where Military Road crosses White River. Up the road was Captain Maloney. Down the road—well, here comes Eaton."

141

"How did it happen? *What* happened?"

"Leschi set up an ambush. A fellow by the name of McAllister, and another guy, Connell, rode right into it. Next thing anyone knew, Leschi and maybe a hundred warriors were whooping down the road after the rest of Eaton's boys. Got 'em boxed up tight in some abandoned log house out on Bitting's Prairie."

"Are they dead?"

"The Rangers?" David shrugged. "Suwalth's spy left about four this morning, before things simmered down, so he doesn't know. But things don't look good."

"They *must* be dead."

"Liza—" David leaned over the table, "—this is just the beginning. Everything we ever feared. Yesterday, the Rangers. This morning—White River. As for Slaughter, no one's heard boo from him. Maybe Maloney found him, maybe not. Now Captain Sterrett tells us Major Rains—for whatever reason— is delayed at The Dalles. Which leaves Maloney*and* Slaughter alone in the filed without Rains."

Louisa gasped.

David suddenly shot backward in his chair, and all but spit in a burst of anger, "Stevens and his whirlwind treaties! He raised the tempest, then left us to ride out the storm!"

Tears burned her eyes.

"It's war, Liza. No one can stop it!"

More tears.

"Suwalth says the Indians around here are strutting like jay birds! They figure Maloney and Slaughter are done for! There's even talk of consortium with the Haida—"

She wished he'd stop. . . .

"But before that can happen, Suwalth's more worried about things closer to home." David eased his chair back onto all four legs. "He's worried that maybe the Puyallup settlers are next. Maybe even tonight. And none of them know to be on guard. They have no idea what happened yesterday on Military Road, or out at White River this morning."

"Can't Chief Seattle do *anything* to save us?" She was clutching the table with both hands.

"He's doing what he can."

She stared at her hands, white from gripping the table edge.

David sighed. "He came over with Doc, to talk the rest of his people into moving over to the reservation at Port Madison. If he can take a thousand of them—"

"Everyone knows you can't tell an Indian what to do," she said quietly. "They don't work that way."

"Chief Seattle's a persuasive man."

"He couldn't stop Leschi—"

"Because he didn't get here in time. Liza—" He leaned over the table again. "Seattle's going to talk with the Lake Washington Indians first. To Tecumseh and his brothers. Then head up to the foothills and spread out through the headwaters." He reached for her hands, still gripping the table. Gently he pried them loose and covered them over with his own large, strong hands. He gave her a smile. "It's not all black. We at least have Seattle on our side. If we didn't, we wouldn't be sitting here talking."

"I know. . . ."

"And he *is* persuasive. Remember Mary's clothesline? At Alki? And all our clothes?" He gave her another smile.

That had been a scary afternoon. She'd never seen anything like it, the Indians racing around in a rush to bring everything back they'd stolen, including Pa's red handkerchief.

"We have Seattle. We have Pat Kanim, too," said David.

"Why *is* he on our side?"

"Pat Kanim?"

"I *know* why he is. He's been to San Francisco. He's seen how many white people there are—*but why Seattle?*"

"I don't know. Probably for the same reason as Pat Kanim. But Seattle doesn't have to go to San Francisco, you know, to read the handwriting on the wall."

143

"I was just wondering," said Louisa thoughtfully, "if it was because he's a Christian."

"Leschi's a Christian."

"He *is?*" She hadn't heard *that* before.

"He was baptized the same day as Seattle."

"Oh."

"Being a Christian only lets you claim God on your side."

"Oh, David, it really *is* war, *isn't it?*"

He didn't answer.

"More people are going to die, aren't they? *We* might die." She started to cry then, exhaustion and fear descending all at once. Suddenly she blurted, "Someone has to find Elizabeth. Someone has to bury her. . . ."

"Let's go to bed, Liza, it's late."

"Someone has to bury her, David."

"It's night, it's dark. Come on, bedtime."

When she climbed in beside him, a few minutes later, he was on his back. "Come here," he said, lifting her so that she lay on her stomach, her head resting on his shoulder and chest, her arms tucked in under his neck. This way they could both feel the new baby move and stretch between them, and fall asleep to the rhythm of their own breathing and the steady beat of each other's hearts.

"We're going out in the morning to bury the dead," he told her in a whisper, rubbing the tension out of her back and shoulders with his hard, strong hands.

"Who's going?" she asked, starting to feel lulled.

"The volunteers. We'll bury the dead, and rescue the survivors, if there are any."

"How long?"

"How long will I be gone?"

She nodded.

"I have no idea. We don't know what we'll find, and we have to blaze a trail as we go." His hands slowed, his touch softened. He was growing sleepy.

"You're not going by river? Charles can't take you?" No, she remembered now, Charles was back east with Lee. There was the *Traveler*, though, the new steamboat. "What about Captain Parker?"

"He's in Steilacoom," mumbled David, yawning. "Go to sleep, Liza."

She reached up to cradle his bearded chin in her hand. "How are you going to do it?" she asked him softly. "Go to White River, I mean. The woods are so dense."

"Jim and George Seattle will go as guides."

"Can you talk Klap-ki-latchi into going?"

"Maybe. But you know how he is around white folks."

"I don't blame him, not after Luther Collins tried stringing him up. If it wasn't for you and Dobbins—"

"George swears there's some trails through there. I hope so . . . Hard work if not . . ."

She let David drift, allowing herself a small moment of happiness in the security of her husband's relaxing arms. Nothing was going to happen to them right now, not tonight anyway. "David?" she whispered in a minute.

"Mmm?"

"The baby's getting bigger and bigger. Soon we won't be able to manage this."

"Mmm . . ."

She was nodding off when the full meaning of David's departure in the morning washed over her like a flooding wave taking her out to sea. *"David!"*

He was asleep.

But if David slept this night, others did not. Out at Connell's Prairie, the rich meadowlands washed by White River and through which the military road ran, contention at the Indian war camp ran hot. The spot itself had been forced upon them. This was where, the day before, Leschi had found himself caught between the soldiers up ahead and Eaton's Rangers hard on his heels. Despairingly, Leschi had painted

145

his face black. *Were white men fools? Didn't they know that every creature, no matter how small or outnumbered, will fight the dogs before they die?*

Word of his successful ambush had electrified the Indians everywhere. Even while he and his braves continued far into the night pummeling the remaining Rangers in the abandoned cabin on Bitting's Prairie, warriors and braves from all points had come to help. Muck Creek, South Prairie, the Upper Puyallup. Four in the morning Puyallup's medicine man arrived breathless.

His son, Kitsap the Younger, he said, along with Kanasket of the renegade Klikitat and Nelson of the Muckleshoot, were plotting to descend White River at dawn—on a killing spree. They intended to kill every whiteskin between the headwaters and Seattle—men, women, *and* children.

White men without honor, yes! He could believe that, thought Leschi. He was used to it. *But his own kind?*

Enraged, he'd called off the firing, abandoning the battle against Charlie Eaton and his Rangers. There was no time to lose! He had to get to White River before dawn! Eaton, he'd take care of later. McAllister, he'd already taken care of! "Get the horses hidden out back! Down in the swamp!" he ordered. "Eaton's *and* mine! I want mine back! *All of them!*"

His favorite pony had been brought up. Briefly they nuzzled noses before Leschi leapt onto her familiar back and told the old Puyallup medicine man to stay with the war camp.

"*Go!*" admonished Kitsap the Elder. "Hurry!"

"I'm gone!"

But he'd not made it in time.

And now tonight at the camp, thirty warriors mushroomed to two hundred in less than twenty-four hours, Leschi berated the three chiefs responsible for the outrages. He circled their fire.

"I gave my *word!*" he screamed at Kanasket, Nelson, and Kitsap the Younger. "I told the whiteskins, 'Stay on your own places and you will not be hurt!' But look what you did! Unarmed men! Women! Children!"

Kanasket, the scar-faced war chief of the renegade Klikitat, sneered into the night for all in the camp to hear, "Who calls you chief, to give *me* command?"

Quiemuth, Leschi's brother, quietly spoke up. "We do."

He referred to Leschi's thirty-one braves, a small enough force but one that would instantly obey him and execute his orders. The other warriors—Leschi looked around in worry at the hodgepodge. The others posed a serious dilemma for him. Few could be relied on. Most were deplorably poor shots, many of them arrant cowards and desperate shirks. The most arrant of all was Kanasket, a man Leschi loathed. Kanasket was also the most feared in the camp, the most ruthless, the most cunning, and, next to Leschi, the best marksman. *He needs to be taught a few manners,* thought Leschi. With a swift kick, he booted his nemesis in the ribs. "Who am I?" he roared in a challenge. "Who are *you?*"

Kanasket came to his feet, howling, "I am war chief of *Klikitat!*" and he lunged for Leschi and would've had his throat had Leschi not adroitly dodged.

Leschi came back around. Contemptuously, he pushed the flat of his hand against Kanasket's chest. "Chief of *renegade* Klikitat," he scorned. "Why are you not with the rest of your band? Why are you not with my cousin Qualchin! Son of Owhi! Fiercest of all war chiefs and lieutenant to Kamiakin! You don't answer? You are nothing but a dog!" and he spit, and with a wave of his hand dismissed Kanasket like a bad dog.

Nelson lumbered to his feet, deliberately stepping between the two quarreling men.

"Out of the way," Leschi told him flatly.

"He is the only one here trained in warfare," said Nelson, gripping his musket. "We are only farmers and hunters. He wishes you no harm. He brought you the child, did he not? To be your son? He could have kept the boy himself."

147

The white boy. They'd taken one of the children to pacify him.

Leschi whirled away from the fire. *Fools! Fools! They saw only the battle, not the war!* And such short-sightedness, he knew, would cost *him* the war!

Kanasket hollered out, taunting. "If you wish to be war chief, you have to go to war!" Leschi flung himself around to face the gyrating war chief, dancing now around the fire and executing a war cry of high yipping screams. Leschi shouted over the hideous ruckus.

"You think killing women and children is war? Do you have the heart of a mouse?"

Sudden silence. Everywhere. And then, from Kanasket who'd stopped dancing and was standing deathly still, "Tomorrow at dawn! The Puyallup! No whiteskin escapes! You hear me? *I* am your war chief! You! Leschi! Go back to your plowing! Only men with courage are *my* braves!"

Leschi strode away. He had his own means to counter Kanasket this night. Let Kanasket think himself victor for now. Let him win this particular battle. *He,* Leschi, would win the war!

14

still nighttime

When the news . . . reached Seattle on that memorable Sunday evening of the 28th, Thomas Mercer was still on his place north of the village. Dexter Horton and William (Bill) Gilliam went out quickly to warn him. Mrs. Susan Mercer Graham remembers how her father talked in low tones to the men outside the cabin; how, stepping inside, he told his daughters not to be frightened but to pack some clothes and bedding, for there was danger from Indians and they must get into town at once.

Stumbling along the dark trail, her hand in Dexter Horton's, Susie began to cry. Mr. Horton told her not to cry; there might not be any Indians lurking about, but then again there might. They must be very quiet.

—Roberta Frye Watt, Katy Denny's daughter
in *Four Wagons West*

There were others who didn't sleep this frightful night of the 28th. Two miles north of Seattle Susannah Mercer woke just after midnight. She could hear her father talking to two men outside. Indians! In just minutes she was hurrying along the road into Seattle with her family, trying hard not to cry. But the night was so cold. The moon so high it cast long scary shadows across the trail before them. And she had to hop and run to keep up with Mr. Horton, who held her hand tightly. A few feet ahead was her father, carrying Alice and holding Eliza Ann's hand. Behind was Mr. Gilliam and her big sister, Mary Jane. But Susannah was only twelve years old, and though she tried, she couldn't stop the tears from dribbling down her cheeks. Nor could she stop the big gulps of air that started coming up, pushing past the awful lump in her throat.

"Shh," whispered Mr. Horton, giving her hand a gentle squeeze. "You mustn't cry, Susie. There might not be any Indians lurking about, but then again there might. We must be very quiet."

They weren't halfway to Seattle when she felt the first sprinkle of rain.

For a long time Johnny King couldn't figure out why the tree kept rubbing his shoulder for there was no wind. It made no sense. He tried pushing it away. Gradually he realized it was Tom, Tom from the woods, Tom who'd brought them here to this lodge. Now Tom was persistently poking his shoulder. "It is time," Tom said to him. "We go now. The moon is high."

Johnny could see this was so. Shining rays fell down through the circular hole at the top of the shelter where he and his sister and brother had been put to bed—though exactly where he was, he had no idea. This was not his world. But he was tired, he knew that much, and was so sleepy he had to keep rubbing his eyes to make them stay open. "Dead for sleep," his mother called such behavior. In the end it was his sister and brother who woke him up for they were positively cross. He pushed them out the flap of the wigwam, got them into the canoe Tom had ready and waiting, and was glad it was dark. Was his mother still alive? Had the Indians come back? He pushed away his tears as inconspicuously as possible with his shoulders. *Oh, Mother!* his little heart wept.

If the night was frosty, the ride downriver was ice. Clad in nothing more than what they'd worn when sitting down to breakfast sixteen hours before, the three children huddled against each other for warmth in the bottom of the cold dugout. Johnny was beginning to think he and the little ones just might freeze to death when, in the muted light of night, a scratchy warm blanket was pushed forward beside him. Remembering his manners—and mumbling between frozen lips and chattering teeth—he said thank-you to Tom then hastily spread the blanket over the three of them, only his own head sticking out so he could watch his kind benefactor, bathed in moonlight.

Naked to the waist without his blanket, Tom knelt in the stern, perched on his heels, and he paddled more vigorously and in quicker rhythm as if to keep from freezing. Under the tent of blanket, however, warmth slowly began to grow and the little ones quieted. Finally they fell into sleep, the canoe bobbing and bouncing faster and faster, hurtling on down the cold river of moonlight. When the little ones woke some time later from hunger, Tom handed them four cold boiled potatoes, all the food he had in the canoe. They ate and fell back to sleep, Johnny too—but only because it had started to rain. To keep dry he squirreled down with his sister and brother beneath the blanket, head and all. There, in the cozy warmth and darkness, and in spite of himself, he at last let go and slept.

In the Puyallup Valley south of Seattle, pioneers leapt from their beds to boots while still asleep, stirred by a fierce pounding on their doors and a frantic message that stopped their hearts but quickened their wits. "Mr. Hayward!" "Mr. Morrison!" "Mr. Kincaid!" "Mr. Woolery!" "Mr. More!" "Mr. Benson!" "Mr. Nix! Hurry, go to the fort! You will be killed if you don't!" Eighty settlers in all lived on the Puyallup, a twelve-mile vale of wooded forests and luxurious meadows, and all through the cold dark night a lone old Indian on horseback thundered down the valley with his warning, plunging into each yard, reigning in and leaping to the ground almost before his horse could stop, banging on each door and shouting over and over. "Mr. Boatman! Get up! Take your family to the fort!" "Get up! Mr. Wright! Get up! This is Kitsap the Elder! Leschi sent me! You're in danger from my son Kitsap the Younger! From Nelson! From Kanasket!" "Mr. Bett! Get up! Get up! Everyone is to be massacred, all the whiteskins! All of you!" "Mr. Meeker!" "Mr. Dunlap! Get up! Quick! Quick! Go to the fort! Hurry! Get up! Get up!"

At Stuck Creek, a tributary of the Puyallup, the warning propelled a frightened widower out of bed, along with his seventeen-year-old son, his daughter, fifteen years old, and five-year-old Joseph. They escaped across the river on a fallen alder log that stretched bank to bank. Mr. Kincaid's eldest son, John, carried the gun, Susan the little boy. The two of them ran like the blazes over the river on that small log while their father, being an older gentleman and not very good at walking so small a log even in daytime, dropped down on all fours and cooned across it. They all went running pell-mell over to Jonathan McCarthy's, the trail between the two homes well trod. McCarthy had just recently married Ruth Kincaid.

Earlier in the evening the lucky groom had forgotten to load his gun. He was just getting out of bed to do so when his father-in-law and his wife's sister and brothers burst through the door. "The Indians are here!" McCarthy got so excited at the terrifying news that he put his boots on backwards. Loading his double-barreled rifle he forgot to put powder in one of the barrels.

Five miles east of Fort Steilacoom, the Meekers—a father, two sons and their wives—were awakened at two in the morning by the furious pounding and frightful summons.

The three families under the one roof couldn't agree what they should do. The two sons insisted their own log cabin, with their own trusted rifles in their own hands, was safer than hurrying to a fort that wasn't truly a fort but an encampment of log cabins and light board houses and that furthermore had no soldiers. But father and women insisted they fly. They flew.

Another Indian rider, his horse dripping with sweat, pounded up to Jim Longmire's farmhouse on Yelm Prairie. Hair stood up the back of Longmire's neck when he heard the news. Quickly he holstered his revolver and went out to the barn to saddle up. High time to join his family already playing it safe at Olympia!

But out in the barn his horse was gone! Frightened, he hightailed it over to McLean Chambers's place, tripping across the furrowed field in the moonlight, scared spitless and figuring any moment he was a dead man. He found Chambers ready to make the run. "So you really think there's something to this scare, Chambers?" Longmire asked, hoping against hope to hear an argument. He got none out of Chambers.

"See you in Olympia, Longmire! Say, what's the matter with you?"

Longmire was frantically glancing about, here, there, slapping at his holstered revolver.

"Longmire!" repeated Chambers. "You got bats in your belfry?"

"I can't believe it, I left my rifle at home!"

"You what?"

"I left my rifle!"

"Forget your tea kettle!"

"I can't walk twenty-five miles into Olympia with only a revolver!"

Chambers swore in exasperation, stood up in his stirrups, swung his right leg back over his horse's rump, and dropped to the ground. "Take my horse. Get your fool rifle, then get back here on the double. I'll be hiding in the hay out back."

Longmire leapt into the saddle and beat a hasty path back to his house, only to find just about everything he and his wife owned strewn across the yard, a graveyard of sorts. The ransacked pork barrels looked like strange headstones in the pearly light of the moon. Inside, the house was worse. Everything torn apart, turned upside down. When he got a match lit and then a candle, and got to looking around, he saw that everything of value was gone, including his rifle. Every stitch of clothing, every cache of food . . . *At least I had the good sense to send Alvira and the boys to Olympia.*

Wondering if he'd ever see them again, he edged back out the door. Revolver drawn and ready to fire in a blink, he mounted his neighbor's horse and put it to a lively run. McLean Chambers was in the hay, just like he said.

"Hate leaving you behind, unarmed and all. Maybe you can hike over to my brother's place?" suggested Chambers. "See if he's got a horse and rifle he can let you have? But for land's sakes, stick to the woods, man!"

"I'll do that, thank you."

But Tom Chambers was gone too. Longmire decided to head over to the Hughes's, and was just coming into the yard, passing a pile of rails so newly cut the scent still sweetened the air, when he heard horses coming up on the trail. Quickly he dove behind the rails, hunkered down, heart pounding in his ears. In just minutes he heard the peculiar "shee-shee" hissing sound the Indians used to drive their stock. *The blackguards are stealing every last horse off the prairie!* Angrily he smote a fist into the ground beside him.

Coast finally clear, he made his way over to the house but found to his dismay that the Hughes, too, had already fled. *Now where do I go? Now what do I do?* he wondered, frightened, stomping cold toes onto the stoop, staring at the silent door and feeling against his cheek the first drop of rain. Ah! George Edwards! Edwards, a former employee of the Hudson's Bay Company, had married a Nisqually woman and gone "American," meaning he'd filed a 640-acre claim under the Donation Act. He'd be home! A man with a Nisqually wife didn't need to fear the Indians!

But Edwards—after stepping outside and quickly shutting the door behind him—shook his head no when asked for the loan of a rifle. "Besides, you'll never make Olympia by sunrise."

"You don't think?"

"Nope. And you can't stay here, it's too dangerous. Well," he relented in the ensuing silence, "I suppose the barn's all right. But soon as it's dark again, Longmire, you best make hay while you can. Hungry?"

"Yes, I think so."

"I'll have the missus bring you some grub in the morning."

Fear was its own catalyst. Having ignited at White River it swiftly enflamed the Sound, and in its brisk devastating path none slept. Those farthest out were the most frantic. They fled house and home with nary hat nor coat. Closer to the settlements, where a larger population presumably lent some sense of safety in numbers, better thought and preparation seemed to prevail. Teams of horses and oxen were gathered by lamplight. Hastily they were put to the yoke. Wherever possible stock was turned onto the open range to fend for itself. Windows and doors were barricaded. Provisions and goods that could be carried were loaded into wagons and, once loaded, silently urged forward. Horse and oxen tugged into their braces. Leather creaked. Wagons rumbled out. Away from lonely cabins into the dark—and, when the fearful night fell into its darkest hours, rain.

Moving out past the settlements the opposite direction, Billy Tidd, blissfully unaware of the panic behind him or the dangers ahead, waded his horse into the milky shallows of the Puyallup River by moonlight, scuffled across its pebbly bed, then plunged again into yet another patch of woods to ascend Elhi Hill. He'd been in the saddle too long and was bone tired, and for a very brief moment thought of pulling over at Mr. Bitting's half-finished cabin to sneak forty winks. But time was of the essence. He'd gotten a late start. Besides, he decided, thundering past the abandoned house, it looked oddly haunted, what with the moon playing swords through the uncaulked logs. He pushed on, into yet another stand of woods, unaware he'd passed the Rangers, who were still holed up and uncertain as to what to do. Make a run for it, or await their reinforcements.

Dusk had drawn its curtain. The high, nearly full moon caused every obstacle of fallen tree, bramble, and quagmire to loom large and formidable. His eyes fairly stung from straining to see what was real and what was not, and he bent low over his horse's neck, the two of them clinging together, dashing between the shadowed fir trunks and hemlock and cedar, Tidd whisking his "off" leg away to avoid amputation, dodging the boughs that drooped across the "road." *Fine enough road,* he grumbled to himself irritably, fatigue blunting his normal good humor, *for men on foot or driving a mule train!* But for a rider trying to make time? The biggest stumps had yet to be grubbed. They stood shin to knee-high with sharp spires and splintered edges—death for any horse. Laming caltrops, saplings, and briars that once grew in the trail but which gave way to folks riding through, were now torn up and thrown into rigid heaps; a bristling, unyielding hedge that could only be skirted or leaped. As far as he was concerned, it seemed a belt of forest had been unmade and nothing made, and it seemed to him that guys like Finnell and Lemmon and Ogle and Connell, guys who lived along this miserable stretch of the road, really ought to see to things. But maybe they figured the army should.

Military Road suddenly dropped him into a heavily timbered swamp, a mile-deep jungle of standing and fallen timber, brush, and deep bogs that filled with water after every rain. "Whoa, whoa!" he hollered suddenly, his horse shying and pulling back.

They stood quietly and very still for a moment while he peered nervously into the moonlight, searching for sight, for sound. Nothing. Only the roaring torrent of White River two or three miles off. "Come on, old girl," he finally whispered, "we haven't got all day." But a few yards on she balked again. "Whoa! Whoa!" He reined in hard, listened hard, tried hard to decipher the shadows rippled by moonbeams. He missed entirely the two bodies. He was looking for Indians crouched behind trees or hiding under briar clumps, not two dead white men. "Come on then," he urged. "This is no Sunday stroll, old girl. There you go, eas-sy now. . . ."

Half an hour later they approached the river crossing where Military Road intersected White River. Rapid, turbulent, treacherously deep, the river rushed formidably off the high mountain peaks and ran so deep all the way down to the Duwamish that only a few places were at all fordable. The water gleamed white from the powder ground by the glacier rock farther up, and was so turbid at this first crossing that the boulders—as big as a man's head and bigger, and worn round and smooth and slippery—were invisible even by day, and made uncertain footing for man and beast. A misstep meant, in all probability, fatal results.

Tidd hesitated but a moment at the roaring edge between land and river before urging his horse in, the thunderous roar of the water all around obliterating every sound but itself. A hundred yards away was the sleeping war camp, as oblivious to Tidd's passing as he to their presence.

He and his horse entered the water by pointing their noses upstream lest the urgent current, bearing against their broadsides, douse, if not drown, them. He felt the first icy cold of the water when it embraced his ankles. Almost at once it soaked through his moccasins, numbing his feet, then climbed high up his shins until his teeth fairly chattered. His horse held steady, though. Floundering at times,

157

but always recovering herself, she stoutly carried them both on through. If the footing became too uncertain, she'd stop stock-still, test the riverbed with one foot, finally reach out carefully until she could find more secure footing, then move up a step or two. This instinctive nature of his horse reassured Tidd, and when they scrambled up onto the other slope, icy water streaming off their legs, he was wide wake, his horse ready to run.

"Ah, burr-rrrr! How many more like that before the summit, old girl?" he asked exuberantly, now that he was wide awake. "A dozen, you say? Not talking? All right then."

At the next river crossing the moon clouded over. Great! Tidd shoved his chin down inside his coat collar and pulled his woolen toque down around his ears. He kneed his horse, urged her faster up the ever-steepening trail. "I expect you went and forgot the umbrella?"

Louisa listened to the rain beginning to fall against the cedar shakes overhead and into the trees beyond her four walls. She listened, too, to the sound of David's deep, even breathing. *Tomorrow he'll be gone.* She slipped her fingers into his hand, slack with sleep. Tears filled her eyes. She felt them run down off her temples, into her ears. The rain picked up. Three in the morning and it was drumming on the roof, leaking through, dripping onto the stove. Had she ever heard such rain?

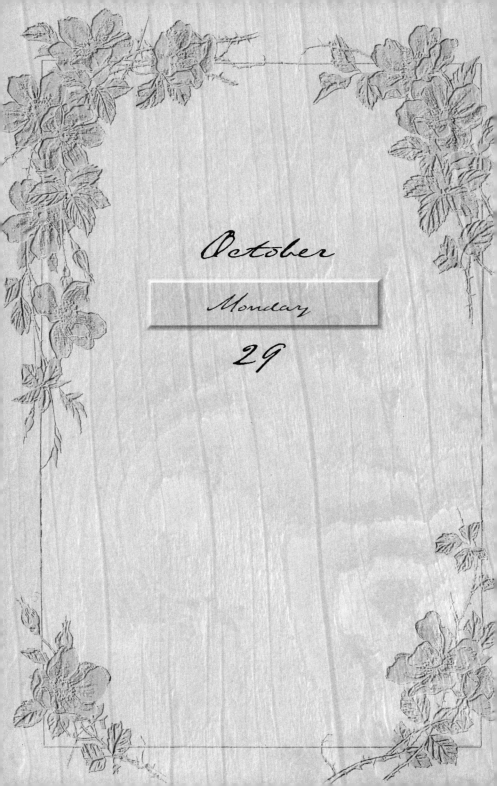

October

Monday

29

15

morning

This influx into the towns meant an extreme hardship for the farmers, for in this climate the fall harvesting had not been completed. Henry Van Asselt told in after years how he and Sam Maple and Dr. S. L. Grow cared for their crops and stock and slept in the woods at night. . . . Mr. Mercer remained in a little house in town, but drove out to his farm by day.

—Roberta Frye Watt, Katy Denny's daughter
in *Four Wagons West*

By morning the pounding downpour had stopped. The sun came out with surprising energy and warmth to catch the rash of battered Conestogas lumbering and jouncing with all possible speed along the narrow roads of the Upper Sound.

The narrow roads led into Military Road like creeks flowing into a river; narrow, crooked little creeks flooding a river of roots and holes and ruts and mud. This morning, after last night's hard rain, the road couldn't have been worse. Thick mud sucked on everything that came along.

Hopping beside the splattered wagons or trying to catch up from behind, children by the dozens drove sheep and hogs and geese through the mud while the men, eyes bloodshot from fatigue and worry—though this did not stop them from keeping a sharp lookout—herded their cattle with impatient prodding and occasional bellowing. At the Puyallup River, those living on the far side were forced to endure a nerve-wracking wait on the bank, shuffling and peering over their shoulders as their wagons were ferried in pieces to the far shore. Following the reassembling of the wagons, they too joined the mad dash down muddy Military Road to the fort, chicken crates and children bouncing along on the top of the load and sometimes off.

In no time at all Fort Steilacoom beggared description. Settlers arrived on foot with scant clothing and no food. Others came with their wagons piled high with furniture, everything from footstools to spinning wheels to pianos and plows. Some had their chicken coops piled higgledy-piggledy in with other effects, tailed by a menagerie of cattle, sheep, and swine—all of which could not possibly be cared for at the fort! Some came with horse teams, some with oxen, others with pack ponies. Many a mother came packing her youngest child on her back, leading her other children by the hand. All day long this never-ending stream, supplemented in the afternoon until late in the night, and then again the next day by those living farthest out.

A sorry mess, the fort. By eight in the morning timid women and children were crying, some brutes of men were cursing and swearing, oxen bawled, cattle lowed, sheep and goats bleated forlornly, dogs were barking, ducks squawking, geese honking, chickens screeching, children lost from parents, wives from husbands, a world without order. In a word, utmost *disorder*.

Second Lieutenant Nugen, left in charge of the fort that wasn't a fort, hastily wrote Acting Governor Mason in Olympia for he was alarmed not just by the tidal wave of humanity and livestock invading his fort but by the rumor accompanying the panic.

A rumor to the effect that McAllister and nine others of the Rangers were killed on the Puyallup, and that the Indians were advancing toward this post 250 strong. *I am unable to say how true this is, but fear it is all too true. . . . I have nearly all the women and children in the county at this post, and will of course protect them,* he wrote.

In Olympia, the territorial capital, the same panic prevailed. Settlers from miles around were fast crowding into the small village and every available shelter was being sought to protect the women and children. Two and three families crowded into one small room, others found shelter in woodsheds and outbuildings. It was apparent to all how utterly vulnerable and unprepared they were, and men and women, with blanched, terror-stricken countenances, appealed to each other for help and protection. Their lack of arms and means of defense; the uncertainty as to the number of hostiles and where they were; the sparsely spread settlements; the restricted means of communications; the soldiers gone to fight elsewhere—all this combined to accelerate their runaway panic.

In a concerted effort to protect the town from whatever and however many Indians had broken out, Acting Governor Mason and Isaac Hayes, captain of Olympia's "Home Guard," (brother to Captain Judge Gilmore Hayes of Company B already in the field with Captain Maloney), moved quickly. Isaac Hayes picketed sentries on the hills above town while Mason had every piece of firearm—of *any* use—hunted up and loaded. The price of powder and shot went sky high. One volunteer paid forty dollars cash for a small Kentucky rifle that didn't cost above six dollars at the factory. Another man laid out twenty-four dollars for a secondhand Colt revolver not worth two dollars. Most weren't that lucky. Within an hour or so there wasn't a gun to be had at any price and Mason, desperate for weapons, sent a dispatch to the

Hudson's Bay Company at their nearby Fort Nisqually with a requisition for whatever arms and ammunition they might have on hand.

Seattle, north sixty miles, was spared this chaos—but only because two useless roads led into town: Mercer Road servicing but two families—Uncle Tommy Mercer's farm and David Denny's claim to the north—and Beach Road to the south, a wretched, sorry excuse of a road that hugged the shoreline around Elliott Bay to the Duwamish River mouth and over which no wagon could *ever* be driven. The trail, for this was all it could legitimately be called, crawled up steep hills and down again. Sometimes it fell away altogether into the sea, necessitating yet another bridge of sorts to be built, only to wash out again on the next high tide. Consequently, the pioneers fleeing to Seattle had to do so by canoe and could take precious little. Likewise, farmers coming from the south, along the beach, were limited, able to bring into town only what they could carry on their backs and in their hands. This spared Seattle the chaos, also the urgency and panic accompanying clutter and confusion. Too, they had the *Decatur*, a reassuring presence.

Perhaps too reassuring. The farmers who lived within walking distance—and finding themselves once again in Seattle without their effects and crops still begging harvest—were tempted by the calm light of day and cleared skies to return home.

Uncle Tommy Mercer was one. He had a bumper crop of potatoes and onions, and though Louisa and David tried to persuade him to stay in town where he and the girls might be safe, he adamantly insisted upon going back.

"At least leave the girls," David pleaded.

"Do," urged Louisa. "I worry about them out there. And we'd love to have them as our guests. I could use the company, what with David leaving today. . . ." Her voice trailed off and she said no more.

164

The two littlest of the four Mercer girls jumped up and down silently while their father debated. But in the end Uncle Tommy demurred, deciding instead to rent a small board cabin next door to Dr. Williamson's mercantile on the Point. He got the girls settled into housekeeping, then took one of his horses and rode back out to the farm.

Uncle Tommy owned the only two horses north of Steilacoom: Tib, a glossy black mare, and Charley, a snowy white gelding. Normally Tom stabled them at Plummer's Livery down near the sandspit on the Point so that his partner in the transport business, Dexter Horton, after having tallied figures all day at his store, could use them to haul lumber over to the mill. Or to take shipments coming in by sea up to the four stores on Commercial Street. But today Uncle Tommy split the team to take Tib, a nervous beast with a sixth sense for danger, with him. He put in a full day's work at the farm, turned right around, and rode the two and a half miles back into town where Mary Jane, his eldest, sixteen years old, had supper ready and waiting. For a whole fortnight this would be Uncle Tommy's routine, ceasing only when his crops were at last cellared and stored.

Other men felt compelled to return as well. Dr. Henry Smith—warned by Mr. Plummer during the night and having paddled in from Smith Cove with muffled oars—ensconced his mother at "Plummer's Post," his sister's fancy mansion across from her husband's livery stables. Satisfied both his mother and sister were safe, he hired a couple of "harum-scarum"—as he described them—deserters who, at some point in time, had jumped ship when their sea captains weren't looking. Henry paddled them out to his orchard on the Cove where the three of them took turns picking apples and standing guard—always with a sharp eye and loaded rifles. Many a time, hearing the bushes crack behind them, their faces would blanche and they'd spring for their rifles only to discover that the crackling brush was nothing more than a deer passing through. At night they barred the

165

door and slept in the attic, hauling the ladder up after themselves. Sometimes the deserters, pranksters at heart—and always egged on by Henry who enjoyed a good tale—told bloodcurdling stories until they became panicky by their own eloquence. One morning they woke to find fresh moccasin tracks circling the house. After that, Henry had a hard time keeping the boys. He managed by opening his pocketbook, and two weeks later his crop too was cellared and stored. At a cost considerably higher than he'd anticipated.

Henry Van Asselt, Sam Maple, and Dr. Grow on the Duwamish River did something similar on their farms, rotating days at their different claims, trading off work and guard duty with each other, sleeping each night in the woods.

Luther Collins, like Henry Smith, hired deserters to help him out. His farm was the first in the area and was in its fourth season of production. There was seemingly no end to his beets, his peaches and pears and cherries, his potatoes, his onions, his parsley, carrots, turnips, rutabagas, squash, pumpkins. On and on.

George Frye, brought in from his timber camp, was up and gone at the crack of dawn. Worried the Indians might have stolen his oxen, he hurried all the way. He found them; but in a high state of nervous agitation, lowing miserably and straining at their ropes—an oddly typical reaction for oxen on the Sound whenever they smelled Indians. The instant he loosed them they were gone, charging up Beach Road. The whole five miles into Seattle they lumbered pellmell, lurching side to side in their awkward gait, heads low, tails high, bawling in confusion, cow bells clanging with every lurch and lunge—George right behind and hard after them. Breathing fast. Hat gone. Hair streaming straight out.

Captain Sterrett, on deck of the *Decatur,* was surveying the comical scene through his spyglass, and he laughed right out loud.

His lieutenant, leaning on the ship rail beside him—the two men waiting for eight bells and breakfast—thought the laughter peculiar considering the cloud of worry they were under.

Sterrett, still chuckling, handed over the glass. "Take a look at that, Lieutenant."

Lieutenant Drake, a tall man with a fair complexion and ink black hair, found himself smiling a little. "Didn't know oxen could run that fast!" he said. "Say, how old do you suppose the kid is anyway?"

"Twenty?" guessed Sterrett, a shorter man, bulkier, about ten years older than his lieutenant.

"Oops," said Drake.

"What?"

"Someone else is coming in." He passed the spyglass back to the captain.

"Where?"

"Yonder—on the bay, coming off the river mouth." He pointed.

Sterrett fiddled a little with the glass, then held still, breath held. "Coming mighty fast . . . whoever he is. Here, take another look, Drake. That look like an Indian to you?"

16

still morning

The oldest of the children, little John King, almost seven years of age, told the settlers enough to convince them that a hideous massacre had taken place. The gruesome details they discovered later.

—Roberta Frye Watt, Katy Denny's daughter
in *Four Wagons West*

When Johnny King awoke, the rain had long since ceased and they'd come to a place where the river divided itself around an island. Tom steered into the right channel, paddling harder but going slower. *"Salt chuck,"* he grunted when he saw Johnny watching him. Tidewater.

The river met itself again and widened, opening like a fan, melting into a sea all of its own. A luminous gray sea, pink glazed, spreading far away to a distant shore—though not so far that Johnny couldn't see that the shoreline went almost straight up into high hills, and that beyond the forest, on the hills, the morning had broken open with pink in her sky.

In his nostrils there was the strange, exciting smell of salt-water. Against his cheeks the morning breeze was fresh and stinging cold. The water that stretched away from the canoe seemed to him to dance, every little sharp wave a graceful leap, twinkling pink in the silver. Tom was paddling easily now, slowly drifting at the river's mouth, his eyes intent upon something moving to their right. Then Johnny saw it was another canoe, paddled by another Indian, coming directly toward them. Tom and the stranger hailed. The two canoes drifted together. The two men jabbered. Tom pointed across the bay. The other Indian nodded, but argued. Johnny could see he'd been fishing. Hooks and lines and three slithery wet cod were tangled in the bottom of his canoe.

"You go with him," said Tom at last to Johnny. "Indian Dave will take you to Seattle." No more was said. The stranger lifted the two sleeping children into his canoe. Johnny made the transfer himself, a little nervous because the canoes were tippy and he wasn't sure about those hooks. After the children were settled in, the canoes separated. Tom started to paddle back up the river. Johnny waved good-bye, and was glad when Tom turned around and waved too.

The new Indian started across the rippled water toward the high distant shore, paddling swiftly with long, clean strokes, leaving behind tiny swirls of funneling water each time he lifted his paddle to dig back in. For a long time Johnny sat mesmerized by this, until he noticed a large ship ahead, anchored but a few rods offshore from a small peninsula.

The ship was a great black one. With muzzles of big cannons poking out the gun ports. Above were three towering masts with black yards, like crosses, against the sky. The peninsula near which it floated, Johnny now saw, was like a high island, but connected to the mainland by a strip of yellow sawdust. On the high part of the peninsula, and on the mainland too, scattered cabins and houses of a village peeked out among the trees.

Seattle. He remembered being there.

169

They came closer to the ship. Johnny squinted, the rising sun in his eyes. Several men stood on deck. And then he saw the gun. Pointed straight at him. He screamed—"MOTHER-R-R-R-R-R!"—one long high-pitched cry of terror and threw himself onto the bottom of the canoe amongst all the lines and hooks and sliding fish, hands over his head, and he could not stop screaming.

In town, everyone rushed to their windows. At the little "Mercer" house on Commercial Street (where David and Louisa lingered to see the girls properly settled before returning to their own affairs—both terribly anxious about David's imminent departure for White River), Louisa and the girls hastily, breathlessly, pressed their noses to the dirty windowpane. David yanked open the door. Suddenly laughter joined the wild cry, a burst of mirth more startling than the scream itself, and the effect was not unlike that of an unrosined bow screeching across a violin string, immediately accompanied by the low tones of a playful bassoon rollicking through the scales. But after a few more bars of the colliding music, the violin petered out, as if embarrassed by its discordant outburst, while the bassoon played on in merry quick rhythm. The screaming had ceased. Only the amazing laughter remained.

All through town the pioneers, looking to each other for explanations not forthcoming, finally braved their fear and headed for the wharf. By the time David and Louisa got down to the waterfront with Emily Inez, Mary Jane, Eliza Ann, Susannah, and Alice Mercer the story had been told and retold a dozen times. Three children from White River had just been brought in by a friendly Indian, their approach across the bay monitored by Captain Sterrett through the spyglass. The eldest—some said he was six years old, others said seven—happened to look up as they approached. Having just seen his parents shockingly and swiftly murdered by the Indians he'd thought the spyglass bearing down on him was a gun. This unexpected danger, just when he thought himself safe,

170

had struck him with terror. But the laughter? So soon following? The child's terror juxtaposed against something so harmless as a spyglass was apparently—to Indian Dave—a hilarious joke. As for the boy, once given the spyglass to examine, he forgot his embarrassment and, once aboard the *Decatur* and finding himself surrounded by a company of uniformed marines, his fear.

The story he told, however, struck terror into the hearts of everyone else. Their worst fears were realized. There'd been a massacre of horrific scale. Friends were dead, and they needed only to look around to find out who was not with them—the Brannans, the Kings, the Joneses—the three families farthest out.

While Indian Dave went ashore hoping to hawk his glassy-eyed fish, the men of Company H determinedly and grim-faced dispersed to collect what they could in way of shovels and pick axes, hatchets, handsaws, crowbars, anything useful to cut through the forest. The women stumbled home in sick dread to gather what they could in way of provisions for their men while fighting their tears and trying to answer their children's many anxious questions. "Why's Pa leaving?" "Is he coming back?" "What will happen to us?" "Did the Indians kill a whole lot of people, Ma?"

Mrs. Butler relieved David and Louisa of their self-imposed charge of the Mercer girls, and led them back to the Point like Mother Goose with four goslings. Her full Virginian dress swung through the mud and sawdust like a luminous flower waving cheerfully in the gloom.

Because Arthur wasn't a volunteer and wouldn't be going, Mary Ann was able to help Louisa pack a hastily emptied flour sack for David. She needed help. Johnny King's horrifying story kept ringing through her ears and reverberating through her heart until she was fairly sick with apprehension, shuddering at every thought of David going out to the scene of such outrages. What kind of evil compelled men to gun down a woman and her children while they were seated at their Sunday morning breakfast? *And where were those same evil men now? What further murderous plots were they hatching?* These were the questions that plagued her, and she sat at her own table, listlessly, staring at the growing pile of supplies Mary Ann laid out on the bed.

Two blankets.

A loaf of bread.

Dried venison.

Cheese.

Several tea bags.

A pie.

Dried blackberries.

A tin pot.

A tin cup.

A tin spoon.

Sulfur matches.

"I have some dried clams," said Mary Ann all of a sudden. "He likes clams."

"Yes," said Louisa quietly.

"Nora," Mary Ann told her eight-year-old, "run home and get down some of the clams for Uncle David."

"I don't know where they are, Ma."

"Katy knows, ask her."

Katy was minding the other children next door, and as soon as Nora was gone, dashing lickety-split over the trail between the two homes, Louisa began to cry. "I don't know what I'm going to do, Mary," she said, weeping softly, "if he doesn't come back to me."

Mary Ann put down the bread and went over to her sister. "None of us will know what to do, Liza, if he doesn't come back."

"I shall die, I think. Oh, Mary, it just keeps getting worse. And now David is going out there? To face how many Indians? With only murder in their hearts? I shall die, for I can't bear the idea of life without David."

Mary Ann sighed deeply. "Maybe it's best we don't think about such things until we need to."

"I can't help it, Mary." Louisa used her apron to dry her eyes. "He's everything to me."

"But you have Mynez to look after . . . and the little one coming."

Louisa looked out the window. The sea stretched into the sky, everything gray. Odd that the water was so calm while her soul felt so troubled. "Now I know how it was for Ma when Father died," she said sadly.

"Lonely?" guessed Mary Ann.

"Poor Ma. It must have been terrible for her until she met Pa." She looked back over to Mary. "Do you think so?"

Nora stomped in and plopped the long string of clams onto the table. "Ugh! They stink to high heaven!" she declared, wrinkling her nose in utter disgust, her soft brown curls bouncing around her animated face.

"Such exaggeration," sighed Mary Ann, getting up from the table. "She's getting more like her sister every day."

"They do stink, Ma! Don't they, Auntie Louisa? Say yes, Auntie! Please! Ple-eease!"

"Yes, Nora, they stink."

"See, Ma? I told you!"

Down on the Sawdust, Captain Hewitt and Lieutenant Neely detailed the tools coming in while Mr. Yesler bustled around with brand-new burlap sacks, bundling things up, carefully balancing weight and bulk so none of the "soldier boys" had to carry too much. Captain Sterrett, seeing that the loosely organized militia was determined to proceed with or without sufficient ammunition, sought out Arthur to make arrangements with him to purchase eighteen stands of arms—the very last that could be spared from the *Decatur*. The two men were overseeing the final load from the sloop of war when a sudden shout erupted at the cookhouse.

"Looks like a scuffle," said Arthur. Both men hurried off the wharf and crossed the Sawdust to the cookhouse.

"What's going on, Wyckoff?" Arthur asked breathlessly, pushing into the hastily gathering crowd and squeezing in next to Seattle's blacksmith. "Whoa! How'd David get mixed up with the likes o' Ben Wetmore?" The leader of the Do-Nothings had his fists up and was dancing around David like some kind of mad man. "What the deuce . . . ?"

"Some Indian," said Lewis, "was getting a bucket of water over at the pump. Wetmore didn't like it. Kicked the bucket, water and all, sent the whole thing flying. Should have seen it, Arthur. Whoa, water everywhere! Must have been near plumb full when Wetmore came along!"

"And then along came David," said Arthur, figuring the rest out for himself.

Wetmore was still circling, punching the air. "You been the dandy telling us Injuns is no-good devils! Now they're murderin' white folk and yer stickin' up fer 'em? Come on, Denny, git yer hands up, ye yellow-bellied kissup!"

Arthur shook his head in disgust. "Twelve hours ago the man was saying the Indians were as happy as clams. Now, because some of them have taken to the warpath he figures they all have?"

"You should have seen him! He went wild, Arthur—soon as David rescued that bucket and handed it over, nice as you please, to that Indian. Whoa, just look at him! He's been itching to fight your brother! Now he's got his chance. He won't let this one slip by."

"Looks that way, doesn't it," said Arthur, watching curiously. Would David fight? Walk away? Would he even try to reason with the crusty old goat? If so, it would be a complete waste of time.

"You want to fight?" shouted David all of a sudden.

"Yeah, I wanna fight you yellow-bellied—"

"We fight on my terms then!"

"Name 'em!" snarled Wetmore.

174

David pointed to the bay.

Wetmore, and everyone else, gazed stupidly at David. "You want to fight," gasped Wetmore, "in the water?"

In way of an answer David started for the beach, and kept on walking.

The leader of the Do-Nothings rubbed his knuckles into his eyes. Suddenly he spit. Arthur half expected him to paw his feet like some bull taking on a challenge. Instead he swore, real mean, and started for the beach himself. He stormed into the water after David, splashing and cussing so fiercely the men standing about had to send their wives and children off home. For a second Arthur recollected himself; guiltily he looked about for Mary Ann and the children. *Oh that's right,* he remembered. *They're helping Louisa.*

David was standing chest deep in the frigid cold water, moving his arms a little over the rippled surface to keep his balance, and watching Wetmore come in after him. Arthur could see David was laughing—not out loud, but shaking way down inside where nobody could see, as if he knew exactly what was going to happen when Wetmore got a few more feet out where the water would cool him off. As it was, water was creeping up past Wetmore's hips and into his back pockets before he decided he wasn't half as mad as he'd thought. He turned back as meek as a lamb, and looking a might sheepish.

"Mmph," grunted Captain Sterrett at Arthur's elbow. "There's a man who knows how to fight with his head."

The first Louisa knew anything of the fight was when David showed up at the house dripping wet and sneezing. His appearance—new blue flannel shirt stuck to his skin, seaweed hanging off his boots, water dripping off the coils of his curls at the back of his neck—did nothing to calm her already fragile state of mind. He saw this the instant he crossed the threshold; but before she could emit any kind of a stunned cry, or throw herself into his arms, he held out his hand and firmly said—as firmly as he could between chattering teeth, "I'm all right! Just help me get these clothes off, something dry on. Please."

An hour later, eleven o'clock by Mr. Yesler's mill clock, he and the others were finally ready. Even with the eighteen additional stands of arms from Captain Sterrett, fifteen of their number headed for White River shouldering nothing more than rusty relics, defective and with missing parts, carried only for morale and show.

David, his well-oiled rifle in hand (so familiar to his palm and fingers that it felt more an extension of his arm than anything separate) and Louisa's flour sack slung across his back, kept himself moving and did not look back. Once he got his feet going he kept them going, afraid that if he turned around he might follow his heart instead of his head and responsibility. Louisa had been fine and brave, but at the last—when Reverend Blaine prayed for the company's safety—she'd broken down completely. In tears, she'd clung to him and begged he be careful.

"Of course, I'll be careful!"

"We'll have our whole lives together if you just promise to be careful!"

"I promise, I promise," and he did promise. "I will come back to you."

The others had started off ahead of him. Both he and Louisa knew he had to go too, so it was a relief to them both when Arthur finally intervened. But now, trudging down Beach Road for the Duwamish River mouth, David felt as though he'd left life itself behind. And then he knew. He had. For without Liza and Mynez and the new baby coming in the spring, what was there?

17

daytime

Maynards took charge of the orphaned children and wrote a blistering letter to the War Department saying it was time to get over the idea that a handful of whites could outfight a host of Indians. "The number, valor and prowess of the Indians have been greatly underrated."

—Thomas Prosch
in *David S. Maynard and Catherine T. Maynard*

ix miles of Beach Road behind them and Luther Collins's ferry slip just around the bend, David stared across the snaking Duwamish River to the dark wall of forest. For a moment his heart betrayed him. Somewhere out there was a force of Indians meant to kill every last white man. And according to the boy, Harvey Jones's stepson, at least one of those forces had been led by Nelson. A man he personally knew. A man he liked.

The Company ferried over on Collins's raft. Large enough for two wagons and caulked with strips of old clothing dipped in pitch pine, it was serviceable enough, but nothing to boast about. Large wooden pulleys carved out of seasoned birch had been fastened to two short ropes fore and aft of the raft. Through these was threaded the long guide rope, *its* ends snubbed to secure pilings each side of the river.

They crossed in three shifts, twenty men each, a fourth for the supplies, each time the ferry angling into the current at a twenty-five degree angle and getting swept along. At the end, everything said and done, there were a lot of high whoops and hollers.

Captain Hewitt left in way of payment a promissory note jammed down through a dangerously sharp cut in the lid of an old rusty tin can Collins had nailed to a piling for just that purpose. Lieutenant Neely remarked that Collins probably preferred cash. David wondered if Luther Collins even knew what a promissory note was. *He'll figure it out.*

Where was Collins anyway?

Another mile saw them to Henry Van Asselt's, and they entered the dark wall of woods at a point just south of his farm. But no sooner did they commit themselves to the woods than the sky darkened. At first only a light sprinkle of rain reached down, here and there—like scouts testing the terrain. Apparently finding things to their liking they called out the troops, reserves too, for the rain began to fall in earnest, a steady drumming; a rain so cold it went straight to the bones and ate at a man's innards. Rain worse than the night before, if possible. Rain—a new enemy.

The volunteers slugged it out, following their three Indian guides deeper and deeper, ever deeper, into the wet, dark trees. Wet boughs slopped icy spills of water down their necks, wet stinging branches slapped their heads and cut their faces. Soaking-wet underbrush drenched their pants. The excess dripped down into their boots and puddled their socks and numbed their feet. *Elliott Bay,* thought David, teeth chattering, *had been warmer than this!*

The forest grew yet denser, tighter, closing in. In pairs the men took turns at the front, wielding ax and hatchet against the brush and forestfall to carve out a narrow defile through which the others could follow. When their arms gave out—and they ran risk of whacking off their own toes—they passed off the ax and hatchet to the next pair of men and fell in behind. For a while they enjoyed the easier walk at the tail. But at the tail there was no backbreaking labor to stir heat into their limbs and soon they were so stiff with cold they could hardly walk at all; and with every deluge of water spilling off the trees onto their heads, their strength and warmth and courage seemed to bleed right out of them. Rain—an enemy they couldn't disarm.

The earliest anyone in Seattle expected the men to return was late Wednesday, November 1st—two days out, two days back, a minimum of four anxious days. Maybe more. To ease their wait the women decided to reconvene their September prayer meetings at Widow Holgate's house. How fine and reassuring it would be to be together and to pray for the safety of their fathers and husbands!

Things started awkwardly. Catherine Maynard brought Princess Angeline. Louisa, teary-eyed and missing David so badly it hurt, couldn't help but notice, however, a few raised eyebrows and Kate Blaine's tight, prim mouth. *Too bad,* Louisa thought even as Widow Holgate opened their meeting with a list of the many things they might pray for. The fate of Lieutenant Slaughter. That Captain Maloney get the news of Rains's delay in time. The safety of Eaton's Rangers—and *all* the volunteers, everywhere. "Anything else?" she asked, her cheerful manner almost an irritant to their collective despair and disconsolation. Nonetheless, it was her cheer they clung to.

"I think we need to pray for Mr. Mason," said someone quietly.

"Yes," agreed Abbie Jane Hanford, Widow Holgate's married daughter. "And Lieutenant Nugen at the fort."

"Certainly!" agreed her mother. "Poor man must have his hands full!"

"We can't forget Chief Seattle," said Catherine Maynard. "He's gone out to persuade all his tribes to go over to Port Madison. If he can do it, that's a thousand warriors *not* fighting us."

"There's Pat Kanim, too," added Mary Ann. "I don't know how many of you know this, but when Lieutenant Slaughter first left for Yakima he complained that Pat Kanim was causing him trouble. Mr. Mason ordered Captain Sterrett to arrest Thlid and John, Pat Kanim's brothers—as well as all the other Snoqualmie men on the Point."

"What's wrong with that idea?" asked Kate Blaine.

"What's wrong," said Mary Ann, her usual gentleness strained, "is that Pat Kanim's been nowhere near Military Road. He's up at Steilaguamish River, and to arrest the Snoqualmie right now would be, as Arthur says, tantamount to signing our own death papers. So Captain Sterrett's graciously allowed a messenger to be sent north, asking that Pat Kanim come down and verify his whereabouts. He has, I think, until the second or third of next month—"

"Next month!" gasped Mrs. Butler. "But that's a long time away!"

"Only five or six days, Mrs. Butler."

"Oh, yes, how silly of me," and Mrs. Butler laughed self-consciously. "Getting old, when I can't keep track of where we are in the month!"

"So I'd like to pray," finished Mary Ann, smiling over at Mrs. Butler, "that Pat Kanim gets the message, and can get down here in time. I really do worry about what might happen if he doesn't."

Everyone prayed, even Angeline. All the while the rain poured down, making the cozy little house feel warm and safe. When the last amen was said, Widow Holgate opened her Bible. "I found a passage that might give us hope and encouragement."

"Oh, do read it," said Ursula. "Do! I've been chewing my nails to the nubs all day. We sit here praying, but I'm still afraid. I see Indians in every shadow." She stopped, and apologetically turned to Angeline. "I'm sorry. I meant *bad* Indians, not you."

"I know what you say," said Angeline. "I see bad Indians too."

Everyone smiled thinly. Even Kate Blaine. The tissue pages of Widow Holgate's Bible rustled softly as she turned to the verses she'd marked.

"I'm reading from 2 Kings, chapter 12. Where the King of Syria—" she paused, and looked over her reading glasses at them all. "He had a bone to pick with Elisha, one of Israel's prophets, and sent out a great army to have him seized. I'll start reading from there. Let's see, that's 2 Kings, chapter 6, verse fifteen.

When Elisha's servant rose in the morning and went out, behold, an army with horses and chariots was round about the city. And the servant said, "Alas, my master! What shall we do!" Elisha said, "Fear not, for those who are with us are more than those who are with them." Then Elisha prayed and said, "O Lord, I pray thee, open his eyes that he may see." So the Lord opened the eyes of the young man, and he saw: and behold, the mountain was full of horses and chariots of fire round Elisha.

Abbie Jane Hanford dabbed at her eyes. "That's wonderful, Mother. We forget, don't we, the bigger army of God?"

"Louisa!" breathed out Sally Bell excitedly. "It's like you said! When Suwalth came out in August? To bring us into town? Do you remember?"

"No. . . ."

"You said we needed to remember the small ways in which God saves us. That it's little things—invisible things, if you will—that God uses to bring us through."

Yes, she remembered saying *something* like that.

"I don't understand *anything* you're saying," said Diana Collins, the very stout wife of Luther Collins, all of a sudden.

"I think I do," said Ursula pensively. "It's like—" She broke off suddenly and got up and went to the window.

Everyone sat up straight. Mary Ann dropped her knitting and rushed over.

"What is it?" someone squeaked out.

"The *Haida*," whispered Ursula, growing white.

Louisa could see her sister swallow tightly.

"I think," her sister said, turning away from the window and speaking softly, quickly, "we better do what we can to get the children into the blockhouse. As fast as possible. There seem to be a lot of them—"

Surprisingly, everyone moved with utmost order, calmly picking up their rain hats and coats and calling to their children in the back room, where Olivia (17), and John (15), Widow Holgate's two youngest children, entertained the little ones.

"What is it, Mama?" Katy asked her mother, realizing instantly that something serious and urgent was afoot.

"It's the Haida. Darling, if you'll see to Orion. Nora, help Rollie. That way I can help Mrs. Bell with her baby."

"I can help Mama with Austin," said Laura Bell quickly.

"Thank you, Laura. Sally," said Mary Ann to Mrs. Bell, where the consumptive woman sat in the chair closest to the fire. "If you let Laura manage your baby, I can help you along. Do you have any rain gear?"

"Thank you, Mary. And yes, it's by—No, here comes one of my precious ones now with it. Thank you, my darling Virginia," she said, then looked up at Mary Ann with a heart-piercing smile. It was obvious to everyone in the room Sally Bell wouldn't live through the winter.

"I'll help," said Ursula, rushing over.

"Ma, where're we going to go?" George Junior asked, for once quiet and restrained.

"To the blockhouse," his mother answered.

"Are they going to kill us?" A plaintive voice suddenly cut through the odd calm. Louisa and everyone else spun around. Johnny King, with his little sister and brother, had come out of the back room, and they stood frozen, a trio of faces peaked with terror. Suddenly, in a rush, they were all over Catherine Maynard, clinging to her, climbing on her, seizing her—for it was Catherine and Doc who'd taken them this morning. Kate hurried to take the baby. Mrs. Butler helped herself to the little girl. But Johnny wouldn't let go of Catherine. He held fast to her, his freckled face buried in her skirts.

"There, there, it'll be just fine," Catherine told him reassuringly, stroking his head. "Come now, Johnny, be a brave boy. We need to go where it's safe."

They all left the house together, one of the few homes high on the hill. They were coming down out of the trees and passing Dobbins and Anna's old house, rented by the Bells just now, when Louisa, in a jolt of horror, realized just how many Haida there were! Through the downpour, she could see two large war canoes nosed into shore—at *least* a hundred warriors! They crowded all through the mill, swarmed the Sawdust like ants! A third canoe was coming in around the prow of the sloop of war. Her knees buckled. Fortunately, Diana Collins was right beside her and shot out a steadying arm.

"Thank you," whispered Louisa, gulping, eyes fixed on the horde of war-painted Indians.

"Now you stay by me, Mrs. Denny. There's a lot o' me to get around afore they can go after you, you're such a wee mite of a thing. You got that child o' yours held hard?"

This was the most in one breath Louisa had ever heard out of Diana Collins. Like Louisa, Diana was a refugee—though her husband was still at their farm, bringing in the last of his crops. "Remember, Mrs. Denny," Diana cautioned her, "don't let them know you're afraid."

"Yes, Ma'am," was about all Louisa could manage to say, and she had to look down to get her feet moving right. Diana tugged on her elbow, and somehow she was moving again.

"Begory, but there's the marines!" said Diana all of a sudden. "Can you see? Moving in, through the trees! Well, I'll be, if it isn't Widow Holgate's version of God's fiery horses and chariots."

"What? Where?" asked Louisa.

"Can't you see? The marines, coming out from everywhere! The trees, the cookhouse, the blockhouse—Oh! Look! On the warship—Yon! The captain!" declared Diana. "Guess he's not scared o' much!"

Captain Sterrett, shrouded by the gloomy fog and rain, was leaning over the rail, talking down to two painted warriors standing up in the center of the huge canoe come alongside.

"Now you're doing real good," said Diana. "We got just one more block to go, Mrs. Denny."

BOOM!

The roar of cannon going off filled the air like a clap of thunder and shook the earth so soundly and so forcefully Louisa stopped dead in her tracks, the reverberations rooting her fast. The sloop of war had half her thirty-two-pound guns pointed into the Sound; smoke spewed from the ends of the gleaming barrels, blackening the sky.

At the first volley the two Haida speaking to the captain and standing in their canoe at the prow of the sloop of war collapsed to their knees. The rest of their crew frantically laid into their paddles, making off through the overwhelming noise and smoke, bent on safety.

On the Sawdust, the landed Haida screamed and raced for the beach, howling and stumbling over each other in their frenetic haste to clamber into their canoes and make their own escape. Panicked, they could scarcely get hold of their paddles.

184

The spectators in Seattle watched in astonishment as the warriors, after many false starts, finally got underway and headed out to sea. They tore like the wind after the fleeing canoe ahead, all of them making off, afraid for their lives, not one daring to look back as they slowly disappeared from view. Why the Haida came into Seattle, no one knew, *but it was obvious to the youngest child why they left!*

Louisa was still standing agog, dazed, when word came up from the wharf that everyone could go about their business now.

"Just a little scare, folks," called out Captain Sterrett. "Theirs!" And he laughed. Everyone else did too, nervously, and people started wandering off. Finding each other, they pooled into huddled wet groups to convince themselves it truly *was* over.

Louisa and Diana splashed through the mud, their legs still shaking and feeling weak, to join Widow Holgate, Princess Angeline, Catherine Maynard, Mrs. Butler, and Kate Blaine. The Jones children, holding fast to reassuring hands and skirts, gaped in wonder at the *Decatur* and smoking air. "Wow," breathed out Johnny King.

"Wow is right," said Catherine. "Widow Holgate," she scolded, laughing happily and as breathlessly as everyone else, "I don't think anyone's ever going to forget your little Bible lesson today!"

"I bet you planned that on purpose," accused Catherine, teasing her.

"A little object lesson?" said Mrs. Butler, laughing, bobbing nervously under her umbrella, "to go along with your verses?"

Louisa laughed too, and hugged Emily Inez in her arms, who, amazingly, hadn't uttered a cry the whole time. *Oh, dear God, just bring me back David!* she prayed, and then she felt guilty. Wasn't it enough to see God's almighty hand? To know she had reason to hope in God? No. Because faith alone would never ease this terrible emptiness inside, her David gone from her.

The volunteers heard the cannon fire and stood frightened and uncertain in the drowning rain, looking to each other for explanation or assurance. There *was* none. For David there was only one thought, *Louisa!*

In time, the echoes gave way to the sounds of rain.

"What was *that?*"

"Has to have been the *Decatur.*"

"Why?"

"Haida?"

Should they go back? Should they carry on? It was Hewitt's decision, and David listened with sinking heart as their solemn-faced captain explained they'd be going on. "I know we all have families, but they're in better hands than ours," he said.

This was true, and it was only this that could induce David to carry on. This and his prayers.

Another six miles. Forever. But finally, twelve of their twenty lay behind them. Dusk fell and they entered a wide glen carpeted by moss, canopied over with towering cedars. Here the rain fell less. Captain Hewitt didn't hesitate. "Pitch camp!"

As corporal, David—along with his best friends Jim and George Seattle—marked off four different spots for the campfires, divergent one from the other. Silently, they drove four three-foot stakes in a square around each of the fire locations: silently because long-standing practice rendered words between them unnecessary. Dave Neely and John Henning, despite wet foliage, got the fires started.

Chief Seattle's sons, men in their midtwenties, shoulder-length hair parted down the middle and falling loose, showed the other men how to tie blankets between the stakes. When the blankets were stretched out and their outer ends weighted down, four lean-to tents then faced each other around a single fire. Over the fire was a big square opening for the smoke to escape, and around the fire were four sloping tents which reflected the heat like Dutch ovens. With a second blanket spread over them—and with two and three men under each awning and as many as a dozen clustered around each of the four fires—everyone was able to corral some warmth and get a much-needed sleep, anxiety notwithstanding.

For David, this took a while. Listening unwillingly to the disruptive snoring of his comrades, he tried desperately to forget his reason for being here. Tried to forget, too, the danger he and the others faced—perhaps even now, imminent and invisible to the eyes of their standing guard! Most of all he tried to forget the danger Louisa and Mynez might be in.

He listened to the sound of the rain, falling onto the blanket above his head, and wondered if this might be the most comforting of all sounds between the meeting of nature and man-made things. Certainly it sang of welcome shelter. His last thoughts were of Louisa. There'd been no more sound of guns. *She must be safe,* he decided. *No Indians can compete with sixteen thirty-two pounders.*

So did she stay in the cabin, he wondered, *or did she succumb to my bidding and go over to Arthur and Mary Ann's?* If so—he tallied up—the house would be a full one. Arthur and Mary and the four children. Irene Neely, her three boys and baby daughter. Louisa and Mynez. On second thought, and smiling to himself, he knew the answer. His Louisa would be at home, waiting for him.

18

night

The express rider, William Tidd, had left Steilacoom and in some unaccountable way passed over the road where McAllister and Connell lay and through the prairie unharmed, and safely delivered his dispatches to Maloney on the 29th.

—Ezra Meeker, pioneer and historian
in *Pioneer Reminiscences*

*U*nable to sleep, and almost regretting her decision to remain at home alone, Louisa stared wide-eyed at the rafters overhead and the bunches of onions and turnips and beets. The rain beat against the shingles, freshly sealed with tar. Somewhere in the day's excitement Arthur had come over to plug the holes. *David? Where is David?* She could hear the wind, rustling the thick branches surrounding the house, a lonely sound. *What a terrible night to be out. Is he warm? Is he safe? Does he miss me? Is he safe? Where is he? Is he . . .*

A wolf howled. The howl was taken up and spread through the trees. A cougar screamed. She recalled how a marine once asked how a person could tell the difference between a cougar's scream and that of a woman being murdered: It was a sound no one ever got used to. An animal suddenly crashed through the undergrowth right outside and she started up!

She held a mortal terror of cougars. Their second winter on the Sound, David had shot the hugest cat anyone could ever remember seeing. Nine feet long! Tail to teeth! The very next winter a cougar had jumped *her*, and knocked her into the snow, shredding her winter coat clean through. Fortunately the cat had only been after the venison she'd been trying to cut down from the tree. But that same winter, a starry, snowy night, a cougar had actually killed a child. Ursula Mc-Conaha Wyckoff's little girl, only six or seven at the time, she'd gone out to the necessary house.

Remembering the awful tragedy, Louisa realized that she herself had to go out. Oh, but she didn't dare! What a fine pickle I'm in, she thought, easing down into the covers and holding on as long as she could. The more she tried to forget things, though, the worse things became.

Finally she muttered, "This is ridiculous!" She flung back the covers and dragged herself out of bed, groping about in the cold for her shawl. She was in such a hurry by now she very nearly didn't bother to add another log to the fire . . . but she knew she'd want the warmth when she returned!

Two sticks of wood. A pitchy pine knot laid over the embers. The pine knot sizzled and flamed up almost instantly. "Come on, Watch."

What's this? Firelight? Not a wink of sleep for a hundred miles, and having just picked his way through the wretched ink of night and come down the first treacherous descent east of Naches Pass, Billy Tidd wondered if he was seeing things. The trail he'd followed had been abysmally narrow and frightfully high above the Naches River gorge, made all the worse for the snow that lay over the rocky ground. But now, what was that? Winking firelight through the trees?

189

Ah! If the men sitting around that cheery fire will let me lie and sleep but ten minutes, I'll forever be their servant! Though I'd take it better, he prayed, *to find friend, not foe. If you don't mind, Sir,* he added.

At first the flame was but a cloudy glimmer, then flicker, soon a broad and welcome light. And though the fire couldn't conquer the surrounding darkness it was luminous enough to show a pathway *out*. In relief and gratitude Tidd left the snow-covered trail to follow this beckoning path of light. His horse, as fatigued and famished as he, slowly, clumsily, worked her way forward while behind them the western pines of the forest dimly closed.

"Sorry, Old Girl," Tidd mumbled when they stumbled into, and were enmeshed by, a tangling thicket. "Easy there, *eeeeasy*. Round about, there you go . . ." he encouraged and soon they emerged from the thicket, coming onto the bank of a rumbling stream. "Must feed into the Naches River," mumbled Tidd, rubbing his weary eyes. A belt of reflected crimson lay over the stream, and every ripple and breaker of the water's surface tore at the red light, riving it into rags and streamers. Yet still the shattered girdle of crimson remained undestroyed, constantly made and remade by the red light of the fire across the way.

A small collection of men—*white men* Tidd noted with a quick prayer of thanksgiving to his Maker!—were grouped about the fire, red hot flames circled by a ring of cold white snow fading into the surrounding black of night. At his first crashing approach the men sprang to their feet, alert, automatically reaching for their weapons. Now they moved nervously in the glare of the fire against the oppressing gloom.

"Best not dally on the brink, Old Girl," whispered Tidd, "lest they think an ambush and point those dread guns at our souls." He was close enough to give a hearty halloo. The effect—trumpeted so loudly it startled even him—stirred both men and beast alike. The men sprang to the stream's edge, his horse as well—and she dashed with a last reserve of energy into the crimson pathway, carrying him over and across to the astonished officers of the 4th Infantry waiting on the shore.

Tidd fastened his bloodshot eyes on the young captain standing forefront. Wearily he handed off the dispatch.

"Tidd?" questioned Captain Maloney in alarm. "What's happened?"

"Rains is standing you up, Sir. Got some bee under his bonnet."

"He's not coming?" snapped Captain Maloney.

"If he is, he ain't left yet! Sir? Could I bother you for a bed? Whoa!" He jerked up straight. *"Slaughter?"*

"In the flesh," greeted Lieutenant Slaughter, giving Tidd a smart salute and a boyish grin.

Tidd all but tumbled off his horse to shake the young man's hand. "Boy am I glad to see you! And your wife? She'll be tickled pink! Though I suppose if you and Maloney keep on—" He thumbed east, over his shoulder. Then made motion of scalping himself. "I mean, without Rains—"

Slaughter laughed. "You look half dead yourself. Need some sleep?" he asked kindly.

"Just point me to a bed. Beggars can't be choosers, I know, but if I could have one by your fire I'd feel truly blessed." He fell asleep listening to the officers discuss their dilemma. Ordered to meet Rains. But no Rains to meet. A delicate situation.

As she returned to the cabin, the wind and rain tore at Louisa's hair and slapped the wet hem of her gown against her shins. Watch, beside her, suddenly stopped and growled. Simultaneously Louisa heard a scramble along a high branch directly overhead. She froze, icy hand laid suddenly against her heart!

Not Watch. He leapt straight up, snarling and barking, leaping again! A shadow cascaded out of the tree into another! The bough cracked under the weight. Watch broke into a high-pitched barking, then both shadow and dog were leaping from tree to tree, snarling, barking, growling, and snarling again! Louisa found her feet and started to run. The cougar, pressed by Watch, dropped onto the house roof just as Louisa flew through the door. "Watch!" she screamed.

For a fraction of a second, Watch debated. In that moment, Louisa heard the scrambling of claws over Arthur's newly patched shingles, and then the huge cat thrust his head and shoulders down off the roof. Watch went wild, snarling and jumping up and down on the stoop, trying to reach the monstrous cat that pawed and lunged down at him from the eaves. Inez awoke screaming. *I have to save us! I have to drive that cougar off! How? How?* Louisa wondered frantically, seizing her head with both hands. *How, dear God? How?* She glanced all around. *What do I do? Tell me what to do!* Her eyes fastened on the pine knot she'd thrown into the fire on her way out.

In an instant she was across the floor, the long shaft of the blazing pine knot seized in her hands. She ran for the door! She thrust the torch into the gleaming green eyes of the lunging black shadow! An instantaneous, tortured scream! So stunned, so terrified was she by the unearthly howl that she very nearly dropped the firebrand. The shadow hurtled off the roof, a muddy yellow color flashing through her narrow band of firelight. Thud! She lowered the torch. The huge cat staggered.

Watch was on it in a wink, yapping and barking. The cougar howled, their bodies tangled. *"Watch! Wa-a-a-a-tch!"* Without thinking, she tossed her flaming pine knot into the air—underhand—up, up, and out—launching the torch in an arc of fire through the night. Down it came, knifing toward the thrashing animals. Watch saw it first, leapt back. The firebrand crashed onto the cougar's shoulder. The stink of singed fur, the sound of a wounded scream, and the sudden peppering of gunfire all came at the same time.

Louisa and Watch collided, trying to get back through the door. Louisa heaved the door shut. She threw the bolt. Emily

192

Inez was out of bed and into her arms before Louisa could even think.

"Louisa! Are you all right?"

Arthur!

"Yes, yes!" Sniffing back her tears and wiping her cheek with the back of her hand, she tried pulling back the door bolt. But it jammed tightly and the night was so dark, only shadows. She couldn't see, but she couldn't put Inez down—There! The bolt gave.

The cold breath of rain swept in. Arthur too. He pushed past, rifle in hand, and went straight to the table. In just seconds he had the lamp lit. She understood now. Watch's frantic fuss had brought Arthur and others running, guns in hand.

"You get the cougar?" Louisa asked him, staggering over to the rocking chair with wobbly legs and sitting down, pulling Emily Inez in close and trying to hush her.

"Either me or one of the marines." He took the lamp over to the door and stepped out. Louisa craned her neck to see. A half dozen uniformed men were prodding the dead cat with the toe of their boots.

"Just a cougar!" someone hollered. "Plugged full of holes! Looks like Swiss cheese! You can all go back to your posts now!"

"Shh, shhh," Louisa whispered to Emily Inez. "It's all over now. Uncle Arthur and the soldiers killed the big cat."

Arthur came back in and closed the door. "You all right, Liza?" he asked, worried.

"I'll recover."

"You look a little peaked."

She gave him a weak smile. "Thanks for coming to my rescue."

"Looks like I didn't need to. That was pretty quick thinking, Louisa, driving off that cat with fire. And then throwing that torch like that? Giving us a clear target? Don't know as I could've done better!"

193

She eased her back into the rocker, Emily Inez heavy in her arms, the baby inside all stirred up and kicking. She dropped her head onto the high backing of the chair and closed her eyes, toes pushing up on the earthen floor to start the rocking. "Coming from you, Arthur," she sighed, "I'll take that as a compliment."

"What's that supposed to mean? Coming from me?"

Eyes shut. The smooth motion of the rocking lulling her. She felt heavy, but light too. And safe. Emily Inez started to settle down, thumb in her mouth. "Well it wasn't exactly a compliment, you know."

"It was."

"No it wasn't." She opened her eyes, turned her face to his, and gave him a smile. He was perched against the table edge, arms crossed, ankles crossed. "It's not a compliment when you set yourself as the measuring stick. If you want to compliment someone, Arthur, do them a favor and leave yourself out of it." Suddenly she was tired. She'd be able to sleep now, soon as he left.

"You don't like me, do you."

"Like you?" She sat forward, caught off guard by the question. "Well of course I like you! You're just irritating is all."

"In what way?"

"Well . . . like now. You made out like you were giving me a compliment! When all you really did—if you're going to be honest—was remind me one more time just how much better you are than me."

"I certainly did not!"

"Arthur, you did too."

"I did not! Louisa, you're so exasperating! I pay you a compliment and look what you do! Create a federal case!"

"You did *not* pay me a compliment." She was *not* going to give in to him. "Actually, you *were* doing a fine job until you said, 'I don't know as I could have done any better.'"

He pursed his lip. "You want to come over to our place?" he asked abruptly, changing the subject.

194

Rocking. Eyes shut. "No. But thank you. I think we'll be all right here. As long as I don't go outside," she added, smiling to herself.

"Suit yourself." She heard him get up to go. "By the way—"

She looked up. His hand was on the door bolt.

"First thing in the morning, Louisa, I'm buying you a chamber pot. I don't want you going out anymore once it's dark."

"Thank you! That's real—"

"Go back to bed and get some sleep. You look awful."

"—sweet of you." She kissed the top of Emily Inez's head. "He's frustrating and cantankerous sometimes, but he loves us just the same."

October

Tuesday

30

19

daytime

After two days' hard work we reached the house of Mr. Cox (one of the settlers who had escaped to Seattle) which we found robbed. We next went to Mr. Jones, whose house had been burned to the ground; and Mr. Jones, being sick at the time, was burned in it. The body of Mrs. Jones was found some thirty yards from the house, shot through the lower part of the lungs, her face and jaw . . .

—Captain Christopher Hewitt, Company H
in letter to Acting Governor Mason

It was a grim experience for these volunteers to come upon, one by one, the mutilated bodies of their neighbors and friends whom they had sheltered so shortly before.

—Roberta Frye Watt, Katy Denny's daughter
in *Four Wagons West*

Sunday the 28th the Upper Sound Indians struck their blow.

Monday the 29th pioneers everywhere raced in a panic for safety.

Tuesday the 30th Company H of Seattle stumbled onto the remains of their White River friends, friends they'd sheltered only a short time before.

First, however, Captain Maloney and Lieutenant Slaughter had to bid Billy Tidd good-bye. Allowed but a few hours sleep (though given an ample breakfast of oatmeal and blackstrap), Tidd was back in his saddle and gone before the crack of dawn—with dispatches for Nugen, Mason, and Rains tucked into his breast pocket and six men riding out behind him, each having his own reason for returning in advance of the main column.

Also, Charlie Eaton's nine Rangers, having made up their minds to make a run for it, and then losing their bearings and being exhausted from two days and two nights in the wilds, had to first stumble into Fort Nisqually of the Hudson's Bay Company with their garbled account of McAllister's and Connell's deaths.

And Major Rains had to first strike out from The Dalles. Mollified by his "hocus-pocus" title of Brigadier General, bestowed upon him by Acting Governor Mason, he'd consented at last to let the Oregon volunteers bring up his tail. Ironically, he headed out at sunrise with his 350 regulars and 6 companies of the Oregon boys, for a total of 750 men, all mounted and with provisions to last twenty days—*even as Maloney and Slaughter struck camp and headed home!*

None of this movement was known by or even material to Company H, however. They traveled southeast most of the morning, slashing their way through the heavy thickets and seeing nothing but trees, and more trees. The rain let up, but the foliage remained wet, chilling their hands and making progress deplorably slow. Too, worry for their families made everything worse; every mile twice as long, twice as far, taking them ever and farther away from those they loved and who might be suffering danger with them not there to help. This, David learned, was harder to fight than the rain and the impenetrable trees.

Finally, just before noon they came to their first abandoned cabin. Everything indoors had been torn apart, and when David got poking about the clutter he suddenly realized it was the Russell's place. *This took a lot of work to make*, he thought, peering into the dark tunnel.

Seattle's sheriff, Tom Russell, picked up a chair rung. "Guess Ma and Pa won't be needing any kindling for a while," he commented. He dropped it back into the rubble.

Someone else picked up a piece of jagged glass. "Too bad, looks like it was a nice mirror."

"It was," said the sheriff.

The rest of the cabins were all ransacked in one way or another, the robbery and destruction increasing in extent and violence the farther they went. By the time they came to the Coxes' homestead no one was surprised to find the house in ruination. A sorry sight. David surveyed the ravished furnishings and prayed for strength for what might lie ahead. It wouldn't be the buildings bearing the worst marks of depravity anymore.

They came first into the orchard belonging to Harvey Jones, Johnny King's stepfather; row after row of second-year fruit trees bowed to the night's beating rain. Suddenly, through the dripping leaves, the house, a blackened heap of smoldering ash, desolate, with a stench of death not even the cleansing rain or the forest humus could cover. The task of sifting through the wet, but still warm, ash for what remained of Mr. Jones's charred body proved revoltingly difficult, and when someone found Enos Cooper's body a hundred and fifty feet away from the house, shot through the lungs, a few of the men were detailed to begin digging the graves. David, with Dave Neely and Lewis Wyckoff, circled out, looking for Eliza, though David wanted only to go home. Home to Louisa, to put this—all of it—from his mind.

"You hear a dog?" Lewis asked suddenly.

The two Davids cocked their ears.

"Not barking," said Lewis. "Nothing that loud. More like whining. Whimpering might be closer to the mark."

David Denny heard it, a mournful, weak cry. He veered through the tall wet pasture and found both Eliza and the dog—Eliza lying in a circle of trampled grass, the dog shivering on her woolen skirt. Mrs. Jones's face had been hideously mangled—crushed by what looked to be a violent blow from the blunt end of an ax. Her nose rammed in. Mouth hidden by ripped skin. Jaw slack, askew. The malevolence of such an action caused David to involuntarily cry out. The dog snarled a sharp warning.

"Hey, hey, it's all right." He held a hand out to the pup and motioned for Neely and Wyckoff to come on. The dog laid back his ears. David went down on one knee and continued to speak softly, carefully, watching to see if he'd be allowed to feel the woman's neck for a pulse without getting his hand bitten off. There was no need. Eliza was stone cold, and David snatched his hand back. The dog, apparently deciding David was a friend, dragged himself from his pathetic nest, and David, thinking Johnny King might like to see his dog again, picked up the thin, shivering mutt and tucked him into his wet jacket.

"Dear God—" Lewis Wyckoff snapped off his hat and bowed his head. "I hope she was dead before they did that."

"I doubt it. They usually do this kind of thing to finish them off."

"She was shot then, do you think?"

"Lower left lung and dying slowly."

Dave Neely came up.

"Say nothing of this to the boy," David Denny asked his friends, buttoning his coat around the dog. "Johnny doesn't need to know they came back to do this to his mother."

"No, I expect he doesn't," said Dave Neely sadly.

Farther on the carnage was worse. The house still stood— a good, small log cabin—but it bore evidence of horrific struggle: broken windows, door, shattered furniture, scattered implements. And inside, the body of Will Brannan, lying in a deep pool of blood, gave mute testimony to unspeakable violence.

The earthen floor around his mutilated body was covered with shreds of clothing and tufts of hair. Both his hands were lacerated, as if he'd seized the knife with which he'd been stabbed, trying desperately to wrench it away from his assailant. His right hand bore two long slashes, cut clean through the flesh of his fingers and palm, exposing the bones. His left palm bore two deep punctures. His arms and legs were so badly cut that his shirtsleeves and pantlegs draped his muscular limbs in bloodied ribbons. Captain Hewitt counted fifteen separate stab wounds to his back, most of them a little below his left shoulder.

David squatted down. Gently he closed his friend's eyes. Jim Seattle squatted too, and took up a limp hand. *"Klikitat,"* he told David.

"What's he saying?" Captain Hewitt wanted to know. David motioned him to wait.

"This wasn't Nelson," continued Jim, speaking in Duwamish. "He didn't do the direct killing anyway. See here?"

David pulled his eyes away from the smooth, angular features of his Indian friend to look hesitantly at the cruel wounds mutilating his white friend. *Nelson?* In league with the *Klikitat?*

"See?" said Jim somberly, spreading open the pieces of Will's hand. "Klikitat have a favorite close-quarter weapon. They grind a saw file to a point. They sharpen the long edge. Makes a fierce, deadly thing. Slices clean, see? But then tears out the flesh when it's withdrawn. Klikitat did this. Maybe they were here while Nelson was over at the other place, no?"

David relayed the information to Captain Hewitt.

"Let's wrap him up, get him buried," was all the captain said.

203

Some of the other officers helped David wrap a blanket around the body to carry it outdoors to where others dug the grave.

"Can't find the wife or baby," someone said.

"Keep looking," said Captain Hewitt, "they're bound to be around here somewhere."

David remembered his protestations to Louisa. Over and over he'd assured her that not even the Klikitat would hurt Elizabeth. So where was she? What had happened to her?

They started lowering Will into the muddy ground. *You poor fool,* he thought sadly, heart breaking. *Friend, why didn't you listen? Why did you come back here? Why? When Arthur told you, when I told you? And where is Elizabeth? What have they done to your wife?*

"Spread out!" hollered the captain. "We're not going on until I know what's happened to the missus and the wee one!"

A shadow suddenly emerged from the trees and David, in a sudden faint, nearly keeled face-first into the half-filled grave. The emerging shadow was Will's brother and the strong resemblance between the two men made David think he was seeing a ghost. In a way he was, for Joe stumbled toward the staring observers looking like something dead himself.

"You won't find her," Joe said woodenly to them all, his gaunt, haunted face devoid of expression. "I've already looked. She's gone. The devils took her."

The scouts argued, insisting Elizabeth was either alive and hiding—or had been accidentally killed and her body hidden. This wasn't something David had considered, Elizabeth caught in the crossfire.

"She's not alive, that's certain," said Lewis.

"How so?" someone asked.

"She'd have come out of hiding."

"Okay, for argument's sake," said Captain Hewitt, holding up his hands, "let's say she's dead. Why isn't she lying out in the open like everyone else so far?"

Because, Jim Seattle explained, no Indian would ever deliberately harm a King George. But if Elizabeth had gotten in the way? And was wounded? or worse? Then those responsible would have made every effort to hide their crime. On this all three scouts agreed.

The men spread out, determined to find some clue. Joe Brannan sat inert upon a stump. "I came for church," he said to no one, "we have service on Sunday."

Bill Gilliam spotted blood glistening off a path of flattened grass leading to the fence, and for a moment the men thought they were onto something. But when David saw the amount of blood, both on the ground and fence, and after following it for some distance, concluded this was nothing more than a wounded Indian being hauled away by his friends. Far too much blood. "Looks like Will at least gave as good as he got," he muttered to Dave Neely.

Back they went to the yard, to search again, looking everywhere. David sat on one of the yard stumps to survey the homestead critically, and started to notice how clean the yard was. The house too—if they didn't count the damage done by the fight inside. Everywhere else, though, there was no sign of wanton destruction. Which reinforced the scouts' position—and his own understanding—that Elizabeth was undoubtedly dead. That the culprits viewed her unintended death as murder, themselves guilty. That they'd cleared out fast, not lingering to do further mischief. *So where would I hide a body if I wanted to get away fast?*

The rest of the company was searching *under* things now. Under the stoop, under the house, under the woodpile, under the chicken coop, under the compost. Suddenly he remembered something Louisa told him. Elizabeth said she'd kill herself and Doris before ever letting the Indians touch them. This warranted some thought. He ambled over to the well and leaned against the low stone surround, out of the rain, to run everything through his mind one more time. *The Indians arrive. They go for Will. Maybe she gets in the way, maybe she doesn't. Maybe she's wounded, maybe she's not. Either way, she seizes the baby, she runs.* David pushed a fist into his thigh. This *still* puts me back full circle! Even if she *did* kill herself and child, the Indians *still* had to hide the bodies! So where? *Where?*

One minute he didn't know, the next he did. It was as simple as that. He whirled around and looked down, leaped to his feet as if struck, and whirled again. *Oh, my God,* he prayed, looking down the well and feeling sick. She was there. Upside down.

When he and two others pulled her out, the baby was in her arms—without clothing and not a mark on her. Elizabeth herself had been stabbed through the back to just beneath her left breast—not necessarily a fatal wound. One of the men understood this, and swore. *"You mean those filthy buzzards stuffed her down there while she and the baby were still alive?"*

Most everyone turned away, the idea too gruesome to face. But David didn't look away; he had questions, and he wanted answers. Had the Indians done this? Thrown her and the baby in, head first, while she was still alive? Or had she, wounded and thinking she and the baby were both to be killed or worse, run for the well and with unbridled resolve and panic thrown herself and the child headlong down into their watery grave? The haunting questions went unanswered.

The Kings' place was the worst. The house had been burned to the ground with Mr. and Mrs. King in it, and their roasted bodies had been partially devoured by hogs. Scattered over the yard was more of their charred, gnawed bones and half-eaten, blackened flesh.

Suddenly Joe Brannan was talking. He stood by the pile of horrifying bones Mr. Holderness was trying to sort through in order to make some kind of accounting. "Mrs. King, she killed two redskins before they got her," he choked out, wringing his hands and staring at the roasted flesh. "They cut her to pieces for it. . . ."

David and the others glanced at each other in horror. *Joe was here? He saw?*

"I was coming by," said Joe, voice breaking again. The story came out in fits and starts, in great gusts of grief. He and the Kings were to walk to his brother's. He was just coming into the clearing when he heard the cries. Without a gun he could do nothing. He saw them killed, mutilated, the house torched, the bodies thrown onto the fire. He stood by the bones, helplessly telling; the rest of them knelt in the ash and debris, helplessly listening.

Knowing more of the treachery that lay behind this sickening spectacle of death that stained their hands and turned their stomachs brought new fear. This nightmare of brutality through which they waded was not restraint snapping under injustice, not an eruption of rage. This was evil, carefully orchestrated and executed. Suddenly it seemed to David that to try and remember the Indians' side only confused matters. The only way to right the wrong was to forget what led to the trouble and *punish* the Indians for these terrible things! Hunt them down! Keep on hunting! Hunt them until the very last was dead! Gone! Erased from the very face of the earth! Oh, he understood now why some of the pioneers had cheered the headlines of the *Pioneer & Democrat*. "WE TRUST THE YAKIMA WILL BE RUBBED OUT—BLOTTED FROM EXISTENCE AS A TRIBE!" Why, Joe Brannan, standing by the bones, swore in a voice that grew stronger with each word he uttered that he'd never rest, he'd never veer from his course, until he'd seen eye for an eye. Until he'd found justice for his brother, his brother's wife, and their child.

Jim Seattle squatted next to David. "I'm appalled. My heart hurts with shame."

"You and me both . . ."

"Anyone seen anything of the boy?" Mr. Holderness suddenly hollered.

"What boy?" asked George in alarm, coming up to his brother and David.

"The Kings had a five-year-old son," David explained.

"But," said Jim, looking puzzled, "I thought Indian Dave brought him into town before we left. No?"

"No, no, that was *Johnny* King, no relation to these people."

"Oh," said both Seattle boys at once, and they twisted around to view the desolation.

"If he's not here," said Jim flatly, "they took him."

"They *took* him?" gasped David.

"A little white boy," George said, "would make a good son. For a chief who has no sons."

"What chief has no sons?"

"Leschi."

Nelson, the Klikitat, now Leschi. The vortex of evil grew, sucking everyone into its whirlwind of madness, and David, looking into his own soul and reactionary thoughts, *terrible* thoughts of revenge and punishment, wondered how a man withstood this seduction of evil beckoning him to do wrong in order to make things right.

Contention in the war camp ran white hot. For two days Kanasket had been sparring for chieftainship, decrying Leschi's warning to the Puyallup settlers—"Whose side is he on?"—and boasting his feats of bravery, his distinctions in warfare, his skill at marksmanship, his prowess at combat. What had Leschi to offer in comparison? he scorned to everyone who would listen. *Leschi is nothing but a coward and traitor, a farmer!*

To these vain boastings and insults Leschi had listened patiently enough, until he saw that Kanasket was coming perilously close to fragmenting the entire camp. Now, dusk falling, this second day of their quarrel, Leschi was seated

208

beneath a large cedar tree with his braves. They'd built a blazing fire and were molding bullets. His lieutenants, just in from scouting, reported sixty men from Seattle in the vicinity of Kanasket's massacre. It was time now to settle the question—once and for all—before things were made worse over another wrong target!

"Come!" Leschi called loudly, leaving his companions and stalking over to where Kanasket sat with his own following—Nelson, Kitsap the Younger, Coquilton of the Puyallup, Klowowit of the Puyallup. "Let's us see," he proposed to Kanasket, "whether you can shoot better than me! Winner is war chief!"

Though evening had fallen, the moon was high enough and bright enough to distinguish objects at a considerable distance. Taking his gun, Leschi withdrew the wooden ramrod, walked out to where the shadows melted into the night, and struck his rod into the ground, as far away as it could be seen.

Kanasket had a brand-new Halls rifle. It's shiny barrel gleamed and glistened in the moonlight. He fired and let out a crow.

"That was but a glancing blow," said Leschi calmly, taking his place at the firing line. When he fired, he cut his rod in two.

For a moment all were still. Kanasket rubbed his throat. *Would he acquiesce?*

"After my brother Quiemuth, you are next lieutenant," Leschi told him, making it easy for Kanasket to save face. He hurried on, seeing it wasn't enough. Right now he'd give Kanasket anything, except chieftainship, to keep them all together. "There are white men at White River. I want to know what they're doing. If they carry guns, and come after us to make war, to you I give the honor of winning our first battle. Is it good for you?"

"If I can appoint my own lieutenants."

There could be no quarrels between them now. He said, "Yes."

209

October

Wednesday

31

20

morning

Minutes of Legislative Assembly, Olympia Dec 5, 1855. Territorial divorces granted: 1) Diana Collins of Seattle.

—*Puget Sound Courier*
December 7, 1855

omorrow David might be home! Happily, and feeling in better spirits than she had for a long time, Louisa was tying on Mynez's moccasins this last day of the month when she heard a tiny, shy knock. "Miss Mynez-Inez," she said, lifting her daughter onto the ground, "can you guess who might that be?"

"Katy?"

"Maybe."

The little girl climbed up on the chair to look out the window.

"Ma asks," piped up little Rollie the minute Louisa cracked the door, "can you please help clean the chicken coop?" He beamed ear to ear, so pleased to be the messenger!

213

Louisa smiled down at her three-year-old nephew and drew him in from the rain and fluffed up his golden red curls, like fine spun gold, all over his head. "Isn't your ma going to prayer circle today?"

"Mama, she said—um . . . *after* circle. Pa thinks the sun will come out!" Another happy grin, so *full* of smiles!

"That'll be nice! It's been so long since I've seen the sky. Rollie, I've forgotten! What color *is* the sky?"

"Blue!"

She pretended to whack her head for being so stupid, and he laughed in pure joy. "Yes," she said, "you can tell your ma, of course I'll help. But can I have a clothespin?"

"Why do you need a clothespin?"

"To plug my nose. So I don't have to smell all that chicken doo!"

He laughed so happily she lifted him right off his feet and gave him a kiss. "Rollie, would you like to take some cookies back to your house? One for each of you?"

"All of us, Auntie?"

"Yes! You, Orion, Nora, Katy, Jonathon, Joe, Sammy, Salinthia—Anyone else? Did I miss anyone?"

"I don't think so."

"So you will take some to everyone?"

"That would be real nice," he said politely.

"My too?" chirped up Emily Inez.

"Yes, you too."

Prayer meeting went well. The previous day, much of their time had been spent with all the excitement over Louisa's escape from the cougar. Mrs. Bell had wanted to know who would get the skin. Louisa said she thought Arthur should have it. Kate wondered if it could be given to Captain Sterrett—in appreciation for everything he was doing for them during these perilous times. "No," Mary Ann had said, "it's much too riddled to be of use. Arthur gave it to Mr. Wetmore. Perhaps he and Mr. Woodin can get enough pieces to make a pair of boots." Everyone's spirits had been so bolstered, too, by the previous day's show of arms and, now comical, flight of the Haida, that they'd spent the rest of their time sharing with each other the many ways they could now see where God had aided and protected them. Each had at least one story to tell!

Today some of that same excitement still prevailed, though after three days of missing their men, their loneliness and uncertainty were beginning to tell.

"I thought we could pray specifically for each of our men today," said Widow Holgate, beginning their time together with a smile. "And has anyone anything about Lieutenant Slaughter? No? Captain Maloney? Has he—"

"Even if he does get news of Major Rains's delay," pined Mrs. Blaine, "what can he do?"

"Perhaps he'll come back?" whispered Mary Jane Mercer.

"Yes!" cried Ursula, swinging around to face the eldest Mercer girl, sixteen years old. "I'd not thought of that! But of course! He can come back now! He—"

"No," argued Mrs. Butler, shaking her head, little curls bouncing around her plump face. "I reckon the only thing he can do is sit tight. He's under orders."

A glum silence fell over the room.

"Mary Ann?" said Widow Holgate. "Has your husband gotten any word from Pat Kanim?"

"No, not yet."

They prayed a long time. Fifty-five names were a lot to get through. Louisa's mind must have wandered because suddenly she heard the last "amen" and everyone was getting up and casting about for their coats. Mary Ann came over and squatted down beside her.

"What do you think, Liza, about my asking Diana Collins for lunch today? She looks so sad. And I was remembering our first Christmas, over at Alki, when she and Mr. Collins and the others came over."

"Am I invited?"

"What a question." Mary eased to her feet. "Ohhh," she grimaced. "That's getting hard to do."

"The old gray mare ain't what she used to be?"

"Oh, stop."

The cookies Louisa had sent home earlier with Rollie were not enough. He'd proudly brought them out after lunch, and now, over tea, the nine children—Irene Neely's four, Mary's four, Louisa's one—were licking the sugar off their lips and sighing with regret.

"I'll go home and get some more," offered Louisa, scooting back from the crowded table. "I made two batches."

"You're spoiling them," said Irene Neely, a pretty woman with honey blonde hair, luxuriously wavy and always spilling out of her hairpins.

Louisa laughed. "I spoil my nieces and nephews shamelessly, Irene. I might as well include your children. Mary, why don't you put on another pot of tea? We could *all* have another cookie. And if we're really going to tackle that smelly coop we do have to have our fort-i-fi-ca-tion! Can you spell that, Jonathon?" she asked Irene's eight-year-old on her way out the door.

A few minutes later, while cleaning up the dishes, it was decided that Irene would take the children down to the Point for some new hay. During the summer, David and Tom Mercer had harvested fifty or sixty hay bales from the Swale, winter feed for Tib and Charley. It was all stored at the livery. Mary Ann and Louisa could do the nasty stuff: muck out the soiled straw. Diana Collins said she was an old hand at this. If they didn't mind her staying on, she didn't mind helping out.

"Mind?" laughed Mary Ann. "You're hired!"

Not a pleasant task, to be sure. But Arthur, as usual, was right; the sun was out, revealing a rare blue sky, and the three women started right in, glad at least for the fresh, bright day.

Tools were plentiful. David had brought from the Swale his own rake and shovels, and for fifteen or twenty minutes the women worked hard, jabbing into the coop's nooks and crannies and drawing out the dank-smelling straw.

"This is good for me, keeping busy like this," puffed Louisa, stopping to brush the hair out of her face. "Yesterday I thought I'd go out of mind all by myself, missing David like some foolish schoolgirl."

"We all miss David," said Mary Ann. "Where's that footstool? I need to get up and look in the nesting boxes. Never mind, I see it. You know, I don't think there's been a moment gone by these last three days," she told Louisa, fetching the stool, "that I'm not praying for his safe return. I guess I've managed finally to 'pray without ceasing'? Oh, ugh!" she gasped, reeling backward. "I can't *believe* I've let things get so deplorable in here! Whew-*eee!*" and she waved her hand back and forth in front of her nose. "What about you, Diana? Do you miss Mr. Collins?"

Silence.

This was the wrong question. Louisa felt it immediately. Diana stopped sweeping. She stood rigidly in the middle of the floor, staring steadfastly out the door, away from them.

"Diana?" asked Mary Ann hesitantly, her hand freezing midair, whisk broom poised.

"Diana, are you all right?" breathed out Louisa, afraid to move.

Diana Collins didn't answer. She stood motionless, the only movement coming from her huge body being some rapid blinking as she tried to stop her tears.

Mary Ann stepped off the footstool. "I didn't mean to upset you, Diana," she said, going over and peering with worried concern into Diana's troubled face. "Is something wrong?"

Diana nodded. Her whole body quivered.

"Can we help you? Oh, Diana, you're crying! Louisa, *help me!*"

They got her outdoors even as the big woman's tears began to flow and sobs came up from her chest.

Nervously Louisa said, "We haven't swept anything out yet, the stoop's reasonably clean. You can sit here." She felt so stupidly helpless—and overwhelmed by Diana's sudden breakdown. She was a virtual stranger. True, they'd known each other from the beginning. Diana and her husband had settled up the Duwamish River a couple of months before David had arrived on the bay. But because they'd always lived so far apart, they'd never really had a chance to know each other. But now here they were.

Mary Ann squeezed in beside Diana, somehow finding space on the stoop. "It's about your husband, isn't it? Is he all right? Is there something we can do?"

"Ain't nobody can help me!"

Mary Ann wrapped a comforting arm around Diana's back. Diana burst into fresh tears, pushing her hands over her eyes to try and stop the flow. "Nobody can help me. Exceptin' if someone could skin my husband good. You think someone can do that?" she asked Mary pitifully.

"I'll fetch some handkerchiefs!" volunteered Louisa, running off. But not fast enough.

"An *Indian* mistress!"

When Louisa got back Mary was asking, "But do you still love Mr. Collins?"

Quickly Louisa thrust the hankies into Diana's hands. Tears flooded her eyes like something had sprung loose inside.

"Yes. No. I don't know. The man's sat on me so many times he's done squeezed out all the love I had for him long ago."

Louisa eased around the two women and crept back into the coop, stricken through and through. Luther Collins? Who hated Indians? Who'd personally hung three and gotten everyone living in Seattle into perilous trouble for it? *He'd taken up with an Indian girl?*

218

She tried not to listen, but couldn't help it. Mr. Collins was lying to everyone, Diana said. His crops were in. He was staying on the claim so he could be with his Indian. *How do such things go on and we not know?* wondered Louisa. She swept quickly, gathering all the refuse into a pile. *Do our blessings blind us to other people's suffering?*

"I'm sure Arthur can get you a territorial divorce," said Mary Ann all of a sudden, "soon as the legislature convenes in December."

"Mary!" gasped Louisa.

Mary turned around and gave Louisa an angry sweep of her eyes. Louisa gulped. She was to stay out of this, obviously. *Oh, heaven help me! My very own sister, telling someone to get a divorce!*

"If you'll just read Deuteronomy 24, Diana, one through four," Mary was saying, "you'll see that when a man doesn't want his wife God *requires* he give her a bill of divorce."

Never did a chicken coop get so clean so fast! Louisa fairly flew around, raking, sweeping, even dusting out the last bits of leftover dross in the nesting boxes with her hand. All the while Mary and Diana talked and talked, Diana's crying rising and falling like a tide.

"Oh, Diana," sighed Mary Ann after a while, her voice so full of compassion it almost made *Louisa* cry. "How much God must love unhappy women. How much he must love *you*, Diana, to take such care to protect you."

At that, Diana threw herself into Mary Ann's arms. *Was she going to suffocate Mary?* wondered Louisa, truly worried. But Mary managed, and rocked the grief-stricken woman like a baby, letting her cry and continue to cry, Louisa sweeping and sweeping, and when the children at last could be heard far down the trail, Louisa edged out the door and hurried away to divert them—only to be jarred horribly when she realized they were running pell-mell up past the blockhouse screaming, "Indians! Indians! More Indians are coming!"

21

daytime

On his return Billy Tidd was accompanied by A. Benton Moses, Joseph Miles, George Bright, Dr. Burns, A. B. Rabbeson and John Bradley. This party arrived at the crossing of White River near Connell's Prairie early in the afternoon of Wednesday, October 31st, and were surprised to find Leschi and a large camp of Indians there.

—Clinton Snowden
in *History of Washington*

In looking over my diary as kept in 1855, I find the following account of a trip from Captain Maloney's camp to Steilacoom . . .

—A. B. Rabbeson, pioneer
in *A Small World of Our Own*

avid and the others trudged all morning back through the forests, making little headway. Noon had come and gone and they weren't even to the Russell's. David finally had to admit to himself that getting home was going to take a lot longer than he'd hoped. Days maybe; he might as well settle to it. Captain Hewitt—fortunately or unfortunately, depending on who was looking at it—had brought along some hammers and nails and they were fixing things up as they went along. "While we're out this way," the captain had explained over morning coffee, "we'll board up what cabins we find. Do what we can to protect folks' belongings."

Easier said than done. The ravished homes required consummate work before they could be secured. Scattered implements had to be gathered and put back indoors. Furniture, if in one piece, turned upright. Broken glass and china Hewitt wanted swept out of the way. Clothes had to be folded onto shelves, towels and jackets hung on nails. Pigs had to be set loose. Sometimes a cow or two had to be milked and fed, then added to the small herd they were collecting to drive into Seattle. The trail was almost impossible to traverse and Johnny King's dog was earning his keep, snapping at the cows whenever they balked, which they did frequently. As for covering the broken windows and doors, the men resorted to taking the doors off the outbuildings. If this wasn't enough, they'd wrench a cedar slab or two off the privy. But all this took an extraordinary amount of time, an agony to David who wanted only to be home with Louisa. Was she all right? What of Mynez? Did she miss her father? Did she wonder where he was? Would they never get there? Just how long had they been gone anyway? He counted on his fingers. The 29th, 30th, the 31st. Three days? That was all?

Worse, at each cabin horrible memories of the Jones' and Kings' gutted homes replayed themselves, and he began to worry if the ghastly images would ever leach from his mind. And when he thought of his own home out on the Swale? The pretty golden log house he and Louisa had so lovingly built, and into which they'd poured their dreams and all of their joys? Somehow, thinking of it now, the image came to him differently, like a half-remembered place. It wasn't the Swale though, he knew, that had been altered. Something within himself was changed. Broken. The events of the last few days had undone him in a way he couldn't yet define.

In a way, he and Louisa had lost their home just as the Muckleshoot, the Nisqually, even these barbarous Klikitat were losing theirs. He didn't know who to blame. Stevens? No. He blamed the Indians more. A man can be wronged, but he still had a choice. The Indians had chosen to wantonly kill and savage innocent men. Knife a woman to death. Plunge another and her infant into a well. To smash in the face of a dying woman.

Louisa was expecting their baby in the spring. What kind of world was it when women and children weren't safe from savages? Such beasts had to be stopped. Until then, there wasn't any use thinking of home and land and children growing up.

The narrow trail widened a little. Lewis squeezed in next to him. "How much of this, if any, are you going to tell Louisa?"

"How much are you telling Ursula?"

"Seems a good idea not to overly distress her with the details."

"It's going to get around."

"I wonder . . ." Lewis paused. "I wonder what it's going to do to the orphans, when they hear?"

"That's the worst," said David, ducking under a low branch.

"You been hearing any talk of building another blockhouse, down on the Point?" said Lewis. "I wasn't so sure at first. Now it seems a real good idea."

"I know what you mean. I've been thinking for weeks of building Liza and Mynez a place closer to the Cherry Street blockhouse. After this, I know I am."

"You believe in ghosts?"

"Why?" asked David, surprised by the question.

"I don't know, but I've been feeling strange all morning, like something's following us. I keep looking over my shoulder."

222

"The Indians would tell you it's the *stick siwash*."
"What's that?"
"Ghosts."

Billy Tidd's small party of seven, far in advance of Maloney's column, galloped up hard to Connell's Prairie. They saw first the burnt house, its lonely stone chimney standing like a skeleton, then rode head over heels into the war camp. It was hard to say who was more surprised, the Indians, or the express riders.

Clearly, the Indians hadn't expected anyone to approach from off the mountains. They'd posted no sentries that direction, and Tidd suddenly found himself amongst women and children and painted warriors every bit as flabbergasted as he. He hardly knew what to do. He pulled in hard on the reins and came to a stop. But he'd no more said *kla-how-ya* when Dr. Burns, a hot-headed Scotsman and physician for the volunteers, said, "I have him!" Mistaking a nameless youth for forty-one-year-old Leschi, Burns wrenched a pistol from the astonished young man's hands and very nearly blew his head off before Tidd and the rest could restrain him.

Stupid, foolish man! Livid, Tidd tried to seize the precarious moment by diverting to something less threatening. Casually in Chinook he inquired if he might purchase a pair of moccasins.

Someone was sent to bring over three klootchmen. The bartering began. Nonchalantly, in an effort to determine the Indians' true position, he inquired if anyone knew why Mike Connell's cabin happened to be burnt to the ground.

They had no idea. They'd really only just gotten here themselves, to catch some salmon and graze their stock. They were peaceful Indians, they said—though every word they spoke belied the paint on their faces. Their *tum-tums hyas copa Boston*—their hearts were right toward the Americans. Maybe, suggested a middle-aged man wearing a hat and coat, it had been burned by accident?

223

Tidd squinted at the flat, passive-looking face under the war paint and hat. Leschi?

The whole exchange had the quality of an uneasy dream. The Indians made no show of fighting, yet they were obviously as eager for the intruders to be gone as the intruders were to go. When Tidd tied the moccasins—for which he'd paid too much—to his saddlehorn and steered Old Girl back onto the road there was a collective sigh of relief on both sides.

Military Road made a long detour around a stand of timber before heading west across the prairie into a swamp thick with brush and fir trees. The riders, following the road, disappeared, coming out ten or fifteen minutes later to start across the prairie.

At the swamp Military Road narrowed, a cut barely wide enough for one wagon to pass through so closely did the fallen timber and underbrush crowd from both sides. After the recent heavy rain the road was, in some places, flooded with water and mud. *This is where Old Girl shied three nights ago,* Tidd realized with a start, and he got a funny feeling in the pit of his stomach. Joseph Miles pushed on past, into the foliage. Nothing to be done but pray and plunge on.

A quarter of a mile in, where skunk cabbages grew thickly, and the horses struggled hock deep in the soupy mire, the Indians, having beelined through the timber to beat the white men, unleashed a volley of musket fire from less than thirty yards away. Joseph Miles toppled backwards off his horse into the mud. Tidd frantically angled in beside the riderless horse, snagged the bridle.

"Grab your stirrup leather!" he screamed over the whiz of bullets and balls. A bullet struck his head with startling pain, nearly twisting his head clean off. "You got it, Miles?" he bellowed in frenzy of rage, pain, and terror.

"Yes! Go! Go!"

Tidd spurred his horse. With supreme effort Old Girl managed to drag Miles out of the mud and around a bend. Tidd pulled to a frantic stop, leaped down, Rabbeson right behind him. They found Miles so faint from a bullet through his neck that it was impossible for him to mount his horse.

"Leave me, make your escape, if possible," Miles gasped. "No hope for me. . . ."

The other four men—Burns, Bradley, Bright, and Moses—sped on by. Moses in the rear was obviously hit but managing to stay in his saddle.

"Let's get out of here!" shouted Rabbeson over to Tidd. For another quarter mile the six remaining men thundered down the muddy, gooey road before any of them realized the firing had ceased. There was only the sound of the horses' hard breathing and the slap and splash of the horses' hooves in the mud.

Are we in the clear? Tidd thought.

Two bullets whizzed past. Another thudded into his head with familiar, shocking pain. He didn't need to urge Old Girl into high gear, she was on her way. Amazingly, they swept through the second ambuscade, all six men and their horses; and were almost out of the swamp when Moses, falling farther and farther behind, hollered after them, "I am a dead man!"

They turned back even as Steilacoom's sheriff slumped forward and sideways out of his saddle. Tidd reached him first. The bullet had gone through Moses' back and out through his chest. Weak from loss of blood, he couldn't continue. They dragged him two hundred yards clear of the swamp and up off the road to Finnell's Prairie. Tidd did his best to stop the bleeding and plug the wound, then they all wrapped him in their overcoats to keep him warm. "We'll come back for you, soon as we get help," they assured him.

Tidd covered him over with brush. "Just hiding you is all. Moses under the reeds instead of in them," he added, trying to make the terrified man smile.

"If you escape, remember me, boys. . . ."

"We will!"

225

Now only five, they rode full speed out to the cliff above the first crossing of Finnell's Creek—right into a third bunch of warriors. These were the scouts keeping a lazy eye on the road ahead, and before they could gather their wits and get turned around, the riders were dismounted and charging, three to this side of the road, two to that, pitching into the unprepared and startled scouts with murderous vengeance. Rifles emptied of ammunition, Tidd and his comrades drew their sabers and stabbed, rent and slashed at least four of the Indians to death before finally routing the rest. Dr. Burns went hallooing after the fleeing Indians, a one-man avenging army. Though his friends hollered after him to stop, he kept running, declaring he would fight to the death.

A foolish, reckless thing to do. The three remaining men watched the hot-headed doctor enter a stand of fir on the far side of the prairie. Immediately they heard the crack of gunfire three times and an Indian yell.

"He's dead," said Tidd.

"Now what?" asked Bright.

"I'm all for getting back to Maloney," panted Rabbeson, mopping his brow. "I've had enough."

"What? Run that gauntlet again?" demanded Bradley incredulously, looking pointedly back over his shoulder.

Rabbeson, stout, sturdy, thrust his whiskered chin ahead. "There's Indians between us and Steilacoom. Peppering the countryside. I don't know about you, Bradley. Throw pepper in my nose, I sneeze."

"Yet either direction we go we've got Indians," Bright pointed out dismally. "But if we go on, we might get help for Miles and Moses faster."

"I'm with Bright," said Tidd. Gingerly he rubbed his head. Three slugs? How did a man take three slugs to the skull and live to count? "We'll have to abandon the horses and stick to the woods."

"Sorry, Old Girl," he told his faithful horse, kissing her velvety nose. "Stay out of trouble." With that he led the other men into the trees as rain began to fall. Before long they were so cold and so wet that the bullets in their cartridge boxes beat time to their shivers. *Sure glad we gave Moses our coats,* thought Tidd. *It'll ease his dying.*

Suddenly, Tidd prayed, *Let him die before they find him.*

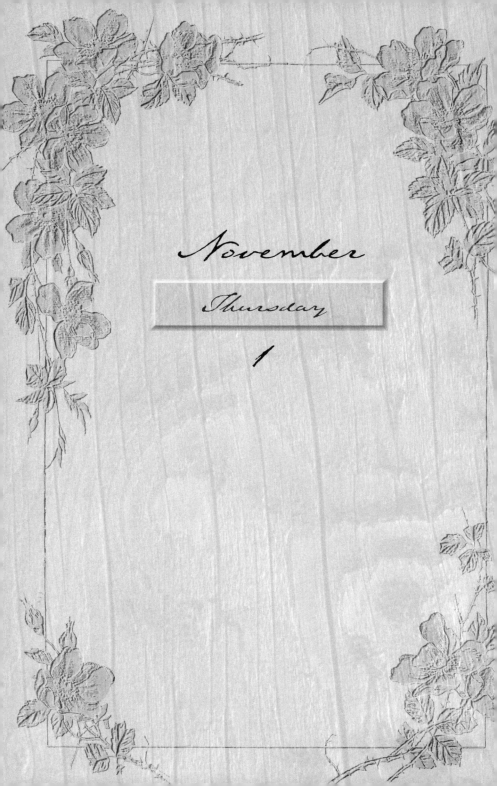

November

Thursday

1

22

morning

I was sent with the Traveler [November 1] to Victoria with a
requisition for arms and ammunition.

—J. G. Parker, Captain of the *Traveler*

I must cordially acknowledge the moral obligation which
binds Christian and civilized nations to exert their utmost
power and influence in checking the inroads of the merciless savage . . .

—Governor Douglas, Victoria, British Columbia
in response to the requisition for arms

*Y*esterday's alarm in Seattle over new Indians in town had
been without cause. The Indians were Chief Seattle's.
"Why ever are you creating such a commotion if it's only
Seattle's people?" Louisa had demanded of the screaming,
crying troop of children when she'd met them on the trail.
"You near scared me—and everyone else in Seattle, I might
add—half to death!"

"But Georgie, he said it was the Indians who killed everyone at White River!" bawled Nora, tears smudging her face.

"Oh, for heaven's sakes!" sighed Louisa, disgusted by the boy's folderol. How ever did Ursula manage?

Another group had arrived during the supper hour, then two more before dusk. Early this morning, the first of November, yet another band had come in. The village, already overcrowded with refugees, was now filled to overflowing with Indians as well.

Some of the settlers, watching two hundred displaced natives crowd in with the Snoqualmie on the Point and the Duwamish near the blockhouse—and starting to feel just a little nervous—called a hasty town meeting.

"There are more Indians around here," Reverend Blaine complained to the commissioners, "than white people!"

"Friendly Indians," said Mr. Yesler from his spot at the commissioner's table.

"Indians nonetheless."

"Umph! Seems to me," drawled Yesler, "sittin' in the middle of three hundred Indians these days is a good place to be. Fellows like Nelson and Leschi can't find you."

Everyone guffawed and that was that. After the meeting, Captain Sterrett hauled Arthur aside. "Hear anything from Pat Kanim, Mr. Denny?"

"Don't worry. He'll be here."

Sterrett laughed. "I didn't want to hear that," he confessed.

Movement outside caught the acting governor's eye. Quickly he glanced up from his desk. Nothing. Back to his review of everything he knew—and didn't know.

McAllister and Connell were dead, this he knew.

Possibly three families from White River, this he knew. He also knew it had been a big mistake on his part. He should have listened to Arthur Denny. War was upon them. A war of the most merciless kind. A war in which a lurking enemy might be anywhere, by the roadside, behind any tree, at the border of the clearing, at the door of a cabin. A war in which those who went to fight had to leave their wives and children, perhaps to be butchered by those they'd once regarded, and perhaps still regarded, as friends.

For such a war, for any war, they were hopelessly unprepared. They were four thousand of them—living amongst twenty thousand natives. And of their four thousand, only sixteen hundred were capable of bearing arms—the majority of whom, as he'd already discovered, had none to their name.

As for the 4th Infantry at Fort Steilacoom? Twenty-five at the fort, two hundred somewhere in the mountains? Depending on whether or not Tidd had been able to catch up with them, they could either be pushing alone into hostile country or they could be standing still, killing time—hoping and praying their provisions didn't run out before hearing from Major Rains.

Or! and on this Mason pondered. Maybe Captain Maloney would take things under his own advisement and head back? Yet why? He had his orders.

This was the biggest problem. Military orders, or lack thereof. What small army they did have on the Sound was being undermined by the politics and incompetency of their two highest commanding officers: Major General Wool headquartered in California—and Major Rains.

Major General John E. Wool, Commander in Chief—seventy-two years old and bearing a bitter grudge against Governor Stevens dating back to the Mexican War—deemed from the start that the trouble was of the settlers' making. Consequently, he not only refused to take seriously Mason's first urgent appeals for help, he sought also to undermine Mason's efforts toward self-defense—to the point of disbanding first the one company, then the other, that Mason had specifically raised to go in search of Governor Stevens.

As to active command, Major Rains was an officer rumored to have "no great capacity," "lacking enterprise," a man "wasteful of opportunities," a man "concerned about matters of form rather than inflicting serious injury to the enemy." And to date, Mason saw nothing to persuade him otherwise.

All this he knew. What he didn't know, but which he feared, was that this second campaign to punish the Yakima would prove another failure. Such repeated disaster would leave the already emboldened Indians all the more so. Worse, it would leave the Sound with only an army of twenty-five and a smattering of untrained volunteers.

Did he know anything else? Yes. He knew that Fort Steilacoom had but four hundred rounds of ammunition. He knew Fort Nisqually of England's Hudson's Bay Company had nothing. He knew of, and was grateful for, the generous shipment from Captain Sterrett. But that would only go so far.

Mason sighed discouragingly and glanced out the window again. Edward Huggins, overseer of the Company's agricultural farm, was crossing the street. Yes, of course! The Company at Nisqually had no weapons. But what about Company headquarters in Victoria?

Hastily he wrote to Governor Douglas of the Hudson's Bay Company and British Territory. Requisition in hand, he hurried into the rain and down to the docks to see what steamer might be tied up. Ah, the *Traveler!* Captain Parker, Mason knew, was a good man and could be counted on.

Dusk and a new shower of rain descended while David and the rest of Company H patched a hole in someone's chicken fence. A fox or a raccoon had already polished off a few of the chickens, and David was raking up the scattered feathers and chicken parts—well picked over by the other chickens still alive—when Captain Hewitt ordered camp. Glad to call it quits, David tossed his last shovel of bones and feathers into the brush and went over to where Jim Seattle was curiously inspecting the little chicken door between the fenced yard and shed. "What do you say we scare up some firewood and make ourselves a fire?"

"This is clever," Jim commented, kicking his foot against the flap and giving it a swing. "Though why would anyone want to go to all this trouble to fence a bunch of birds? All you have to do, when you want one, is go out and shoot one."

David shoved his hands into his pockets and tucked his chin into his wet coat collar. "We like the eggs."

"Plenty of eggs around." Jim gawked up at the dripping trees, swept his eyes through the forest. "If you know where to find them."

"That's just it. We don't."

Jim laughed. "Don't you think it'd be easier to learn than to go to all that trouble?" He jerked his thumb at the chicken coop. "What if a fox gets all your birds? Mm?"

"About that fire?"

Whoever owned the claim had started to build a small barn out back. It stood with a shake and pole roof, and consisted of one sheltering wall held up by big cedar posts set into the earth. Against this wall and under the roof, plenty of firewood had been stored, as well as shakes for finishing the sides of the barn. The shakes made good kindling, and in no time at all Company H had several fires blazing under the tall hemlocks and cedars encircling the yard, the wide sheltering boughs of the trees shielding them from the worst of the rain.

This being their fourth night out, the men worked in well-practiced unison, silently rigging their shelters and stirring up some supper. In David's small group, Klap-ki-latchi, always a quiet man, hurried down to the river to see about some fish. The rest of them fed the fire and started to see what could be done about their wet clothes. Their boots they propped into the hearth stones. Their shirts they wrung out best they could, then hung them off posts imbedded on cross sticks—so close to the flames that one or another of them was always yanking something back that was smoking.

"How many more days do you think we'll be out here?" Mr. Holderness asked of no one in particular.

David answered, shrugging. "Rate we're going, another three days? Four maybe?"

"Things should move along a little quicker, though," said Lewis encouragingly. "Closer we get, the less damage there is."

"I'm just worried about what's going on in Seattle," said Mr. Holderness.

"We all are," said David quietly. Suddenly Jim Seattle cocked his ear to the woods.

"You hear something?" David asked, even as the Jones's dog, curled at his feet, nose on his paws, began to growl.

Mr. Holderness reached nervously for his rifle—of no value except perhaps as a club. "Something out there?"

"Shh!" hissed Jim.

All three scouts had their ears cocked. All David could hear was the rain.

Three Indians crept closer in. Suddenly Nelson held up his hand, waved his companions back. He put a finger to his lips and waved again. Back! Back! So the three men inched away slowly, quietly. As soon as they were out of earshot, Nelson whispered, "We don't hurt them. We tell the others to circle back. No attack at dawn. Time to rejoin Leschi anyway."

Kanasket turned on Nelson in a fury, but before Leschi's "lieutenant" could begin his venomous protest Nelson amazingly stuck his Hudson's Bay flintlock musket in the ugly Klikitat's face.

"Put that down," snapped Kitsap the Younger, making movement to shove the rifle away from Kanasket's face.

Nelson was too quick. He swung the gun over to Kitsap himself. "Don't you two fools know David Denny?"

"No!"

"You should!"

236

"We don't!"

"He speaks our languages. He and his klootchman pay us well for our work, better than Mr. Yesler. And David Denny knows how to guess bones. He could win the clothes off your back—" Nelson jabbed the end of his musket into Kitsap's chest "—and take all your wealth in one night!"

"I doubt that," snapped Kitsap. "I'm the best."

"He's better."

"I doubt it!"

"We do not attack!" hissed Nelson, nostrils flaring. "David Denny is one of us!"

"What's he doing with whiteskins then?"

"To help bury the dead?" Nelson guessed, keeping his musket poised.

"Why all the guns? And you heard Leschi's—!"

"Guns? Didn't you see those pieces of dog dung they're carrying? I wouldn't use one of those to hit a fish over the head! This? A war party?" Nelson feigned laughter.

Kanasket spoke up for the first since having the rifle shoved unpleasantly into his face. "They are Bostons," he said, and in his voice was all the venom of ten rattlesnakes.

"David Denny is Boston, yes," agreed Nelson. "But he is one of us. In his heart he is Indian. Do we shoot our own?" He swung his musket back to Kanasket. "Oh yes, maybe we do," he said slowly, and this time the muzzle nudged Kanasket's brow, between his eyes. "Maybe we *do* shoot our own!" repeated Nelson. "If we kill King Georges, yes, push them into wells, yes, maybe we do!"

Silent words flashed between the powerful war chief and Nelson, the obstinate Muckleshoot chief. Words sharper than a knife. Words Kitsap the Younger understood well enough for himself. Words like guilt. Words like penance.

"Oh," said Kanasket, shrugging suddenly, all malice gone from his voice and face. "Why didn't you say so in the first place? We leave him alone, sure."

237

November

Friday

2

23

morning

The volunteers buried the dead and went back to Seattle without meeting any Indians, hostile or friendly. But on the river they met a mysterious black man who told them that the night before their camp had been surrounded by a hundred and fifty Indians. Hewitt was pleased that they had not attacked his forty-four [55] men, partly because fifteen of the volunteers' rifles were disabled relics carried only for moral effect.

—Archie Binns, historian
in *Northwest Gateway*

David woke Friday morning the 2nd of November to thick fog and muffled voices. Bleary-eyed, he stumbled from his damp bed, stretched, shivered, then squinted curiously over to where he thought he'd heard the voices coming from. Through the wet blanket of air he could see a flicker of flame and then, yes, the shadowy outlines of three or four men.

He was surprised to find sitting with his fellow officers one of the territory's few black men, drinking a cup of Captain

241

Hewitt's very bad coffee. *Is this the man?* he wondered. *Is he the one for whom the Territory had obtained, from Washington City, his right to claim title to his donation claim?*

Everyone looked pretty serious. David said, "What's up?"

"Mr. Bush here says a hundred and fifty Indians had us surrounded last night," Dave Neely answered. "But for some unexplainable reason, withdrew."

Hardly knowing what to think, David sat on a mossy log with his comrades, and after glancing around the circle of familiar faces he could see that his friends didn't know what to think either.

"Well, I's be moseying on, thanks for the coffee," said the mysterious black man all of a sudden. He set his cup onto a hearth stone and pulled to his feet. "Yo's a lucky bunch!" he told the captain. "God sho' enough got his eye on *you* folk."

"What do you make of it?" Captain Hewitt asked incredulously when the forest was quiet again, the stranger gone. Every single one of them were inclined to discredit the story, but when John Henning, who'd gone out to take a look, returned, confirming that large numbers of Indians had indeed left their mark in the woods, there was no choice but to believe the evidence. And fortuitous mercy.

"Last night Jim thought he heard something," said David, remembering now. "The dog even growled a little. But when we didn't hear anything more, we dismissed it. Must have been someone out there after all."

"So why didn't they attack?" asked the captain.

"Maybe it's like the man said—God's got his eye on us?"

Rather than put God to further test, Captain Hewitt ordered a forced march home. No more securing homes. No more feeding stock. He got no argument out of the men. They had their belongings packed up and slung over their shoulders in no time. "What about the cattle, Captain?" someone hollered.

"If they can keep up, fine! If not—Well, I hope they got sense enough to steer clear of the cougars!"

David brought up the rear with Jim Seattle and the Jones's dog pushing the half dozen cows ahead of them. Literally. David leaning on their big rumps, the dog yapping at their heels, both David and the dog determined to move the dumb beasts along the raw narrow trail littered with brush and treefall.

Lewis Wyckoff, who'd gone on ahead, waited. "What *are* you doing, Denny?" he demanded. He was leaning against a moss-coated hemlock when David reached him, his powerful blacksmith arms crossed over his chest. He shook his head with an amused expression on his friendly face.

David, looking up, laughed. "I have a soft spot for these gentle creatures of the earth."

For Louisa it was not the sound of muffled voices trickling through a fog that called her awake, but the clear, sonorous chant of Latin liturgy. *Chief Seattle is back!* She leapt from bed.

Chief Seattle held Mass, she knew, for his people each morning at Port Madison, but she'd never heard it before for herself. Hastily she dressed and got Emily Inez out of bed.

The day promised to be cold, but clear, only a few fog pockets left on the water. Good, no rain. She could see her breath as she hurried along, a very grumpy Emily Inez dawdling beside her. "I got you up too early, didn't I, darling? I'm sorry," she crooned, stooping down. "Come on then. I'll carry you the rest of the way."

At the blockhouse and looking down on the mill she was astonished by the size of the crowd! There wasn't space to stand! Indians were even sitting on top of the cookhouse, looking down from the roof! That Chief Seattle had such influence over so many people, that they should so abruptly move across the Sound at his bidding, was amazing enough. But this! Close to five hundred men and women standing together in prayer and song?

"Tu va remplir le voeu de la tondresse . . ."

243

A hymn, but not Latin. "What language is *that?*" she asked Emily Inez, kissing her daughter's grumpy, sweet face.

"French," said someone coming up from behind.

"Yoke-Yakeman!" cried Louisa in delight, spinning around and giving Arthur's hired hand a pleased smile.

"You happy to see me?" he teased.

"I'd be happier to see Pat Kanim!" she shot back, and the handsome Indian laughed heartily. "*Is* he here?" she persisted.

"Arthur's got him aboard ship with the captain!"

Another prayer answered, thought Louisa gratefully and happily. If only the volunteers were home!

The atmosphere on the Sawdust and Point was one of high excitement. *Like a carnival!* thought Louisa. Pat Kanim had brought with him the remainder of his tribe, plus a cargo of mountain sheep, venison, and horses and hides. Everyone in town was down at the livery to see the magnificent horses; and while Pat Kanim rented them out to eager young riders, Chief Seattle's strongest warriors purchased a dozen cross-cut saws and took to the woods with a view to felling "canoe" trees. The only way to Port Madison was by boat—of some kind, and soon the raspy sound of their saws chewing through two- and three-foot thick cedars riffled down the steep hill to the Point. By afternoon Pat Kanim's horses and Tom Mercer's Tib and Charley were put to better use, hauling the felled trees down to the beaches.

Big fires were started. Everyone milled around, curious about the procedure of canoe making. Indian dugouts were *not* clumsily constructed, hollowed-out logs. They were masterpieces of skill, patience, and design. Doc Maynard liked to boast to newcomers that the Indians had been building their fleets with clipper lines while the English were still building apple-bowed butter tubs!

First, the bark had to be peeled. And how quickly they worked, chips flying! Louisa was fascinated, mesmerized, by their speed, a skill she envied—remembering the hard time

244

she and David had had when building their house. Days and *days* it had taken them to get those logs peeled and all golden in the sun. *But these boys! Whew!* she thought, *they know what they're doing!* Still, it took the greater part of the day, and during the dinner hour people began drifting home, some coming back, some not.

Louisa stayed. Chief Seattle insisted she join them at his fire, along with the Maynards and the orphan children, and so she joined the small, intimate group. She and Emily Inez ate the roasted salmon and wopatoes as hungrily as the rest.

Suddenly, the sharp toot of the *Traveler*—coming into the bay with its weekly newspaper delivery—startled Louisa. Dusk already? Quickly she bid the chief goodnight, and Princess Angeline. She had to get Emily Inez into bed. Suddenly, as she turned to go, the realization that the volunteers hadn't returned overwhelmed her. *Another day come and gone and no David.* Two days into November, and he still wasn't home.

Seattle said something kindly. She looked to Angeline for the translation.

"He say no worry. Jim, George, with him. They come home soon. Tomorrow maybe?"

Seattle had read her mind with the uncanny skill Indians had to see and know and communicate without words. And how dear that he should care! She wished she could speak his language, that she might let him know how very much she appreciated his concern for her, as well as his skillful influence with so many people, his wisdom, his honesty, his willingness to compromise, even if it meant taking the shorter end of the stick to avoid bloodshed. But the Duwamish language to Louisa was an impossible thing. In order to make the harsh, cracking sounds correctly it seemed to her one had to tie their tongue in a knot and then talk fast while swallowing their tongue. She did, however, try a thankyou, a mangled noise. To Angeline she said in English, "Tell him I appreciate very much his watching out for me."

245

She carefully watched father and daughter converse in the growing dusk. They did *not* swallow their tongues.

Up on Commercial Street and standing outside the Maynards' log house, she and the Maynards stood catching their breath. The trail off the beach was short, but they'd taken it at a run. Doc had Emily Inez in his arms, her cheek resting heavily against the black broadcloth of his coat. They started across the road to Plummer & Chase while Catherine went inside with Johnny King and Laura and Frederick Jones.

"What's going to happen to them?" Louisa asked Doc.

"The children?"

"Yes."

"Captain Sterrett sent a letter to some of the Ohio newspapers. Johnny says he has an uncle there."

"Until then, will you keep them?"

"The Russells have asked. Catherine thinks it might be a good idea. It would help Mrs. Russell get her mind off her terror, having someone to watch out for."

"Yes," agreed Louisa.

Captain Parker was already inside Mr. Plummer's fancy store when they arrived. Hired hands were bringing up the bundled newspapers from Plummer's Pier, pushing past the few customers with their heavy loads and stacking them in a corner where Mr. Plummer could cut the tow and start handing them out.

"I'm off to Victoria in the morning!" sang out Captain Parker to a group of new faces coming in. Everyone in town had heard the horn while sitting at their evening fires and come down, anxious to get their copies of the paper and learn the latest war news. "Mason's sending me up!" Captain Parker announced. "To ask Governor Douglas if we can't have some Company guns and ammunition!"

Hopeful smiles came to tired faces.

Captain Parker had other news too, and pretty soon all the men who were left in Seattle were cheering and thumping one another on the back, and whistling. Billy Tidd had come into Steilacoom at three this morning, more dead than alive. Three slugs in his head! *"But he found Maloney!"* shouted Captain Parker. *"Captain Maloney was coming back to the Sound!"* Louisa didn't know who Billy Tidd was, but she knew who Maloney was. She felt her knees sway. Even through her despondency she rejoiced. The soldiers coming back was news too good to be true! *"And he's got Lieutenant Slaughter with him!"* shouted Captain Parker over the roar of huzzas. Only news of David's return could be better news.

She seized her copy of the *Courier,* carefully took Emily Inez, half asleep, into her arms, and bid Doc good-bye.

"David'll be all right," said Doc, reading her mind just as easily as Chief Seattle had.

"Is it that obvious?"

"Go on home, Liza. Get a good night's rest. One of these days it'll all be over. We just have to keep saying our prayers."

"We do, don't we, Doc."

She walked home slowly, the dark pressing from all sides. She passed the mill, lit by lanterns, saw whirling. She moved on, away from the whine, up the slope. Slow steps. Up past the blockhouse, slower yet. She paused at Suwalth's camp. So many Indians now . . . Half-naked children ran in between and around the campfires; shouting, laughing, chasing and teasing each other. When they tired, she knew they would simply curl up wherever there was a corner and fall asleep. Most of the men, consummate gamblers, were playing their bone games—a fascination and obsession she couldn't understand. She passed Sheriff Russell's house. While he was away, his parents were staying there, and through the little window she could see Mr. Russell, Tom's father, reading the paper. Yes, it would be good if the poor orphans found a home there. The Russells were good folks.

Arthur and Mary Ann's house was lit as well. For a moment Louisa was tempted to stop in. But Emily was dead with sleep, she needed to be tucked into bed. *But I don't want to be alone in my forlorn little house,* Louisa sighed to herself. Which was why, she knew, she'd been walking so slowly despite the darkness and late hour. To put off the inevitable.

With great effort she made herself push on, past her sister's cozy house and the happy sounds leaking through the thin windowpane to her own little cabin. When she pulled the latch and pushed open the door, the room was just as lonely and cold and empty as she'd known it would be.

24

evening

We crossed the Nisqually and took the immigrant trail direct to Steilacoom, and arrived at Mr. Tallentire's on Friday morning at 3 o'clock, all very much exhausted, having been three days and nights without food. George Bright became so much fatigued that it was impossible for him to travel any further, laid down and went to sleep, the rest of us being so weak that we could not carry him. On reaching the house we dispatched Mr. Tallentire and a friendly Indian, who was with him, in search of Bright, but he slept so soundly that their hallooing would not arouse him, and the dark being so intense, he could not be found until morning.

After reaching Steilacoom we at once informed Lieutenant Nugen of the above circumstances . . .

—A. B. Rabbeson, pioneer
in *A Small World of Our Own*

*E*mily Inez didn't wake until Louisa tucked her in. At the touch of her soft, fuzzy blanket, laid against her cheek, she stirred. Her eyes flickered open. "Mama, My want my

Papa," she mumbled, then fell back to sleep with a sigh. Louisa kissed her. *Please bring her father home,* she prayed.

Fifteen minutes later, with the fire crackling and throwing sparks up the chimney, her tea made, and holding it carefully lest she spill, Louisa climbed into bed. It felt good to get in, the flannel sheets chilly but soothingly soft. She wiggled down into the covers, and propped her head up against the wall with both her own pillow and David's. A poor advantage of not having him with her, she thought. Slowly she sipped the steaming tea while scanning the headlines and stories.

Lots of news. Hopeful news. Despite her weighted despondency and the eerie loneliness that permeated every corner of the cabin, she found herself feeling less and less depressed. There was so much to be thankful for.

Captain Maloney was on his way home. The newspaper editor suggested he might even be as far as Porter's Prairie.

And Lieutenant Slaughter, she read, had been miraculously spared. Chief Teias, war chief of the Klikitat, was a day in advance of the victorious Yakima, enroute to attack Slaughter, when Slaughter's scout, ignorant of Haller's defeat and trying to determine his whereabouts, rode straight into the enemy war camp! Only the fact that John Edgar was married to Chief Teias's niece—and that he could think fast on his feet—had saved his life, and enabled him to get back to Slaughter with the dire news of the disastrous defeat. Slaughter had wasted no time in turning around. He and his men were, in fact, at Porter's Prairie when Maloney came on them. Together they'd crossed back over the pass. Now here they were, back again. *David will be so relieved when he hears this.*

The express rider who'd brought the joyous news, though, had been ambushed by Leschi at Connell's Prairie in the exact spot where the two men from Eaton's Rangers had been killed. This time three men were dead: Steilacoom's sheriff, a man from Olympia, and a doctor for the volunteers. The express rider Billy Tidd was alive. *So that's who Captain*

Parker was talking about . . . The paper reported he suffered three slugs in his head. A special doctor was being brought up from Fort Vancouver to take them out. How did anyone live with three bullets in their skull? One sad story reported that the horse belonging to Dr. Burns, the dead doctor, still saddled and carrying a medicine bag, had trotted riderless into the fort late last night.

Here was something! Louisa sat up straighter. Eaton's Rangers had escaped! They weren't dead! They were, in fact, with the Steilacoom volunteers right now! Looking for the bodies of McAllister and Connell, as well as the latest dead—Misters Moses and Miles and Dr. Burns!

Watch, half asleep by the fire, perked up, then went over to the door, whining.

"Do you need to go out? No?"

Her dog had returned to the fire and was circling his bed, lying back down, whining.

"You're sure?" she said. One more whine, but he put his nose back onto his paws. She returned to her paper, and blinked in astonishment. Dr. Burns *wasn't* dead?

To Adjutant General Tilton—Sir . . . A letter? From Dr. Burns?

To Adjutant General Tilton—Sir:

Please contradict the report that I was killed by the Indians. I killed 7 with my own hands. They hunted me through the brush for 1 mile with dogs and lighted sticks, and every one who carried the light I shot. The only wound I got was a skin wound in the forehead from a buckshot. I lived in the brush on leaves, and shot an Indian this morning, for his dried salmon and wheat at Mr. Lemon's. Give my respects to Bright and Rabbeson, and let them know I am safe—only I had to throw away my boots and my feet are badly hurt. I lost my horse, instruments and medicine case. My horse was shot in the kidneys in the swamp where we received that murderous discharge of balls and buckshot. Please let Mr. Wiley say I am all right.

I remain respectfully, M. P. Burns, Surgeon Captain Hays's Command.

His horse shot in the kidneys? But didn't— She looked back through the paper. Didn't it just say—Yes, Dr. Burns's horse had trotted into the fort! Still saddled!

Carrying the medicine bag! *What a scamp!* thought Louisa, starting to laugh. *What a liar!*

Company H had crossed the Duwamish on Luther Collins's ferry at dusk and had a despairing time of it. The ropes slipped from their moorings; the cows balked and bawled, raising havoc and causing more than one man to get an unexpected and unwanted dunking. Not a good time to be causing trouble. The men's exhaustion and nerves were stretched to an all-time tautness. Muttered grumbling broke into bitter cursing, and David discovered that only he and a handful of others— namely the Seattle boys and Klap-ki-latchi—had the patience to cope. On their shoulders fell the bulk of the responsibility. Suddenly, out of the growing darkness emerged Henry Van Asselt, Mr. Grow, and Sam Maple on the far bank.

David was never so glad to see anyone in all his life. The three farmers, hearing the commotion, had come out to see what help could be lent. Which was plenty; they knew how to manage the ferry.

"Where's Collins anyway?" barked Captain Hewitt crossly when the horrendous task was done at last, night falling, everyone else busy hunting up and gathering their bags for the final home stretch.

"Haven't seen hide nor hair of him," said Sam Maple. "Probably in Seattle. Everyone's near done out here."

Henry Van Asselt, a middle-aged Dutchman, a man who'd settled the Duwamish River with Luther Collins four years before, hauled David aside. "Somedings smell fishy at de

252

Collins'," he said in a confidentially worried whisper. "He not been oot, ony doze deserters he hired. I'm zinking dat maybe dey done someding to heem? Yah?"

David glanced over his shoulder in the direction of Luther Collins's place, and was ashamed to admit he had no interest in checking on the ornery man. To detour this close to home was unthinkable. "It'll have to wait. I haven't seen my wife for close to a week."

"Yah, dat iz a good zing to do yust now," agreed Henry.

"Hey, Dave!" hollered Lewis. "The others are on their way. Let's get these milk bags moving!"

David shook hands with Van Asselt. "Thanks for coming out. We'd have been here all night, Henry, if you hadn't."

"Yah, I zinc zo."

They both grinned. David hurried over to Lewis.

"Do you think these cows can find their own way in?" he asked the blacksmith.

"I don't know about them! But I sure can! Hey! Wait up!"

They hurried into the dark, leaving the cows to trail. Beach Road opened easily before them, moonlight dropping off their shoulders, playing tricks with their feet and the mudholes. But it was an easy go, compared to what they had been doing five days straight. Up ahead, just around the next bend, David could hear the others; behind, the cattle lumbered along nicely. Johnny King's pup trotted beside him.

"We're moving too slow," he told Lewis.

"I was just going to say the same thing myself."

Simultaneously, they broke into a run.

"Ya-hooo! We're going home!" shouted Lewis into the growing darkness.

David saved his breath to spurt ahead. Lewis caught up. They were still running when they passed the others and the Indian scouts. They were still running when they came down off a high bridgework. Forced finally to slow down, they trudged the dizzyingly high ridge that ran along the Holgate and Hanford claims. When they came to the east half of Doc

253

Maynard's claim, where the road dropped slow and easy to sea level, they picked up pace again until they were half running, half walking. Coming around one of the last bends, the smelly lagoon tucked in behind the Point suddenly popped into view. Moonlight glistened off the water's dark surface. "You know, Lewis," said David, slowing down and panting hard, "don't know as I've ever seen anything so beautiful. I think this means we're home."

"Tide's out. I'm cutting across the spit."

David hesitated. It was almost as fast for him to continue on. Go past Tom Pepper's house, then head into town down Yesler's Skid Road. He wouldn't have to get wet either. Even at low tide, the long narrow spit, hooking over to the Point from this side of the lagoon, would still leave them a ten-foot gap of waist-high water.

"Come on," urged Lewis, already veering off.

"I don't want to get wet!"

Lewis laughed. "You need a bath, Dave!"

David looked down.

Lewis laughed again.

They'd just splashed out of the water and up the east bluff of the Point and were coming around Mr. Plummer's fancy mansion, dripping wet, the Jones's dog shaking off the seawater, when suddenly the pup had his nose to the ground. Snuffing wildly, he darted down the road, tail wagging.

"Smells something," said Lewis.

"Boy, I'll say. Hey, Lewis, does it seem to you we've got a whole lot more Indians around here than when we left?"

Lewis swiveled his neck around, then turned a complete circle. Between the few remaining trees and hundreds of stumps that littered the Point, glowing embers from dozens of dying campfires could be seen. With careful scrutiny, the bulky shadows of rude shelters could be discerned. And with the ever-present sound of the waves lapping the beach below, came pockets of low murmurs, broken occasionally by loud bursts of laughter and then the echo of jovial teasing.

254

"Snoqualmie," said David, catching the language. "Pat Kanim must have gotten in. That's good."

"If you say so," said Lewis. They reached his house and smithy. Lewis had just put his hand on the latch, ready to let himself in, when the dog, kitty-corner across the intersection, started barking and pawing at Doc Maynard's door.

"Well I'll be," breathed out Lewis. "I bet Doc's got the orphans and that mutt's tracked down Johnny King. Amazing. Say, I'd like to have that hound to go hunting with."

"He's a fine dog."

"Night, Dave. See you in the morning."

"Yeah, goodnight." David started across the street to where the dog howled and whined at Maynard's door. The road was empty at this late hour but for a few Indians passing by with their blankets drawn up around their shoulders and heads.

Suddenly Doc yanked opened his door. The dog dove through, nearly knocking him off his feet. "What the deuce—" blustered Doc in his nightshirt. "What the—"

David laughed.

"That you, Denny?" Doc asked, peering into the night. "What in the world was that? A dog? Dave! You guys are back!" he shouted, waking up to what David's presence meant. He stepped out into the street, nightshirt, bare feet and all.

"Yup, we're back all right!" said David, going over to give him a handshake.

"The others? Everyone okay?"

"Everyone's fine. Still coming on though."

"So what was that?" said Doc, scratching his head. "I thought it was a dog, but what would a dog—"

"By any chance, did you take in the orphans?"

"We did, yes."

"Well then, I brought Johnny his dog."

Silence.

"Everything go fine out there?" Doc finally asked, quietly.

255

"A boy is missing, the rest are dead. Joe Brannan's gone off the deep end, he saw some of it."

"Bad?"

"You don't know how bad, Doc."

"Where's Joe now?"

"We tried to get him to come on with us, but he went to Steilacoom. Listen, I'm wet and cold and plenty dirty, and missing Liza. How is she anyway? And what *was* that the day we left?"

"What?"

"The cannon. At least I'm assuming—"

"Oh that. Yeah, the cannon all right. Had a visit from the Haida. Captain took care of them, though. Liza's fine. Pining. Lucky you."

"I'll be going then."

He'd gone a half dozen steps when he heard Doc chuckle.

"If Louisa throws you out until you come in smelling better? You know to come back here, don't you?"

"She won't throw me out!"

"No, I don't expect she will!"

Another half dozen steps.

"Dave?"

"Yeah?"

"Thanks for bringing the dog. It's a hard go for the children."

Dr. Burns was something else, Louisa decided as she sat reading the paper. All kinds of people had something to say about whatever it was that had happened out there.

DR. BURNS FOUND!

Dr. Burns was found and rescued by the Pierce county volunteers, some 4 or 5 miles from the place where he was supposed to have been shot; he had taken refuge in a barley sack, having lost his horse and accoutrements, coat, pistols, boots and hat, but fortunately saving his scalp, and having his ammo dry and carbine ready had remained in that perilous situation FOUR DAYS. A narrow escape, certainly.

That's what the editor had to report. Mr. Hicks, who was riding with the new volunteers, wrote:

> When we crossed the Puy-allup River Dr. Burns saw us and crawled out from under a haystack and joined us.

Another man said:

> Some may inquire, What of Dr. Burns? He was found hidden in a barley sack at Mr. Lemon's place in Puyallup bottom.

Whatever the truth, Dr. Burns was going to have a hard time living this one down. Suddenly the whole thing struck her funny all over again and she got the giggles. Watch lifted his nose, watching her.

"I can't help it," she giggled at her dog. "He's probably going to have to go live in Oregon now."

Watch stretched, pulled to his feet, and went over to the door again.

"*Now* you want out?"

He started to whine, then began to paw and bark, tail wagging. Cougar . . . ! No—she started to relax—not with Watch's tail wagging like that. And then she heard the familiar tune, "Watchman Tell Us of the Night."

She was out of bed in a flash! David! She could hear his voice, strong and beautiful! He was singing! Singing his favorite hymn! Coming home to her! The bolt! Bee's knees, it was jammed! *Come on, come on!* she frantically fussed. She could hear the words now, he was so close! *Come onnnn!* She had so much to tell him! The cougar! How kind Arthur had been—the chamber pot, the tarred roof! And poor Diana Collins! She had to tell him about Diana! He'd know what to do, what the right thing would be! The poor woman was losing her mind; she thought she'd go to hell if she divorced Mr. Collins, but who could go back to that man? That would be hell! *Come on, come on, what's the matter with this latch?* she bemoaned, gritting her teeth and stealing herself for the pain, wrenching hard. The bolt slid back with a bang! She grabbed her hand, fire in her fingers.

And then the door swung open, and she was in his arms! David, David! He was really here, he was home! She couldn't speak for her tears; him either! He held her so closely, so tightly, she wondered that her ribs might break—she didn't care!

He pushed the rest of his way into the cabin and gave the door a shove. Somehow he disentangled himself from her long enough to drop his pack and rifle onto the floor. "Oh, David," she choked out, whispering, "you came back!"

"I told you I would," he said, grinning down at her.

"You came back, you came back to me!"

He stopped her with a kiss, kissing her mouth, her nose, each of her eyes. "Mynez? Is she all right?" he asked breathlessly.

"Yes." Louisa drew away so he could see their daughter sleeping in her little bed.

"I can see her in the morning. Right now I just want to feast my eyes on you," he told her, taking her cheeks in his icy hands and looking happily down into her face with a smile, all his love for her there in his eyes.

"Elizabeth?" she whispered. She had to know.

"You were right. I'm sorry."

She bit her lip, and nodded. She wouldn't ask the details. Not yet. He drew her back into his arms. She didn't care that he was cold! He was here! He was home! she exulted, entwining herself in his fierce embrace and rejoicing in the familiar feel of his body, the firmness, the strength of his arms, the crush of his cheek against hers. *Oh dear God, thank you, thank you!* she cried with all of her heart. *You brought my dear David back to me!* Oh, but he was sooo cold! In fact, she stepped back.

"David, you're soaking wet! What happened to you?"

"I came in over the spit."

"Goodness! Were you trying to catch your death?"

"I was," he said, leaning over the space she'd put between them to kiss her nose, "trying to get home to you."

"Oh, David, why are we standing here? Come to bed, come get warm! Oh my. You are a sorry sight." She started to laugh.

"And you're not? Look at you!"

She looked down. Her nightgown was wet and muddied from his clothes.

He started to laugh.

"I can put on a clean gown," she told him, "but you—" She waggled a finger. "You need a bath!"

"Any water in the reservoir?" He was already shucking off his jacket, tugging off his boots.

"Yes."

"Is it hot?"

"Yes. Oh, David, so much has happened! I have so much to tell you!"

"I have lots to tell you!"

She got down the tub, dragged it over in front of the fire. He did the filling, scooping out the water, piping hot, from the new reservoir on the back of the stove. Quickly he stripped, and stepped in. Carefully he sat. Water on the floor meant more mud. Louisa shivered into a clean gown, then handed him soap and a cloth.

"I'll need the scrub brush!"

She got it off the counter.

"Can you do my hair?"

"Let me get a cup."

She told him all about everything while she shampooed his hair. Captain Maloney and Lieutenant Slaughter, on their way back, the cougar, Diana—he didn't say much about it, but looked sad and worried—the flood of Indians coming in.

"Pat Kanim must have come in?"

"This morning."

"You say Seattle got here yesterday?"

"Yes." She told him about the women's Bible study too, and the big scare with the Haida. "We don't know who was more scared in the end, them or us," she said laughing, rubbing his hair dry and watching all his long curls spring to life when she took the towel away.

"Come here." He took the towel from her. She leaned in close. "You take my breath away, Mrs. Denny."

She smiled. "Maybe you better finish your scrub, Mr. Denny?"

"Bedsheets warm?" he teased.

"They were," she teased back.

"See what you can do."

She leapt into bed. Burrr-rr! But in a minute he'd be here, sliding in next to her! Together they'd warm things up. Two logs always burned brighter than one!

"I still can't believe you're here," she whispered a few minutes later when he blew out the lamp and climbed in, tangling his legs with hers, to be as close to her as possible. "It's been so long, forever and ever and ever. I thought you'd never be back!"

"I didn't either. We had to board up all the cabins—Oh, Liza, never mind all that. I'm back and you're here, just like I knew you'd be." Gently he kissed her. Sweetly, so softly, his cold lips, amazingly, warming her skin.

"It doesn't seem like there's a war going on, does it?" she whispered. And for the first time, she realized, in a long while, that was just the way it felt.

"There is, though."

She put a finger to his lips. When he tried to speak, she shushed him. "You said, never mind all that. So let's never mind. Let's pretend there is no world but our own."

He took her hand away. "I know what I said, but there is another world. We can't forget, I can't. If you saw what I did, if you—"

"David."

"Yes?"

"You don't think God can be trusted both sides of the grave?"

Through the light of the crackling fire, he gazed down at her, a smile slowly growing on his face. He let go of her hand and traced her lips with his finger. "You are an amazing woman . . ."

"Why?"

"What you just said. Trusting God both sides of the grave. That is how we're going to get through this, isn't it?"

"Yes, I think. That *is* our hope," she told him.

"Come here."

"Aren't you glad that we're married?" she whispered, snuggling up to him again. "And that we're so happy, and that we have each other? Right now? This very minute?"

He jerked up.

"What is it?"

"I don't know," he said nervously, easing back into bed. "I suppose I've just gotten used to hearing sounds that aren't there. Where were we?"

"I was asking—"

"I know what you were asking!" he laughed, tracing her lips again with his finger, and making her shiver. "You were asking if I was happy—"

A sudden knock on the door startled them.

"David, let me in! It's me, Arthur!"

"Arthur . . ." moaned Louisa. "Oh, David, he is *so* maddening!"

"You have to admit," he whispered, kissing her mouth quickly, and sneaking another quick kiss, "he's getting better. At least he's not just barging in like he used to do."

"I don't care, and whatever he wants, it can wait until morning."

"David! Come on, open up!"

"Don't go!" Louisa reached to grab his wrist.

261

"We have to get rid of him."

The minute David cracked the door, Arthur pushed in. "Sorry, Louisa, but Dave Neely just got in. He says everyone's back. Welcome home, Dave."

"Thank you. Goodnight, Arthur."

"Glad to see you! Neely says—"

"Goodnight, brother Arthur."

"Oh, right, never mind." Arthur grinned. "Mary sent me, to get Mynez."

"She's asleep!" objected Louisa, sitting up. "You'll—" She stopped abruptly. Quickly she slithered back down into the covers and pulled them up over her flaming face.

Arthur chuckled. And then he laughed out loud when he noticed the darkened room. "You don't waste much time!"

"Arthur," said David. "I got here ahead of everyone else— Lewis and I— Oh never mind."

Arthur chuckled again, and Louisa, hiding under the covers, could hear David lifting Mynez from her bed. She could just picture his soft kiss to her lips, the tenderness with which he would pass her over to Arthur, his hesitancy in letting her go.

"Arthur?" She sat up quickly at the sound of the door opening again. "Did you remember her hat?"

"Does she need one?"

"I'd rather. She's fighting a cold."

David reached for the back of the door, grabbed the little bonnet hanging between Louisa's and his own muddy wet cap. Cold air snaked into the room.

"Tell Mary Ann thanks," David whispered.

"I will. Goodnight, Louisa," Arthur called over to her.

"Goodnight, Arthur."

David gave the door a good shove. He jumped back into bed. "Where were we?"

"I think," said Louisa, laughing at him, "I was asking if you were glad we were married? That we're so happy and that we have each other?"

"Do you have any idea how much I love you, Mrs. Denny?"

"A lot?"

He nodded. "Do you love me?" he asked, holding back a smile.

"I don't know . . . I have to think about that."

He chuckled and slid his arm in under her and drew her close. "Liza, if I ask a question, will you answer me honestly?"

It was the old, old question. She smiled and snuggled her nose into his cold ear.

"Why did you marry me, Liza?"

She laughed right out loud. "You know why!" she said, playing along.

"Tell me anyway!"

They were both laughing by now.

"Because there was no one else about!" she cried, flinging her arms around him. "I had to marry you!"

On top of them the blanket was warm, its faded squares and patches hidden in the night. And on the door, still swinging from the jolt of David's push, hung the two hats, her sunbonnet and his cap.

Bibliography

Anderson, Eva Greenslit. *Chief Seattle.* Caldwell, Idaho: The Caxton Printers, 1943.

Bagley, C. B. *History of Seattle: From the Earliest Settlement to the Present Time.* 3 vols. Chicago: S. J. Clarke, 1916.

_____. *Scrapbook.* Vols. 1, 5, 12, 15. Seattle: University of Washington, Northwest Collections.

_____. *In the Beginning: Early Days on Puget Sound.* Seattle: The Historical Society of Seattle and King County, 1980.

_____. *Pioneer Seattle and Its Pioneers.* Seattle, 1928.

Bancroft, Hubert Howe. *The Works of Hubert Howe Bancroft.* Vol. 31: *History of Washington, Idaho, and Montana.* San Francisco: The History Company, Pub., 1890.

Bass, Sophie Frye. *Pig-Tail Days in Old Seattle.* Florenz Clark, artist. Portland: Binford & Mort, 1937.

_____. *When Seattle Was a Village.* Florenz Clark, artist. Seattle: Lowman & Hanford, 1947.

Bennet, Roberta A., ed. *A Small World of Our Own.* Walla Walla, Wash.: Pioneer Press, 1985.

_____. *We'll All Go Home in the Spring.* Walla Walla, Wash.: Pioneer Press, 1984.

Binns, Archie. *Northwest Gateway: The Story of the Port of Seattle.* Portland: Binford & Mort, 1941.

_____. *Sea in the Forest.* Garden City, N.Y.: Doubleday & Co., Inc., 1953.

Blaine, David and Catherine. Letters 1849–1856.

Blankenship, George E. *Lights and Shades of Pioneer Life on Puget Sound.* Olympia, 1923. Facsimile reproduction, Seattle: The Shorey Bookstore, 1972.

Bonney, W. P. *History of Pierce County, Washington.* Vol. 1. Chicago: Pioneer Historical Publishing Company, 1927.

Boring, Mel. *Sealth—The Story of an American Indian.* Minneapolis: Dillon Press, 1978.

Brewster, David, and David M. Buerge. *Washingtonians: A Biographical Portrait of the State.* Seattle: Sasquatch Books, 1989.

Broderick, Henry. *Picturesque Pioneers.* Seattle: Dogwood Press, 1967.

Buchanan, Laura D. *Souvenir of Chief Seattle and Princess Angeline.* Portland: Binford & Mort, 1909.

Buerge, David M. *The Man We Call Seattle.*

Carpenter, Cecelia: *Fort Nisqually: A Documented History of Indian and British History.* Tacoma, Wash.: Tahoma Research Center, 1986.

_____. *Leschi: Last Chief of the Nisqually.* Tacoma, Wash.: Tahoma Research Center, 1986.

_____. *Tears of Internment: The Indian History of Fox Island and the Puget Sound Indian War.* Tacoma, Wash.: Tahoma Research Center, 1996.

_____. *They Walked Before: The Indians of Washington State.* Tacoma, Wash.: Tahoma Research Center, 1977.

Cleveland High School. *The Duwamish Diary.* Seattle: Seattle Public Schools, 1949.

Conover, C. T. *Pioneer Reminisces.* Seattle: Museum of History and Industry, n.d.

Denny, David. *David's Diaries.* Seattle: Museum of History and Industry.

Denny, Emily Inez. *Blazing the Way.* Seattle: Rainier Printing Company, 1909.

Dorpat, Paul. *494 More Glimpses of Historic Seattle.* Seattle: Mother Wit Press, 1982.

_____. *Seattle Now and Then.* Seattle: Tartu Publications, 1984.

Downie, Ralph Earnest. *A Pictorial History of the State of Washington.* Seattle: Lowman & Hanford, 1937.

Dryden, Cecil. *Dryden's History of Washington*. Portland: Binford & Mort, 1968.

Dunbar: *Scrapbook*. Vols. 5 & 6. Seattle: University of Washington, Northwest Collections.

Eckrom, J. A. *Remembered Drums: A History of the Puget Sound Indian War*. Walla Walla, Wash.: Pioneer Press, 1989.

Edson, Lelah Jackson. *The Fourth Corner: Highlights from the Early Northwest*. Bellingham, Wash.: Cox Brothers, 1951.

Eide, Ingvard. *Oregon Trail*. Rand McNally and Co., 1972.

Emmons, Della Gould. *Leschi of the Nisquallies*. Minneapolis: T. S. Denison & Co., 1965.

Evans, Elwood. *History of the Pacific Northwest: Oregon and Washington*. Vol. 1. Portland: North Pacific History Co., 1889.

Evans, Jack R. *Little History of Lenant F. Thompson*. Seattle: SCW Publications, 1992.

_____. *Little History of North Bend—Snoqalmie, Washington*. Seattle: SCW Publications, 1990.

Fonda. *Scrapbook*. Vol. 1. Seattle: University of Washington, Northwest Collections.

Franzwa, Gregory. *The Oregon Trail Revisited*. St. Louis: Patrice Press, Inc., 1972.

Frisbie. *Scrapbook*. Vol. 1. Seattle: University of Washington, Special Collections.

Glassley, Ray H. *Indian Wars of the Pacific Northwest*. Portland: Binford & Mort, 1972.

Grant, James. *History of Seattle, Washington*. New York: American Publishers and English Co. Pub., 1981.

Green, Frank L. *Thomas M. Chambers Collection*. Tacoma, Wash.: Washington State Historical Society, 1972.

Guie, Dean H. *Bugles in the Valley*. Yakima: Republic Press, 1956.

Hanford, Cornelius. *Seattle and Environs*. 3 vols. Seattle: Pioneer Historical Pub., 1924.

Hawley, Robert Emmett. *Skqee Mus: Or Pioneer Days on the Nooksack*. Bellingham, Wash.: Miller & Sutherlen Printing Co., 1945.

Hemphill, Major General John A., and Robert C. Cumbow. *West Pointers and Early Washington*. Seattle: The West Point Society of Puget Sound, Inc., 1992.

Hilbert, Vi. *Huboo.* Seattle: University of Washington Press, 1980.

James, David. *From Grand Mound to Scatter Creek.* Olympia Wash.: State Capital Historical Association of Washington, 1980.

Johansen, Dorothy O., and Charles M. Gates. Empire *of the Columbia.* New York: Harper and Row, 1967.

Johnson, Jalmar. *Builders of the Northwest.* New York: Dodd, Mead & Co., 1963.

Jones, Nard. *Seattle.* New York: Doubleday, 1972.

Judson, Katharine Berry. *Early Days in Old Oregon.* Portland: Binford & Mort, 1916.

Judson, Phoebe Goodell. *A Pioneer's Search for an Ideal Home.* Lincoln: University of Nebraska Press, 1984.

Karolevitz, Bob. "Seattle Transit." *Seattle Times,* 24 May 1964.

Kelly, Plympton. *We Were Not Summer Soldiers: The Indian War Diary of Plympton J. Kelly, 1855–1856.* Tacoma: Washington State Historical Society, 1976.

Leighton, George R. *America's Growing Pains.* New York: Harper & Brothers, 1939.

Litteer, Loren K. *Bleeding Kansas.* Kansas: Champion Publishing, 1987.

McDonald, Lucille. "Seattlites Recall Cable Car Days." *Seattle Times,* 19 September 1955.

_____. *Washington's Yesterdays.* Portland: Binford & Mort, 1953.

McDonald, Norbert. *Distant Neighbors: A Comparative History of Seattle and Vancouver.* Lincoln: University of Nebraska Press, 1987.

McDonald, Robert. "Railroading in Seattle." *Seattle Sunday Times,* 31 December 1944.

_____. "Seattle's Mayors." Bellingham Public Library vertical file: Seattle History.

Meeker, Ezra. *Pioneer Reminiscences of Puget Sound.* Seattle: Lowman & Hanford, 1905.

_____. *Seventy Years of Progress in Washington.* Tacoma: Allstrum Printing, 1921.

_____. *The Tragedy of Leschi.* Seattle: Lowman & Hanford, 1905.

Meany, Edmond S. *History of the State of Washington.* New York: The MacMillan Co., 1910.

Metcalf, James Vernon. *Chief Seattle*. Seattle: Catholic NW Progress, n.d.

Monaghan, Jay. *Civil War on the Western Border*. Lincoln: University of Nebraska, 1985.

Montgomery, Elizabeth. *Chief Seattle—Great Statesman*. Champaign, Ill.: Garrard Pub. Co., 1966.

Morgan, Murray. *Skid Road: An Informal Portrait of Seattle*. Seattle: University of Washington Press, 1951.

Museum of History and Industry, Manuscript Files:

"Battle of Seattle"

Denny, A. A. Memorial album.

Denny, Emily Inez. "By the Blazing Shore."

———. Biography of Princess Angeline.

Denny, John. Biography.

Denny, Louisa Boren. Manuscript.

———. Interviews.

Denny, Sarah Latimer. *Bass Collection*.

Graham, Susan Mercer. "Fort at Seattle."

Kellogg, David. Manuscript.

Russell, Alonzo. Memoirs.

Smith, D. H. "Early Seattle."

Wyckoff, Eugenia McConaha.

Wyckoff, George McConaha Jr. Letter to mother.

Yesler, Henry. Letters.

Yesler, Sarah. Letters.

Neils, Selma. *The Klickitat Indians*. Portland: Binford & Mort, 1985.

Nelson, Gerald B. *Seattle: The Life and Time of an American City*. New York: Alfred A. Knopf, 1977.

Newell, Gordon. *Totem Tales of Old Seattle*. Seattle: Superior Pub., 1956.

_____. *Westward to Alki*. Seattle: Superior Pub. Co., 1977.

Oates, Stephen B. *To Purge This Land with Blood*. Amherst, Mass: University of Massachusetts Press, 1970.

Pacific Telephone & Telegraph Co. *Growing Together*. Bellingham Public Library vertical file: Seattle History, July 1958.

Paine, Lauran. *Conquest of the Great Northwest*. New York: Robert M. McBride Co., Inc., 1959.

Peltier, Jerome. *Warbonnets and Epaulets.* Compiled by B. C. Payette. Montreal: Payette Radio, n.d.

Phelps, T. S. *Reminiscences of Seattle: Indian War of 1855–1856.* Seattle: The Alice Harrison Co., 1880.

Pierce, Frank Richardson. "The Bell Rang Nine Times." *Seattle Times,* 9 September 1962.

Pioneer & Democrat, 1852–1856. Seattle: University of Washington, Suzalo Library,

Post-Intelligencer. Seattle, Washington.

Potts, Ralph Bushnell. *Seattle Heritage.* Seattle: Superior Pub., 1955.

Prater, Yvonne. *Snoqualmie Pass: From Indian Trail to Interstate.* Seattle: The Mountaineers, 1981.

Prosch, Thomas. *A Chronological History of Seattle.* Seattle: Museum of History and Industry.

_____. *David S. Maynard and Catherine T. Maynard.* Seattle: Lowman & Hanford, 1906.

Puget Sound Courier, 1854–1856. Seattle: University of Washington, Suzalo Library.

Raymond, Steve. "Remember When Seattle Had Cable." *Seattle Times,* 8 August 1865.

Records of King County Clerk: Third Territorial District Court 1852–1889. RBD Washington State Archives, Regional Depository at Bellingham.

Redfield, Edith Sanderson. *Seattle Memoirs.* Boston: Lothrop, Lee and Shepard Co., 1930.

Richards, Kent D. *Isaac I. Stevens: Young Man in a Hurry.* Pullman: Washington State University Press, 1993.

Rucker, Helen. *Cargo of Brides.* Boston: Little, Brown, 1956.

Sale, Roger. *Seattle: Past to Present.* Seattle: University of Washington Press, 1976.

Sanderson, Edith. *Seattle Memoirs.* Boston: Lothrop, Lee and Shepard Co., 1930.

Seattle, Chief Moses. *"How Can One Sell the Air?"* Summertown Tenn.: The Book Publishing Company, 1992.

Seattle's First Physician. Clinics of the Virginia Mason Hospital. Dec. 1932, Vol. 12.

Seattle Times. Seattle, Washington

Smith, Helen Krebs. *With Her Own Wings: Historical Ketches, Reminiscences, and Anecdotes of Pioneer Women*. Portland: Beattie & Company, 1948

Smith, Herndon, ed. *Centralia: The First Fifty Years*. Centralia, Wash.: The Daily Chronicle & F. H. Cole Printing Company, 1942.

Snowden, Clinton. *History of Washington*. New York: The Century History Co., 1909.

Speidel, William. *Doc Maynard: The Man Who Invented Seattle*. Seattle: Nettle Creek Pub., 1978.

_____. *Sons of the Profits*. Seattle: Nettle Creek Pub., 1967.

Stewart, Edgar I. *Washington: Northwest Frontier*. Vol. 2. New York: Lewis Historical Publishing Company, Inc., n.d.

Tavo, Gus. *The Buffalo Are Coming*. New York: Alfred A. Knopf, 1960.

Thompson, Margaret. *Genealogical Notes—Denny Family*. Seattle Public Library, Main Office.

Trotter, F. I.; Loutzenhiser, F. H.; and Loutzenhiser, J. R., eds. *Told by the Pioneers*. Vols. 1–3. U.S. Works Progress Administration, 1938.

Walkinshaw, Robert. *On Puget Sound*. London: J. P. Putnam's Sons, 1929.

Warren, James. *King County and Its Queen City: Seattle*. Historical Society of Seattle and King County. Woodland Hills, Calif.: Windsor Publications, 1981.

Watt, Roberta Frye. *Four Wagons West*. Portland: Binford & Mort, 1931.

Winthrop, Theodore. *The Canoe and the Saddle*. New York: Dodd, Mead and Co., 1862.

Wright, Robin K. *A Time of Gathering*.